Tea with Jam & Dread

Kensington Books by Vicki Delany

The Tea by the Sea mystery series

Tea & Treachery

Murder in a Teacup

Murder Spills the Tea

Steeped in Malice

Trouble is Brewing

Tea with Jam & Dread

Tea *with* Jam & Dread

VICKI DELANY

KENSINGTON PUBLISHING CORP.

KENSINGTON BOOKS are published by

Kensington Publishing Corp.
900 Third Ave.
New York, NY 10022

ISBN: 978-1-4967-4730-3

Printed in the United States of America

The authorized representative in the EU for product safety and compliance is eucomply OU, Parnu mnt 139b-14, Apt 123
Tallinn, Berlin 11317, hello@eucompliancepartner.com

To Alex Delany: Afternoon Tea Companion

Dramatis Personae

THE CRAWFORDS

Edward Crawford, 10th Earl of Frockmorton; deceased

Elizabeth Crawford, Dowager Countess of Frockmorton, Lady Frockmorton, widow of EDWARD; the birthday girl

Robert Crawford, 11th Earl of Frockmorton, eldest son of the late EDWARD and ELIZABETH, and thus the current earl

Annabelle Crawford, Countess of Frockmorton, wife of ROBERT; the current countess, and don't you forget it.

Julien Crawford, Viscount Darnby (and don't you forget that either), only son of ROBERT and ANNABELLE; eldest grandchild of ELIZABETH

Carmela Crawford, wife of JULIEN; at least for now

Lady Jacqueline McLeod, only daughter of ROBERT and ANNABELLE

Alastair McLeod, husband of LADY JACQUELINE; not a "Sir," but a dentist. The family is coming down in the world

Zoe and **Katy McLeod,** twin daughters of JACQUELINE and ALASTAIR; great-granddaughters of ELIZABETH; very cute but always underfoot

Thomas Crawford, second son of the late EDWARD and ELIZABETH; escaped to Canada to get away from his family

Emma Crawford, daughter of THOMAS; wishes she could be a Lady one day, but has to work as a school teacher

Amanda Crawford, daughter of the late EDWARD and ELIZABETH; deceased

viii Dramatis Personae

Katherine Waterfield, youngest child of the late EDWARD and ELIZABETH

Unknown Waterfield: Presumably Katherine had a husband at one time, but he is never seen and never mentioned.

Anthony (Tony) Waterfield, son of KATHERINE AND UNKNOWN WATERFIELD; grandson of ELIZABETH; manager of Thornecroft Castle House and Hotel

Susannah Reilly, née Waterfield, daughter of KATHERINE AND UNKNOWN WATERFIELD; granddaughter of ELIZABETH; a legal secretary, definitely coming down in the world

Ray Reilly, husband of SUSANNAH; a firefighter, even further down in the world

Two Unnamed Little Reillys; children of SUSANNAH and RAY REILLY; great grandchildren to ELIZABETH; disappointed to miss all the drama

Lissie (Miss Lister), white Persian cat; very cute, but always underfoot

STAFF OF THORNECROFT CASTLE HOUSE AND HOTEL
Ian Carver, head chef
Dr. Alicia Boyle, kitchen maid, but only for the day of the party
Beth, receptionist
Irene, waitress
Jason, waiter
George, farmer
Mrs. Beans, former cook, when ROSE was in service; alcoholic (presumably deceased)
Plenty of Unnamed staff; it is a hotel, after all.

PARTY GUESTS
Reginald (Reggie) Hansen, retired Thornecroft stable hand; dreams of wooing Rose shattered when she met Eric Campbell

Josh Hansen, grandson of REGGIE; farrier

Bert Kellogg, annoying guest

**Assorted friends, aquantances, frencmies, hangers on;
maybe even an enemy or two**

AMERICAN VISITORS

Lily Roberts, owner and pastry chef of Tea by the Sea,
North Augusta, Massachusetts

Rose Campbell, née Walker, grandmother to LILY; owner
of Victoria-on-Sea; former kitchen maid at Thornecroft
Castle House; widow of ERIC CAMPBELL

Bernadette Murphy (Bernie), "of the Lower East Side
Murphies"; computer whiz, wannabe novelist; LILY's
friend

Matt Goodwill (AKA Lincoln Badwell), bestselling true-
crime writer; neighbor to ROSE and LILY; BERNADETTE's
paramour

NEIGHBORS, ACQUAINTANCES, PASSERS-BY

Simon McCracken, gardener at nearby Garfield Hall;
LILY's paramour (or is he still?)

Dennis Pembroke, retired Yorkshire cop; desperately trying to be relevant

Alfred, retired Yorkshire jewel thief; also desperately trying to be relevant

Joanie, doctor's receptionist; bossy elder sister of ALICIA;
knows more about Alicia than Alicia does

YORKSHIRE POLICE

Detective Inspector Ravenwood (DI)

Detective Sergeant Sophia Capretti (DS)

**Various unnamed uniformed officers; watching everyone
and everything.**

Chapter 1

I never thought it would end like this.

"We're going to die! We're all going to die!" my best friend screamed, as she threw her hands up to cover her eyes.

"Do restrain yourself, Bernadette," my grandmother said, from the back seat. "Lily is in perfect control."

I was anything but in perfect control. In fact, I agreed with Bernie. The end was nigh. I clenched my teeth with as much force as I was clenching the steering wheel. I would have also liked to cover my eyes, but that would not have been a good idea. Instead, I focused and refocused as I tried to trace the fading lines on the road in front of me, but with the rain and my own nerves, that wasn't easy.

Vehicles of all sizes zipped around me, throwing up spray. Rain pounded the windshield, the wipers barely able to keep up.

"I've missed the exit. Again. I need you to read those signs for me," I said to Bernie.

"Rerouting," said the cheerful voice of the car's GPS.

"They go by so fast," Bernie said.

"What lane do I need to be in?" I asked.

I was trapped in three lanes of fast-moving traffic. Round and round the roundabout we went. Vehicles came from all directions. The exit signs had so many names on them, by the time I read them, I was already driving past. The GPS wasn't helping all that much. I was expecting it to give up and shut down at any moment.

"Okay." Bernie took a deep breath. "I'm back. Momentary overreaction as my life flashed before my eyes. We can do this."

"I would hope so," my grandmother, Rose Campbell, said, "I don't intend to spend the rest of my life in this car. Like a modern version of the Flying Dutchman, doomed to forever circle a roundabout on the outskirts of Leeds, never making landfall at the next service center. Speaking of which, don't take too much longer to get us out of here, love, I need to use the loo."

"You want the A58. That's coming up," Bernie said, alternately consulting the car's installed GPS and her own phone. "Stay in this lane until you pass the next exit, and then move to the left. The exit we want is the one after the next one."

I maneuvered the car into the turn. A white panel van leaned on its horn as it passed me on the right.

"Ignore him," Bernie said. "You're doing fine. Okay, now move to the left."

"There's a whole line of cars coming up on my left."

"They'll let you in," Bernie said confidently, as she twisted in her seat to look behind us. "Okay, maybe not that guy."

I wasn't so sure, but I pulled left. Miraculously once "that guy" had passed, the other approaching vehicles did slow down, and I slipped into the lane. I remembered to breathe. It wouldn't help anyone if I passed out.

The lane exited, and I was, at last, free of the latest of the cursed roundabouts. It, I feared, would not be the last.

I was now on a highway. A nice normal highway with wide straight lanes and vehicles politely staying in their own lanes—most of them, anyway. According to the GPS, I had several miles to calm down before I had to get off the highway and enter another tumble with a three-lane round-about with seven exits, each of those exits having numerous directional signs. It did not help that I was driving on the "wrong" side of the road.

" 'Let's rent a car,' " I mumbled, as I slowly forced my fingers off the steering wheel and gave them a good stretch in an attempt to return some life to each digit. " 'It'll be so much cheaper than taking taxis, and we'll be able to get around to see the sights easier.' "

"All still true," Bernie said. "Once we're in the country-side, the driving will be so much easier." She seemed to have recovered from her earlier vision of impending death.

I had to admit, although only to myself, that much of this had been my idea. Rent a car. See the area. Enjoy the freedom a personal vehicle offers. What an optimist was I.

Not only had I never been to England before—and thus, never driven on the "wrong" side of the road or even seen a multilane roundabout—but I don't drive all that much in America. I'm from Manhattan. I've never even owned a car. When I need to get around Cape Cod, where I now live, I borrow my grandmother's ancient Ford Focus to embark on the calm, low-traffic trip into town. I'd willingly agreed with Bernie when she suggested we save money by having only one driver registered on the rental agreement. Logically, that one person was me, as Bernie would be leaving us the day after tomorrow.

The rain continued to fall, the windshield wipers moved back and forth, back and forth.

"Stay awake, Lily," Bernie said.

"Fear not," I replied. "I am far too terrified to fall asleep."

"I hope the rain lets up," Rose said. "I'm sure they're planning to have much of the party in the gardens."

"I hope the rain lets up so we can see the view," Bernie said. "Looks like some hills over there, but the clouds are so low it's hard to tell."

Swish. Swish.

"Exit coming up," Bernie said. "Look for the sign to Halifax."

"I see it," I said.

Another terrifying game of round and round the roundabout, and at last we were free of highways and intercity traffic, heading off into the countryside.

"Are people allowed to park wherever they like?" I said, as I twisted the wheel into a sharp right, taking us into the lane for oncoming traffic to get out of the way of a line of cars unexpectedly parked every which way, half of them half on the sidewalk. I had been temporarily disoriented because the cars were facing us, as though I was going the wrong way on a one-way street.

"Isn't that charming?" Bernie asked. "Look at those lovely old houses. I bet they're hundreds of years old. Obviously built long before anyone needed a place to park the car."

I dared a quick peek to one side. The houses were old, a long row of red and gray brick stretching from one street corner to another, thin and tall, dotted with chimney pots, colorful doors opening directly onto the sidewalk. No driveways, no garages, no place to put the car other than on the narrow street.

"Look," Bernie said, "A pub. Our first English pub, Lily."

"We saw pubs in Leeds," I said. "On the way to get the car."

"Yes, but that was a city. It's different. That one looks as though it's been at that spot for hundreds of years. All the neighborhood goes there. It's what they call their 'local.' Oh my gosh. Look over there—sheep!"

"Sheep in Yorkshire," Rose said. "What a notion."

We'd been in Yorkshire for all of about an hour. I'd swear Rose's accent was getting stronger with every mile we drove.

"Starting to see anything familiar, Rose?" I asked.

"Hard to say," she replied. "So many things have changed and so much to remember. I'm sure I'll start recognizing places when we get closer."

"You've been back several times, though," Bernie said, "right?"

"Back to Yorkshire, but not to Halifax. My parents moved to Holgate in the 1970s, after my father retired, to be closer to one of my sisters and her family. I haven't been to Halifax for a very long time indeed."

The GPS instructed me to take the next left. I did so, and we drove through more small towns with streets lined by row houses, open fields full of sheep, more than a few pubs. The rain began to slow, and some of the cloud cover lifted. We were climbing steadily, bouncing down a country road lined by rough drystone walls, dark with age. To my left, the ground fell sharply away. I was too scared to pull my eyes off the road in front of me to take a look.

Rose sucked in a breath.

Bernie half turned in her seat. "You okay, back there?"

"I'm okay, as you put it. And there it is. Behold Halifax."

"Don't look Lily," Bernie said. "I'll describe it. We're up way high. The cloud cover is thinning, and I can see a long way down to the valley. Everything is so green. Houses built all up the sides of the hills, the city lies at the bottom. Church steeples and what look like old factories and warehouses. Bridges and train tracks. I bet it looks fabulous in the sunshine."

"It does," Rose said, very softly. "It does."

"Turn right," Bernie said. "According to the GPS and my phone, we're almost there."

"We are," Rose said. Excitement crept into her voice. "Hazel's family lived in that farmhouse. They had three sons. She wasn't needed on the farm, so she worked at Thornecroft."

"Farm looks prosperous enough," Bernie said.

It did. Large stone house, barn and outbuildings built around a courtyard. The sheep didn't bother to look up as we passed.

"Funny how it all starts coming back," Rose said. "I traveled many times down this road going to the shops in Halifax or to catch a train to visit one of my sisters. Hazel and I were friends at first, but then we had a falling out, so I wasn't invited to tea at the farm any longer."

"What did you fall out about?" Bernie asked.

"I don't remember. Goes to show, doesn't it? It must have been dreadfully important at the time, and now, I don't even remember. The McAllisters lived there." She indicated a substantial two-story house set well back from the road. "Doctor McAllister, he was. They dined quite regularly at Thornecroft, as I recall. He was nice enough—good-looking, everyone thought. His wife was a mouse of a woman in public, but she had a horrible reputation below stairs. These days, they'd say he bullied her and she took it out on the servants."

"Here we are," I said at the same time the GPS announced that we had arrived at our destination. "Thornecroft Castle House and Hotel."

Chapter 2

Bernie bounced on the bed. "I can't believe we're actually here. England. Yorkshire. Thornecroft Castle. Rose isn't even my grandmother, but I've heard so much about this place, I've always felt as though I know it. And now I do!"

I turned from the closet, where I was putting away my clothes, to smile at her. "It worked out nicely that you could come. If I was going to drive the car straight off the side of that cliff, I'd want you to be with me."

"Nice sentiment. Not." She bounced again. "Rain's letting up. Do we have time to explore?"

"Do you want me to leave you half of these hangers?"

"One should do. I'll hang up the dress I brought for the party to get some of the wrinkles out, but everything else can stay in the backpack."

I'll never understand how anyone can live out of a suitcase. Or worse yet, a backpack. If I'm going to be in a hotel for more than one night, everything gets unpacked, folded, hung up, tucked neatly away.

"I hate to complain," Bernie said.

"Why should today be any different?"

"This place is mighty impressive, but I would have thought our room would be . . . grander."

I squeezed between the twin bed that would be mine and the desk to take my passport and other things I wouldn't need until we left out of my purse. "Remind me again how much you're paying a night."

"I know. I'm just saying. I was thinking of big double beds with ornate bed frames and heavy velvet curtains. A chaise longue overlooking the perfectly maintained garden and the hills beyond. Red-and-gold wallpaper and tons of gilt on the ceiling. Comfortable chairs around a low table on which to place our tea or a nightcap. A fire in a deep fireplace, big enough to roast one of those many sheep we saw."

"Are you saying you don't want to share with me?"

She grinned at me. "Just getting a rise out of you." She fell back onto her bed and threw out her arms. "We are not honored guests. I'm barely even a tag-along. It was nice of you to share with me, otherwise I'd be sleeping in the barn or the carriage house. Do you suppose they have a carriage house?"

"Almost certainly, although they probably call it the garage." I picked a folder illustrated with a drone photo of the house and environs off the desk and tossed it onto Bernie's stomach. "This'll probably tell you about the history of the house, and I'm sure we can ask anyone."

"Did you catch the accent on that receptionist who checked us in?"

"I could hardly miss it, Bernie. I thought it was charming. This wing looks like a modern addition. It was likely added when they turned the house into a hotel. Thus, we did not get a room in which Queen Victoria once slept."

"Pity, that. What are you going to wear to meet Her Ladyship?"

"Black dress and tights, and that red leather jacket. I'd rather be overdressed than underdressed. You?" I looked at my friend. Close to six feet tall, fit and lean, with a scattering of freckles across her pale cheeks, a mane of wild red curls, flashing green eyes, Bernadette Murphy and I had been best friends since the first day of school. I've always called her the Warrior Princess.

"I only brought one dress, which I'm saving for the party itself. Jeans and a nice sweater and puffy vest be okay?"

"Sure. We don't have time to do much exploring the grounds. Rain's started again, and I don't want to look like a drowned rat when I meet our hostess."

When we checked into the hotel, the receptionist had greeted us warmly. As she handed us our keys, she informed us that Lady Frockmorton had invited us to join her for tea in the drawing room at two thirty.

Lady Frockmorton was Elizabeth Crawford, the Dowager Countess of Frockmorton, owner of Thornecroft Castle House and Hotel. It was her one hundredth birthday we'd come all this way to celebrate; although it was Rose who was here for the birthday. I'd come to assist Rose, and Bernie tagged along because she was meeting her boyfriend, my neighbor, Matt Goodwill, in York, in a couple of days.

Promptly at two twenty-five, Bernie and I left our room. We were on the second floor of the new wing, and Rose's room was below ours. I knocked at her door, and it flew open to reveal my grandmother in all her glory.

"Goodness," Bernie said.

I might have said something along those lines myself. My grandmother is a woman who loves color—the more the better. Today she wore wide-legged black pants splashed with giant yellow sunflowers, a yellow turtleneck sweater accented by horizontal purple stripes, and a length of purple and orange beads, each one the approximate size of a golf ball. Her makeup was thickly applied, most noticeably, the rouge on her cheeks, dark red lipstick on her mouth, and sparkly blue shadow on her eyelids. She held her pink cane.

"I wanted to make an effort to look presentable for tea with Lady Frockmorton," Rose said, when Bernie and I had finally closed our mouths. "Imagine, me, having tea with Her Ladyship, not being the one making it or serving it."

We walked down the hallway to the original house. A white cat, as large and fluffy as a snowdrift, was snoozing on a window ledge. It opened one blue eye as we approached and jumped to the floor. "Who else do you think will be joining us for tea?" Bernie asked. The cat followed.

"The others who've arrived today and are staying here, I expect," Rose said. "Most party guests will likely be from the area, but many will have come from afar. Like us."

The receptionist directed us down two steps on the far side of the lobby, then left to the drawing room.

I was trying to take it all in—the grandeur of the front hall, the comfortable sitting room next to the lobby, the portraits on the walls, the patina on the antique furniture, the bowls of fresh flowers, the grandfather clock dated 1812—all while keeping one hand on Rose's elbow on the stairs and finding our way to the drawing room. Bernie collided with me. Or maybe I collided with Bernie.

At the bottom of the steps, signs pointed right to the bar and the restaurant, left to the drawing room and the reception rooms. A young man, dressed in gray slacks, black shirt, with a badge featuring the family coat-of-arms sewn onto his plum jacket, smiled at us. "Mrs. Rose Campbell and company?"

"That is us," Rose said.

He nodded. "Lady Frockmorton is delighted you will be joining her." He opened the closest door and gestured for us go in.

Still followed by the white cat, we entered what was obviously a public room, as it was full of round tables of varying sizes, set with white linen tablecloths and silver cutlery, surrounded by chairs. Despite that, it managed to maintain the illusion of being in a private home. The ceiling was low, the wood-paneled walls covered with paintings of hounds at the hunt or pastoral scenes of gently flowing rivers and grazing cattle or sheep, all in ornate gilt frames. The mullioned windows were deeply set into the thick stone walls, diamond-shaped individual glass panels divided by rows and columns of lead. The patterned carpet was modern, the design likely chosen to hide evidence left by the passing public. A huge fireplace filled the far wall; small porcelain statues and large bronze plates lined the mantle. On this cold, wet day, logs burned cheerfully.

I scarcely had a chance to take any of it in. Only one other person was in the room. She was seated in a damask-covered wingback chair in front of a low coffee table, close to the fire. She wore a long dress of deep red velvet, a string of pearls around her neck, and more pearls in her ears. Her short slate-gray hair was thin enough to show patches of pink scalp. Her eyes were a startling shade of dark blue, and they sparked with humor and intelligence as she watched us approach. The deep folds of skin around those eyes, and on her face and hands, told me this was the lady whose hundredth birthday was rapidly approaching.

She looked straight at me. "Rose Walker. After all these years."

"I'm not—"

"I know, dear. I haven't totally slipped into the past yet. You are the spitting image of her, so much so, it momentarily took me aback. That heart-shaped face, the lovely skin, the blond hair and blue eyes. A true English rose, our Rose was. And now you." She turned her smile onto my grandmother. "My dear Rose. Please forgive me for not standing, but I'm afraid I can no longer do so without assistance, so I prefer to remain seated and retain my dignity." When we came in, I noticed a walker tucked discreetly against the far wall.

"You never stood for me before, m'lady," Rose said.

Lady Frockmorton threw back her head and laughed. "How well I remember that insolence, and quite fondly. But that American accent you've acquired; that will never do."

American accent? To me, my grandmother had always had an overpowering English accent. It had grown even stronger since we stepped off the plane yesterday morning, and by now it was almost indistinguishable from that of the staff here. Lady Frockmorton's accent was far less pronounced, more London, I guessed, than Yorkshire. More private education than village school.

Rose crossed the room, pink cane tapping on the carpet. She stood in front of Lady Frockmorton and held out both of her hands. Our hostess took them in hers, and the two old ladies looked at each other for a long time.

Bernie and I eyed each other. It was as though we'd simply disappeared.

The door opened, and a woman dressed in a waitress uniform of thick-soled shoes, black skirt, white shirt, and black leggings came in bearing a silver tray. She began laying the low table for tea.

Rose took back her hands. "My granddaughter, Lily Roberts, and our dear friend, Bernadette Murphy."

"Thank you so much for having me," I said. "You have a fabulous home."

Bernie gulped and nodded, as she was not often at a loss for words. Come to think of it, I've never seen Bernie at a loss for words.

Four chairs were arranged around the table. We all sat down. I was absolutely delighted that the tea service was Wedgewood Renaissance gold, a modern design of a geometric oval pattern and gold trim. I own a tearoom, and I adore fine china, although this pattern would be far outside of my budget for the restaurant. The cat settled itself in front of the fire.

"Happy birthday, Lady Frockmorton," I said. I felt somewhat uncomfortable calling her that, but it was her title. Mrs. Crawford might be seen as insulting, and I would never call a lady of her age by her first name without being asked to do so.

"Thank you, my dear. One hundred years, tomorrow. Hard to even imagine what the world was like when I was born. Rose, what are you at now?"

"Eighty-five, next year, m'lady."

"I insist you call me Elizabeth, please. You are here as my guest, not as a kitchen maid. Lily and Bernadette, I hope you will do the same."

Rose tried not to show how pleased that made her.

The waitress returned, carrying a laden tray. She placed a silver teapot in front of Lady Frockmorton and jugs of milk and sugar on the table.

"Thank you, Irene," Elizabeth said. "Shall I pour?"

"Please do," Rose said, and our hostess picked up the pot. The rich spicy scent filled the room.

"Lapsang Souchong," I said. "A favorite of mine."

Her eyes lit up with pleasure as she poured. "You know your teas."

"I own a tearoom. On Cape Cod. I'm a pastry chef by profession, and afternoon tea is my specialty."

Elizabeth put down the teapot and clapped her hands in delight. "How marvelous. An inherited trait, I've no doubt. Rose's scones were widely considered the best in Calderdale."

"Not by Mrs. Beans," said Rose.

Elizabeth laughed. "I'm sure. I see you admiring the china, Lily. A gift from one of my sons for my ninety-fifth birthday."

"It's gorgeous," I said, and she smiled at me.

The waitress brought in a plate of small tea sandwiches and another of miniature tarts. "Will there be anything else, Elizabeth?"

"No, thank you, dear. It all looks lovely."

She left us alone and shut the door behind her.

"The staff call you Elizabeth?" Rose said.

"Only when we are not in public, and I've told them this week is my birthday week, so we are not in public. Times have changed a great deal since you were last here, Rose. In many ways for the better. In some ways, not. Some of the young people working here now are descendants of the staff when we were a private home. Family ties run deep in Yorkshire."

I helped myself to a sandwich studying it before popping it into my mouth. Thin white bread cut into a rectangle. The filling was likely chicken but of a slight yellowish color. I took a bite. Chicken tasting of curry, which would explain the color. It was fabulous, with a rich spicy flavor and a bit of texture from chopped sultanas.

"You're eating that sandwich like the professional you are Lily," Elizabeth said. "How is it?"

"Wonderful. I'd like to get the recipe and serve it at my own place."

"I hope you're not disappointed by the scaled-down offering today. I can assure you Ian, my head chef, will be pulling out all the stops for my birthday tea tomorrow."

"If I may," I said, "I'd enjoy helping him and his staff. If you think they wouldn't mind?"

"Mind? They'd love the help. I'll have a word with Ian later and let him know. Before I forget, we're having a pre-birthday drinks party in the bar tonight, beginning at eight o'clock. People will be arriving at different times, so I didn't think it wise to attempt to organize a dinner party. You're on your own for dinner this evening."

Rose nibbled on a salmon sandwich. "I'm curious about one thing, M'Lady—I mean, Elizabeth. You must have had countless numbers of servants employed here over the years. I don't mean to sound ungrateful, and I will confess that I often think of my own days at Thornecroft, but—"

"But you're wondering why I remembered you specifically. And fondly enough to invite you to my party." She looked between Bernie and me. "If you young women are lucky enough to reach a fine old age, in reasonably good health and some degree of financial stability, you'll find the oddest things stick in your mind. Some of my children and grandchildren were quite appalled when I said I wanted to invite some favored servants to my celebration. Naming no names, but younger people these days can be even more hidebound than us older ones. Comes from insecurity, I believe, as they see the aristocratic families struggling to stay relevant. Not to mention financially solvent."

I next tried a cucumber sandwich. I found it bland. Cucumber and bread; at the very least it needed a touch of salt.

Elizabeth put down her teacup. She smiled at Rose. I could almost see the years fall away behind her blue eyes as memories flooded in. I glanced at my own grandmother. Her gaze was unfocused, her eyes distant. Also remembering.

"How old were you where you came to work here, Rose?"

"Fourteen, I believe. I started as a scullery maid. I was twenty-two when I left to marry Eric Campbell and move to America."

"Were you happy in America? Did you have a good marriage?"

"Very happy. And a genuinely loving marriage. I adored my darling Eric until the day he died, some three years ago, now. I like to think the feeling was mutual."

"It was," I said. "Anyone could see that."

"We had five children," Rose said. "Four boys and a girl, Lily's mother, Petunia. The boys all still live in Iowa where Eric and I settled; Petunia moved to New York City when she was scarcely out of school." Couldn't get out of Grand Lake, Iowa, fast enough, my mother told everyone. Most of her friends and coworkers in the city think her name is Tina, as she refuses to use the loathed name, Petunia. But flower names are the custom in my grandmother's family, and when it was my turn to be christened, Lily it was.

"If you were fourteen, then I was thirty-one," Elizabeth said. "I'd married young, as was the norm at the time. I had children young. About all I remember from those years was being so dreadfully unhappy. I did care for Edward, very much, but that wasn't enough. The war created opportunities for women, but not for the likes of me. My father distinguished himself during the war and was appointed an equerry to King George. He was ruthlessly ambitious but had no skills or talents he could take into the business world. What he did have was an extraordinarily beautiful daughter he could marry into the aristocracy. Which he did. That daughter, of course, was me."

"You were considered one of the great beauties of the age," Rose said. "You don't have to explain anything to me."

"No, I don't. But I am. Don't mistake me, Rose. My marriage to Edward was not an unhappy one. In fact, it was in most part a good one."

"I was sorry to hear about his death," Rose said. "My sister sent me the newspaper clipping."

"Thank you. It was such a blow." She turned to Bernie and me. "Edward, the tenth Earl of Frockmorton, died as the result of a fall off a horse. So sudden. That was in 1965, leaving me with limited income and four minor children. Following his death, I realized we had to do something to monetize the potential of this house, and I began work to turn it into a hotel."

"Pardon me," Bernie said, "but could you do that? I mean, obviously you could, but from what I know from watching *Downton Abbey* and the like, the dowager countess doesn't own the house or much of anything."

"The property in Downton Abbey was entailed." Elizabeth explained. "Entail was done away with in England sometime in the nineteen twenties, but the Frockmorton estate never was entailed. My husband had no siblings and only a scattering of distant cousins who left England between the wars. He left the house and the associated businesses to me, and after I'm gone, it will belong to whomever I decide to leave it to. Which will be one of my children, for them to continue as a family concern. While you're here, be sure and have a look at the castle ruins behind the house. They're owned by the National Trust now but were once part of the much larger Frockmorton estate. An easy footpath leads from the car park to the castle grounds. More tea, Bernadette?"

"Yes, please." Bernie passed her cup to me, and I passed it to Elizabeth, who graciously poured a long arc of steaming, fragrant liquid.

"As I was saying, I had a period of depression in my late

twenties, early thirties. These days, I'd be seeing a thera-
pist and getting the best help available, but back then, one
was told to buck up and get on with it. I got on with it by
spending time in the company of the young, ever-cheerful,
tough, competent kitchen maid."

"I remember," Rose said, "you did seem to spend an in-
ordinate amount of time in the kitchen. Mrs. Beans said it
wasn't proper."

"Ah, yes. Mrs. Beans. She was a drunk, but I suspect
you knew that."

"Everyone knew that. We also knew there had to be a
reason she wasn't fired."

"Sentiment only. Her mother had been cook here before
her, and her mother and Edward's father were . . . shall I
say close?"

Bernie laughed.

"Quite," Elizabeth said. "As I recall Rose, you were
promoted to cook's assistant not long after you arrived. As
the cook, the aforementioned Mrs. Beans, was unable to
prepare the children's breakfast eggs without supervision,
you were the de facto head cook at Thornecroft Castle for
several years."

I'd heard all this before, many times, over the years, but
it was nice to hear Rose's story told in someone else's
voice.

"I admired that in you," Elizabeth said. "I found you
fun to be with. I remember sitting at the big table in the
kitchen with a cup of tea, watching you roll dough for pie
or slicing vegetables for the soup."

"You often helped," Rose said.

"So I did. By then, Mrs. Beans didn't much care if everyone knew Rose was in charge. She snoozed by the fire if
she was having a bad day, or washed dishes and chopped
vegetables if it was a good day. I was most upset when you

announced you were leaving us and moving to America to marry some man you'd only just met."

"Eric Campbell," Rose said, all the love of a lifetime held in those two words.

"I was upset. Jealous, angry. Angry at you for leaving me. As though you had any responsibility to me at all. Jealous because you were going on an adventure. Leaving staid old rainy Yorkshire for the bright lights of America. Something I told myself I wanted to do, if only I had your strength and courage."

"You didn't come down to say goodbye, my last day," Rose said. "I expected you would. I wanted to tell you that I'd miss you. Mrs. Beans, who had the eyes of a hawk for anyone's weakness, told me I was a fool to believe you cared one whit about me. You wouldn't even notice I was gone."

"But I did notice. No, I didn't come down. I never could bear goodbyes. I still can't. What I did, as I watched you walk down the drive with your hat on and your suitcase in hand, heading off to catch the bus to your future, was tell myself I could either find a new life for myself, as you had, or face my responsibilities with the one I had: a kind husband, four children, a beautiful home." She smiled. "I chose the latter. Edward died only a few years later, and a future I didn't want came for me. But I managed, and I like to think I've been happy. I'm sorry I never got to meet your Eric. He must have been a lovely man."

"He was," Rose said, "in every way that truly matters."

The cat yawned and stretched and then began a tour of the room, sniffing at shoes and eyeing their owners.

"You still have Persians, I see," Rose bent over to give it a scratch under the chin.

"For many generations," Elizabeth said. "That's Lissie. We always name our cats after a famous Yorkshire resident. Her proper name is Miss Lister, after Anne Lister, the diarist."

"How are your own children, Elizabeth?" Rose asked, as Lissie jumped onto her lap.

"Put her down if she's bothering you," Elizabeth said.

"Not at all. I like cats. I remember the children well, always running through the kitchen in search of a biscuit or slice of cake. Always underfoot."

"Robert and Katherine are here for the party, along with their families. Thomas lives in Canada and is unable to make it, but his daughter, Emma, has arrived. My Amanda died a long time ago."

"I'm sorry to hear that. I've been fortunate. All five of my children are still with us."

The door opened, and a man came in. He was in his mid-seventies, tall and thin, with sunken cheeks, bulbous nose, out-of-control gray eyebrows, gray hair cut even shorter than the eyebrows, the same blue eyes as Elizabeth. He wore ironed brown slacks and a brown tweed jacket. "Sorry to bother you, Mum, ladies, but Aunt Marjorie has arrived. I thought you'd want to know."

"I do not want to know," Elizabeth said, "but I suppose I must welcome her. Marjorie is the widow of my own much younger brother, and we have never been close. Robert, this is Rose Campbell whom I told you about. Her granddaughter, Lily, and Lily's friend Bernadette. They live on Cape Cod, which I've always wanted to visit. I fear that is no longer in the cards. Ladies, my eldest son, Robert, the eleventh Earl of Frockmorton."

"Pleased to meet you," we said.

Robert nodded politely, but his vacant gaze passed over us. He'd already decided we were people not worth bothering about. "And then you should rest, Mum. It's been a busy few days and will only get busier."

Rose began to stand, and I hurried to help her. Bernie also got to her feet.

"Thank you for the tea," I said.

"I hope to see you in the bar later. Sometime after eight o'clock," Elizabeth said.

We showed ourselves out.

Chapter 3

"A real English pub," Bernie said happily. "Exactly like I've always imagined it."

"Plenty of pubs in North America," I said.

"Yeah, with fake ceiling beams and waitresses in short kilts and someone checking your reservations at the door. No one here even bothered to ask us if we've been having a nice day. There's a table over there."

"Where?"

"Behind that pillar." Bernie darted off, and I followed.

The room was packed, the noise deafening. A real coal fire burned in the small fireplace; wet coats were draped over chair backs or dangled from hooks on the walls.

Bernie shrugged out of her coat. We'd asked the hotel receptionist for a recommendation to a restaurant we could walk to, and she named the White Hart pub. We'd made it about halfway before the skies opened. "All part of the experience," Bernie said, pulling up her hood.

We settled into a table for two, tucked within the dark corner behind the pillar. I looked around me with pleasure. Thick, scarred oak beams holding up the low ceiling, heavily trod wide-plank wooden floors, whitewashed walls. The hotel receptionist told us this pub had been here since 1713. Shelves of bottles lined the wall behind the bar, and the bartenders filled large glass mugs from beer pumps arranged along the counter.

We were lucky to have snagged a table. People were lined up three deep at the bar, and a group of men stood on the far side of the room, holding glasses of beer and roaring with laugher.

"You have a look at the menu," Bernie said, "while I go to the bar for drinks. What do you want?"

"Glass of white wine, if they have it."

She left, and I studied the people in the pub, wondering if anyone was here for Lady Frockmorton's birthday. Hard to tell, as I expected a wide range of ages would be attending the celebration.

The hotel's restaurant was open for dinner tonight, but Bernie and I suggested going out for something less fancy. Rose declined to join us, saying she was tired from the days of travel and wanted a nap before the drinks party later.

I was too wired to nap, and I suspect Bernie felt the same.

I glanced toward the bar to see that my friend had fallen into conversation with a man a few years older than us. He was slightly taller than her and quite good looking, with shaggy blond hair, strong cheekbones, and carefully maintained dark stubble on his jaw. She gave him a dazzling smile and said something in return.

You're outa luck, buddy, I thought. By coincidence, Matt Goodwill, my neighbor and Bernie's boyfriend, was doing research in York. Matt is a hugely successful best-selling author of true crime. His latest book was about seniors who commit murder, and he was at the early stages of gathering information. On Monday, Bernie planned to meet Matt in York. Rose and I would travel home alone later in the week, after allowing some time for me to see the sights of Yorkshire.

It wasn't easy for me to close my business, Tea by the Sea, for two weeks. But late October is a quiet time in Cape Cod, after the main tourist season and before holiday festivities begin. Same for Victoria-on-Sea, Rose's B & B, which at the moment was just a B. We kept the house open for guests at a much-reduced rate—no breakfast provided. Edna Harkness, who helps me in the kitchen, had moved in to keep an eye on the property and attend to guests' demands while Rose was away.

As for the gardens at Victoria-on-Sea, they were barely being maintained at all, that was—

"We've been invited to a party." Bernie said, interrupting my thoughts, as she put two glasses on the table before dropping into her chair. Wine for me and a tall glass of beer for her. "At least, I've been invited to a party. I told him I was with a friend, and he said you can come, too."

"How thoughtful," I said. "I assume you said no."

"Yeah, I did." She took a sip of her beer. "This is good. What are you having for dinner?"

"I haven't even looked at the menu yet." I picked it up.

"I read the specials board behind the bar. Lamb chops should be good. Comes with mint sauce and mashed potatoes and mushy peas. What are mushy peas?"

"I've no idea. Peas that are mushed?"

"Why would anyone do that?"

"I don't know, Bernie." I closed the menu. "I'm going to have the steak pie. Also with mashed potatoes and mushy peas. Do I have to go to the bar to order food, too?"

"Yes. Other people were, anyway."

I got up and made my way through the crowded room.

People stepped aside to let me pass, and several smiled at me. I caught snatches of conversation about things I didn't understand: predictions about tomorrow's match and something unkind about a government official.

"The lamb chops, please, and a steak pie," I said.

"Table number?" the bartender asked.

"I—Sorry, I don't know." I turned and pointed. Bernie had twisted in her chair, and she waved back at me. "That one."

"American redhead. Got it, love," he said.

I returned to our table. "Be right up."

Bernie and I sipped our drinks. The group of six at the table next to us began getting to their feet. Coats and scarves were found and pulled on, good nights exchanged.

Another group descended on the table before it was completely vacated. They were two men and two women, Bernie's blond admirer among them. He gave her a grin and lifted his glass in a salute as he slipped into a chair.

"Like Tony says, closed for a week isn't exactly good business," the second man continued talking as he sat down.

"Come on, Julien, it happens once a century. We can manage," said a woman. She was a few years younger than the blond man, and the resemblance between them was strong: same color hair, same long-legged, slim frame, same facial bone structure. Siblings, I suspected.

"Bankruptcy might only happen once a century too, Susannah," Julien said. "Doesn't lessen the impact."

"We are not going bankrupt."

"The hotel's closed, but we still have guests. That means the staff are being paid. Bar closed early tonight. Restaurant, all day tomorrow. Closed to any income, that is. We're still serving but not charging."

The man doing most of the speaking was in his late forties. English accent, but not the strong tones of Yorkshire.

He wore ironed jeans and a starched white shirt under a navy blue jacket. He was freshly shaven, black hair swept back from the high forehead. Not so much handsome, I thought, as impressive. The sort of man who expected people to pay attention when he spoke. He turned to the person next to him, and I caught a glimpse of large dark blue eyes.

Bernie and I exchanged glances. She wiggled her eyebrows. I hadn't needed to see the color of the eyes, to know some of these people must be Frockmortons. Or should they be referred to as the Crawfords? I didn't know what to call people who had a whole pack of family names.

"It's rather late to be complaining, Julien," the younger woman said. "The party's organized, the guests are arriving. Many of them are already here. The food and drink have been delivered. Granny's not about to change her mind."

"I'm not arguing we cancel the party," Julien said. "As much as I'd like to."

"First time I've heard that," the blond man said, with what I assumed was intended to be sarcasm.

"Enough out of you, Tony," Julien said. "I am simply pointing out that the time has come that something be done about our grandmother's control of the estate."

Bernie and I jumped as a server put plates in front of us. My pie looked fantastic. Thick golden crust, fragrant steam emitting from the small hole cut in the center. It came with a mountain of mashed potatoes, a small bowl of dark, rich gravy, and something green and lumpy that must be the mushy peas.

Good thing the food arrived when it did, before the people at the adjoining table noticed we were listening in.

"Not much we can do as long as she's of sound mind," the young woman said.

"Our grandmother is a hundred years old, Susannah."

"Technically, that's not true. She's ninety-nine. She won't be a hundred until tomorrow."

"Never mind the people she's invited," Julien continued. "Wouldn't be so bad if the MP was coming, some ragged collection of local politicians or important businesspeople. But an upstairs maid? The gardener? A girl who worked reception and went away to Uni? Why not invite that other girl—I forget her name—the one who won all those medals in swimming or something."

"Yes, that one. Something. Granny fired her because she was an incompetent fool. The point is she's invited people who were close to her at one time and—"

"Even a kitchen maid. A former kitchen maid from when Granddad was alive! How could our grandmother have been close to a kitchen maid, I'd like to know."

Our food smelled wonderful, but Bernie and I weren't even attempting to eat it.

"And—" Julien was in full throttle now, barely able to get the words out fast enough. Red faced, spittle flying; he pounded the table. "And because the kitchen maid is almost as old as Granny, she's brought her granddaughter. Another mouth for us to feed."

"Put a sock in it, Julien," said the blond man, Tony. "I might agree with you, but this isn't the place. Or the time." He lifted his glass in a toast to Bernie.

Everyone else at his table stared at us. Bernie grinned. I blushed.

This was going to be embarrassing when they saw us at the birthday party tomorrow.

Susannah got to her feet and picked up her glass. "If all

you lot are going to do is rehash your grievances, I'm not interested."

"I'm not rehashing anything," Tony said.

"I don't have any grievances," Julien said. "I'm pointing out the practicalities, or rather the lack of practicalities around this party, is all."

"Granny's still alive," the second woman said, "for the foreseeable future anyway. When she isn't, which I hope isn't for many years to come, the business, which is the estate and hotel, will go to our parents to run as they see fit." I detected traces of a Canadian accent when she spoke, and remembered Elizabeth telling us her younger son lived in Canada. This must be his daughter, Emma. These, clearly, were Elizabeth's grandchildren. Cousins and siblings to one another.

"Won't that be a mess," Susannah said, "Our parents can't agree on the time of day, never mind how to run the company. You know that, Emma, we all do."

"We don't know that," Julien said. "Let me remind you my father is the current earl, and according to tradition, if no longer law, he is the rightful heir and—"

"I'll thank you not to use that tone of voice with my sister," Tony said. The bantering manner was gone. His words were sharp, his eyes narrow with anger. "You don't have to remind us you're the heir to the earldom, Julien. You never let us forget it."

"It's okay, Tony," Susannah said. "We all care about the future of the family."

"Tradition's important," Emma said. "Our family has a proud and important heritage to uphold."

"Our grandmother owns a hotel and a sheep farm," Susannah said. "These days people pay to sleep in what was once the earl and countess's bedroom."

Emma threw a poisonous look at Susannah. She was a

year or two younger than Julien, about ten years older than Tony and Susannah. Elizabeth was obviously the mutual grandmother they were discussing, unless another dowager countess was having a hundredth birthday tomorrow. Emma was shorter and chubbier than the others in her family, with round pink cheeks, brown eyes, hair an unnatural shade of black, cut in a sharp line at her chin, and heavy bangs that fell below the level of her eyebrows. She peered at the world through a veil of hair.

Julien's phone was sitting on the table. It buzzed with an incoming text, and he read it. "Carmela. Traffic tie-up getting past Sheffield, so she's going to be delayed."

Tony's head snapped up. "What? Carmela? I thought—"

"Carmela's coming?" Susannah laughed. "Surely you're not planning on continuing with that pretext?"

"I have no idea what you're talking about," Julien snapped. "Of course, my wife's coming to my grandmother's party. We didn't travel together as she had work."

"Right. Got it," Susannah said.

"As for the topic at hand," Emma said. "I'm saying it's not our concern. By the time we inherit, if we do, there might not be anything left other than the title. Which I consider to be worth something, even if you don't." She glared at Susannah. "Even if there is anything of value, once it's divided between the pack of us, we might have enough to have a nice dinner out. No place too expensive, mind you."

"That is precisely my point, and thank you for making it, Emma," Julien said. "If the company is going to survive, if our legacy is going to survive, we need to do the hard work now."

"Your legacy," Tony said. "You're the one in line to the title, Julien, not the rest of us. Susannah and I are nothing but the offspring of a lowly daughter and Emma of a second son. As for me, I'll keep on doing what I'm doing, and that means running the hotel to the best of my abilities. For the benefit of us all."

"The title's not worth anything without—"

"Hey, guys. Great to see you." A couple, beers in hand, had stopped at the table next to us. Handshakes and hugs were exchanged.

"The gang's all here," Tony said.

"Looks like it," one of the new arrivals replied. "Going to be a great party."

"Not if Julien has anything to say about it," Susannah said. "That table's coming free. I'll join you. The conversation here's getting mighty boring."

They moved off.

Emma swallowed the last of her wine. "I need to get back. I said I'd do my bit by keeping an eye on the drinks party tonight."

"I'll come with you," Tony said. "I need to check in with the bar staff."

They left Julien sitting alone, not looking at all happy. He left half his beer unfinished and followed his cousins out the door.

"That was interesting." Bernie cut a slice of meat off her lamb chops and slathered it with mint sauce. "Nothing like overhearing people arguing and you know you have absolutely nothing to do with it. All fodder for the writer's pen. Or keyboard, I suppose I should say." She chewed happily. "This is great. How's the pie?"

"As good as it looks," I said.

"I'm thinking of taking Rose, my Rose, and Tessa back to England, what do you think?"

"I think that's an appallingly bad idea, Bernie." Rose, named for my grandmother, and Tessa were the main characters in the book Bernie was writing. Or, I should say, attempting to write. It was a historical mystery, set in New England in the nineteenth century, with Rose as the strong willed, independent-minded daughter of a rich and prominent Boston family, and Tessa the rough-and-tumble Irish immigrant. Bernie was a skilled writer, and the book had, I thought, enormous potential. Except for the fact that she kept dashing off in all directions, plot-wise. She'd changed the time frame and the location more than once.

"Think of the atmosphere it would add," she said. "Crowded pubs, fireplaces, grizzled barmen pulling pints. Lamb on the menu."

"They can do that in America, too, although maybe not with so much lamb. Remember the outline you showed me? It said nothing about an impromptu dash across the ocean. Remember how you promised to stick to said outline?"

Bernie dug her fork into her mountain of mashed potatoes. "An author must go where the muse leads."

"An author must remember that for a book to be published and enjoyed by the reading public, it needs to be finished."

She didn't look entirely convinced as she tasted the potatoes. "Wow. Good. I thought the English were supposed to be terrible cooks."

"A rumor spread by the French, or so I've been told. I'd like to get the recipe for this pastry. If I have to expand the menu over the winter, a hearty meat pie like this one might fit in well."

"Back to more important matters than the petty squabbles of our hostess's family. Or even meat pies. What did Simon have to say when you spoke to him earlier?"

I felt a sudden warm glow in my chest. "I'd love to invite him to the birthday party, but seeing as how not only am I just Rose's companion but I've brought you, I thought inviting yet another person might be stretching Elizabeth's hospitality to excess. I'm going to Garfield Hall the day after tomorrow. He's going to show me around, and we're going to have a couple of days together."

"Nice," she said.

According to Trip Advisor, Victoria-on-Sea is the number-one garden attraction in North Augusta, Massachusetts. There is no number two, but the gardens are truly wonderful and perfectly located next to the bluffs looking over Cape Cod Bay. Simon McCracken worked for us the past summer. His uncle had been the longtime gardener, but when he abruptly quit not long after I arrived to open my tearoom and help Rose run the B & B she'd bought on a foolish whim (in the opinion of everyone in my family), Simon took over. He dug weeds and trimmed roses; I baked. And gradually, slowly, we came together. But then the season ended, along with his contract, and he returned to England to take a winter job at a stately manor house, coincidentally located not too far from Halifax. Although we'd begun a tentative, not too terribly serious (yet) romance over the summer, we made no promises to each other. I was more excited than I was letting on at the idea of seeing him again and enjoying a few days in each other's company. After those few days? Perhaps I'd reassess my feelings.

"Is Rose going to be joining you for those couple of days?" Bernie asked.

I grinned. "Absolutely not. Rose is staying at Thornecroft. What did you think of Elizabeth, Lady Frockmorton? I liked her a lot. She's very much like Rose, don't you think?"

"Yeah, I—" Bernie put a forkful of mushy peas into her mouth. Her eyes opened wide, her face twisted, her mouth puckered. She looked frantically around her searching for someplace, anyplace to spit the mouthful. Instead, she scrunched up her eyes and nose, gathered all her courage, and swallowed. The table almost shook under the force of her shudder as the peas went down.

She grabbed her beer and took a long glug. When she could speak again, she said, "If you add lamb or steak pie to your menu, I suggest you don't include mushy peas. Now I know why the English have a reputation as bad cooks."

Chapter 4

Bernie and I got back to Thornecroft Castle, bedraggled and soaking wet, just in time to get ready for the reception in the hotel bar. We dried our hair, tidied ourselves up, dressed in our party finery, and then we collected my grandmother.

She looked resplendent in full makeup (even more in the evening than the daytime) and a calf-length pink dress covered in silver sequins. She'd styled her short gray hair into spikes and accented the look with a jaunty pink feather attached by a clip to the hair.

"You look . . . amazing," Bernie said.

"Not too much, I hope. I wouldn't want to overshadow the birthday girl."

"I suspect Lady Frockmorton can hold her own," I said.

Rose twirled her cane in reply, and we made our way to the party. People were coming in through the main doors, depositing umbrellas and shaking off rainwater. Most of the guests were in their forties or older, but a few younger people were with them, including some children. Almost everyone was beautifully dressed. Men in suits and ties, or collared shirts under blazers, women in pantsuits or dresses. The children were scrubbed and brushed and tidied.

"Are any of the other servants from your time going to be here, Rose?" Bernie asked.

"Not that I'm aware of. I was one of the youngest then, and—well, time moves on, doesn't it, dear? I asked after my friend Hazel, and Elizabeth told me she moved to London not long after I left."

A small sitting room was tucked away next to the lobby. The paint on the walls was a deep red, the couch upholstered in pink and gold, with matching wingback chairs on either side. The large low table, scratched and marked by decades, centuries perhaps, of use, was covered in local magazines and tourist brochures. A big bouquet of pink roses sat on a side table.

A painting dominated the back wall, a life-sized portrait of a woman standing. She was tall and exceptionally beautiful, with perfect pale skin, full pink lips, huge eyes, and thick black hair piled on her head. She was dressed in a floor-length blue velvet dress, the deeply cut neckline and off-the-shoulder gown designed to show off a necklace and earrings of diamonds and sapphires. Her proud chin was lifted, and her intense blue eyes stared out of the frame at the viewer. "Elizabeth, Lady Frockmorton," Rose said. "As she was when I knew her."

"You said she was a great beauty," Bernie said. "You were not kidding."

"Indeed, I was not."

"Are the rest of the paintings of family members?" I asked. Portraits, some of them stretching back centuries, filled the lobby walls and the hallway to the restaurant and bar.

"I recognize some of them from when I worked here, so likely."

"Old paintings like that should be worth a lot," Bernie said.

"Not necessarily. Not if the subject wasn't a historical figure and the artist is unknown and forgotten."

We followed the crowd down the two steps and turned right, going past a series of small dining rooms into the bar. The room was long and narrow, with deep-set windows and wood-paneled walls, full of small round tables. About fifty people were laughing and chatting and sipping from hefty beer glasses, long stemmed wine glasses, or crystal tumblers. Smiling waitstaff slipped through the crowd delivering drinks. The bar itself was at the far end of the room, behind a solid wooden counter. Wine glasses hung from racks suspended from the ceiling, and the back wall was filled with shelves of bottles, glass panes behind them reflecting the sparkling glass and the lights from the room.

"Oh, my goodness," Bernie said with glee. "An entire wall of gin. Bring it on."

A man approached us as we entered. "Welcome. I'm Julien Crawford, Viscount Darnby, Elizabeth's eldest grandchild."

We knew that—Julien had been at the table next to us at the pub earlier, complaining at great length about the cost of the party. And about Rose being invited. He didn't show any signs of recognizing Bernie and me. Julien must have been intent on making his point to his cousins. Bernie doesn't often go unnoticed.

"Lily Roberts," I said, "And this is—"

"Mrs. Campbell, formerly Miss Walker. My grandmother speaks very fondly of you." Julien took one of Rose's hands in his and lifted it to his lips. The slightest of touches and then he released it. Rose beamed. "Such a pleasure," Julien said. "Granny's thrilled that you came."

Bernie and I exchanged a wiggle of the eyebrows. Nice of him not to tell Rose to get back to the kitchen where she belongs.

"You're the son of?" Rose asked.

"Robert, Granny's eldest, and the current earl. Dad's around here somewhere."

Rose smiled. "Robert. Robbie we called him. Always in the kitchen begging for scraps of unbaked biscuit dough, or the first slice of cake straight from the oven."

"Still sounds like my dad," Julien said. "That's him over there." He pointed to the man we'd met earlier in the drawing room, standing in a circle of men about the same age, all of them dressed in dark suits and ties, holding crystal glasses full of dark liquid. "May I help you to a chair, Mrs. Campbell? My cousin's boy has got the manners of a sewer rat. I'll give him the boot."

"Thank you," Rose said. "Your grandmother not down yet?"

"My grandmother," Julien said, "loves to make an entrance." He waved at an older woman, nicely dressed in a designer suit with pearls. "Allow me to introduce you to my mother, Annabelle, Countess of Frockmorton. Mother, this is Mrs. Campbell, the American lady Granny told us she was inviting."

"How nice to meet you," Annabelle said. She didn't add "—not," but her tone indicated she might as well have. "Thank you for coming." Her gaze passed over us and she wandered off.

"I'll get you a drink, Rose," I said. "What would you like?" As if I needed to ask. My grandmother enjoyed a gin and tonic every evening before dinner. In cases of emergency, such as a murder on the grounds and the subsequent police investigation, she'd have a G&T before *and* after dinner.

"A G&T, love. A local gin would be nice."

Bernie and I joined the line at the bar. A man and a woman were pouring wine and beer and mixing cocktails. A couple of young women slipped through the crowd with laden trays, and Irene, the waitress who'd served our tea earlier, came out from the back, bearing a tray of clean glassware.

I've worked in restaurants and bakeries all my adult life, but never in a bar. The principle is the same, however, and I always enjoy watching a well-oiled operation at work. All around us Yorkshire and London accents flowed along with laughter and the tinkle of glasses.

"Well, this is embarrassing," a man said to us. "If you overheard my sister and my cousins and I squabbling earlier, I hope you've forgotten all about it."

Bernie put her hand behind her ear. "Sorry, Tony, what was that? I have trouble hearing sometimes."

He gave her a big grin. "Not so much trouble that you didn't pick up my name. Which I never gave to you. Anyway, hi. I'm Tony, son of Katherine, Elizabeth's youngest child. Plain old Anthony Waterfield, meaning I am not in line for the earldom, which I don't want in any event."

Bernie introduced herself and me, and she told Tony why we were here.

When it was our turn to be served, Bernie asked for a gin and tonic, and I requested a Negroni and a G&T. "Made with local gin, please, if you have it."

"I assume the second gin is for your grandmother," Tony said. "Jack, see the elderly lady sitting next to Mr. Lancaster gets it."

The bartender nodded as he reached for the shelf behind him.

"Can I take a guess you're more than a guest or ordinary family member at this party?" I asked Tony. "I own my own restaurant, and I've worked in food service all my working life. The way you're watching everything tells me you're supervising."

He chuckled. "I'm the hotel general manager. Paid position. As in the upper classes of old, my destiny was decided for me when I was barely out of short pants, and I was bundled off to uni to get a business degree, and then into hotel management, despite my protestations that I wanted to be a rock star. But I'm not complaining. I like the work. I'm a proud Yorkshireman, and it's a pleasure to work for and with my grandmother and care for this great piece of history. I not only manage this place, I love it on a deeply personal level. However . . ." A cloud passed over his eyes as he looked toward the entrance where Julien was greeting arrivals. Whoever was coming in now was obviously far more important than us. His mother, Annabelle, full of smiles, had joined him.

"However?" Bernie prompted.

"Nothing." Tony turned his attention back to us. "My grandmother owns Thornecroft Castle in her own right. She consults with the family on major decisions and then does what she wanted to do in the first place. I can't help wondering what's going to change when she—is less involved."

"Is this hotel the entirety of the estate?" Bernie asked.

"Not at all. We have some rental properties around the area, including the dowager house next door. You would have passed it on the way in. We still own a substantial amount of farmland around here, which we rent out. Nothing like it was in the glory days of the family, but enough to get by. Your grandmother looks comfortable, so why don't I introduce our honored American visitors to the motley crew that is my extended family."

We gathered our drinks and followed Tony to a crowded corner. Susannah took one look at us and said, "Oops."

"Oops, what?" Emma asked.

"Nothing."

"My cousin Emma Crawford, and my sister, Susannah Reilly." Tony introduced us.

"Anything you might have overheard at the pub earlier was us rehearsing for a play," Susannah said. "Right, Tony?" He ruffled her blond hair, the identical shade of his, and she smiled at him. The affection between brother and sister was obvious.

A scattering of applause began at the entrance to the bar, building as it traveled through the room. I turned to see Elizabeth entering on the arm of her son, Robert.

"Oh my gosh," Susannah said, "are those—?"

"Wow," Emma said.

Elizabeth, Dowager Countess of Frockmorton, was stunningly regal in a long-sleeved, low-necked, blue satin gown, falling in a sleek river down her thin frame, almost to the floor. She wore a heavy necklace of alternating sapphires and diamonds, which looked to be the same as the one in the portrait hanging in the sitting room. The chain touched the bottom of her throat; each individual blue stone must have been about a half-inch square and the diamonds were huge. Matching earrings of diamonds and sapphires cascaded almost to her thin collarbones.

I know absolutely nothing about jewels, but I had no doubt these were genuine. The brilliance of the light they threw off seemed to come from inside them, rather than being mere reflections from the lamps. More than a few people were openly staring at them, while trying not to be obvious about it.

"Nice necklace." Bernie sipped her drink. "Good gin, this."

"The Frockmorton Sapphires," Susannah said. "I've never even seen them. She never takes them out anymore."

"She hasn't worn them since our grandfather died,"

Emma said. "No reason to, I guess. No more balls at the great houses, no more receptions at court. Just hard work to keep the estate and the house from being sold off."

"Tony and Susannah are Katherine's children. Julien's parents are Robert and Annabelle. I didn't catch where you fit into the family tree," I said, wanting to be polite.

"My dad's Thomas, the second son. He'd be called The Honorable, as befits the second son of an earl, if he used his title, which he doesn't. My parents are divorced, and he lives in Canada."

"Canada. I noticed traces of an accent."

"I went to school in Toronto for a while, and I still pop back and forth across the pond regularly, visiting my dad. He broke a leg last week, playing tennis, so he didn't make it."

Robert and Annabelle escorted the birthday girl into the room, as people stepped aside to let them pass. A girl about seven years old, all party dress, bright bows, and shining blond ponytail, was sitting at Rose's table, while an almost identical girl ran around the room talking to everyone. The first girl leapt to her feet as Elizabeth approached and the woman took her place. Robert headed for the bar, and Annabelle hovered near her mother-in-law's table.

Elizabeth smiled at Rose, and Rose returned the smile. The two old women exchanged greetings, and then party guests moved in to chat with the guest-of-honor.

"Oh my gosh," Emma said. "Look at the expression on Aunt Annabelle's face. At last, the sapphires are so close she can almost taste them."

I followed her gaze. Robert's wife was openly staring at Elizabeth's necklace. And yes, the expression on her face might be described as greedy. I assumed the jewels would go to her, as the countess, after Elizabeth's death.

"That's quite the trinket your grandmother has," Bernie said. "Are those stones real?"

"Oh, yes. They're rather famous. The Frockmorton Sapphires," Tony said. "The stones were gifted to the wife of the fourth earl, so rumor says, by her young lover on his return from the Far East, where he stole them from who-knows-who."

"Is that true?" Bernie asked.

"Who knows what's true and what isn't true?" Susannah said. "Myth, legend, fact, it all becomes a blur as time passes. All the great jewels were stolen from someone at some point. You can be sure the fourth Earl of Frockmorton didn't dig them out of the ground with his bare hands. Or even a shovel."

"The story says the earl threatened to kill his wife's lover. Or have him killed, which is more my family's style," Tony said. "To save himself, the young lover handed over the jewels to the earl, who made use of them to improve his family's status. It was the seventh earl, I believe, who obtained the diamonds and had the necklace and earrings made into what they are today."

"I hope you'll pay no attention to my cousins." Julien joined us. "They love nothing more than to gossip about the family."

"I love hearing the stories," Bernie said. "My father's family came over from Ireland sometime in the early twentieth century. We have no exciting stories. No famous jewels, either—far as I know. I'm Bernadette Murphy, by the way, of the Lower East Side Murphys."

Not entirely sure if he was being mocked, Julien said, "Pleased to meet you. Is this your first visit to Halifax?"

"First visit to Britain," Bernie said. "After that drive we went through to get here, and then those mushy peas for dinner, I don't know if I'll be back."

Julien blinked. His cousins snickered. Bernie gave him a

wink and a huge grin. She lifted her glass. "Gin is worth the trip, though."

"I hope you enjoy your stay." He moved on.

"What time are Ray and the kids arriving tomorrow, Susannah?" Emma asked.

"The kids aren't coming. We decided we'd enjoy a nice little vacation without them, and Ray's parents were pleased to have them. He'll be on the early train from King's Cross, getting in mid-morning.

"We live in London," Susannah explained to me, "I came up a few days early to help Granny get ready for the party. My husband didn't want to take the time off work, and we didn't want to take the children out of school at any rate."

"Not that Granny needs any help getting ready for the party," Susannah said. "Tony is completely in control. As always."

"An extra pair of hands never hurts," Emma said.

Tony changed the subject smoothly. "What time's Nigel getting in, Emma?"

Emma's eyes darkened. It would seem, I thought, Tony had unwittingly landed on another unwelcome topic. "I do not know what Nigel is doing, and I do not care. As long as he's not coming here. He's out of the picture."

"Again?" Susannah said.

"Permanently," Emma snapped.

"Again?" Susannah said.

Emma turned on her cousin, but before she could reply, one of the little girls ran up to us, blue eyes sparkling, squealing with excitement. "Uncle Tony, can I have another glass of orange juice?"

"You can if you say 'please' and 'thank you' to Jack," he said.

The girl bounced up and down as she tried to peer over the rim of the bar counter. "Please and thank you, Jack."

"Twins?" I asked.

"Zoe and Katy," Tony said. "That one's Zoe."

"No," Emma said, "it's Katy."

"Are you sure?"

"Not entirely," she admitted.

"They're my cousin Jacqueline's girls," Tony told me. "Jacqueline's Robert and Annabelle's daughter, Julien's sister." He indicated a woman in her mid-forties chatting with guests at the far side of the room, with the fine fair hair and tall thin frame of the Frockmorton (or was that Crawford?) family. "The twins are a total handful, and the only thing that keeps their parents from disciplining them is they're so darn cute. Speaking of being in control, I'm going to do the rounds. Bernie, Lily, I hope to get a chance to talk to you more later." He smiled at me, but his eyes lingered on Bernie.

Emma and Susannah moved away also.

"You need to disabuse Tony of any notion you're available," I said to my friend, once we were alone.

Her green eyes twinkled. "Why would I do that?" The low lights of the bar and the flickering of the electric candles suited her dramatic coloring perfectly.

"Because he obviously likes you, and you're meeting Matt on Monday."

"A little harmless flirtation never hurt anyone, Lily. You should try it sometime. But I take your point. Fear not. If he's the manager of this hotel, he'll be busy all weekend, anyway. Change of subject, I sense some low-level tension in this family. The cousins bicker, and what Emma said about her uncle's wife was downright nasty. No one took her to task for it, I noticed."

"Families," I said. "You should hear my mother when she talks about her brothers."

"As I have. Many times. They all seem fond of their

grandmother, though. Which is nice. Speaking of which, Rose seems to be enjoying herself."

My grandmother looked relaxed and comfortable in the chair next to Elizabeth. As people approached Elizabeth to exchange greetings or offer their congratulations, she introduced them to Rose. A waiter bent over her to ask if she wanted another drink, and she shook her head.

"It's nice of Elizabeth to make her so welcome," I said. "After all these years, never mind the disparity of their positions at the time Rose lived here."

"Might be a matter of two old ladies, the last of their kind, seeking comfort in each other." Many of the guests may have been in their late seventies, but Elizabeth and Rose were by far the eldest present.

"There's an old guy now," Bernie said.

Two men had come into the room. They stood together, looking as though they didn't know anyone and weren't sure of what to do now. The older one was approaching his nineties, if not already there. His hair was still thick, his eyebrows, equally so. His face was a network of deep lines, and the permanent tan indicated a man who'd spent his lifetime outside or outdoors. Even in England. The topmost joint on the first two fingers of his left hand were missing. He gripped a cane in his right hand and leaned heavily against it. His back was bent, and his thin legs quivered under the strain of standing. His suit was about forty years out of date, and I could almost smell the mothballs from here. His white shirt, however, was so new it had fold marks from the packaging. The younger man accompanying him kept a strong hand on his arm.

One of the waiters waved to the new arrivals as he passed, and the younger man laughed.

They made their way across the room to Elizabeth. She clapped her hands in delight when she saw them coming, her smile broad and welcoming. A woman at their table leapt to her feet, and the younger man helped the older one sit. Elizabeth gestured to Rose and the old man grinned a mouthful of stained and broken teeth. He reached out his gnarled and damaged hand to pat my grandmother's knee. Rose roared with laughter.

All around them, people were smiling as they watched.

Children and the extreme elderly. We do like seeing them happy.

The young man went to the bar and ordered two pints. He saw us watching him and gave us a nod, and then he carried one of the drinks over to us. "Mrs. Campbell's granddaughters, I presume. Come from America for the festivities."

"I'm the granddaughter," I said. "This is just my friend."

"Just a friend," Bernie snorted. "I hope I'm far more than that. I'm sort of an honorary granddaughter to Rose. I'm Bernie, and this is Lily."

"Josh Hansen. My granddad, Reggie, was a stable hand when your grandmother worked here. He doesn't remember a lot of things these days, but he remembered her well enough. He says she's the one who got away. He was working up his nerve to suggest they step out sometime when she announced she was leaving Thornecroft and going to marry an American she'd just met. Broke his heart, she did."

Josh's eyes twinkled as he told the tale. He was a lightly built man in his mid- to late forties. Short dark hair and olive skin. Not particularly handsome but with huge brown eyes and a warm smile. "Not that he ever said that in my *nona*'s hearing. She was Italian, and she could wield a frying pan to great effect." The smile faded. "I miss her every day. Your grandfather?"

"Also gone," I said. "Just a couple of years ago. They

had five children, and I've got more cousins than I can count."

"Do they still have stables here?" Bernie asked.

"Do you like to ride?" he responded.

She visibly shuddered. "I'm from Manhattan. The carousel at Central Park is more than enough danger for me."

"Nothing like it once was, back in my granddad's day, but they keep a couple of horses Elizabeth is too sentimental to part with. I'm not full-time on staff—no one is anymore—but I help out now and again. I'm a farrier."

"A blacksmith," I said, delighted. "I've never met a blacksmith before."

"Not a lot of call for farriers in Manhattan," Bernie said.

"Now you've met one. Enjoy the party." He crossed the room to talk to some of the other guests.

Bernie and I stood together, sipping our drinks and watching people. The room was full, the mood friendly and upbeat. Besides the twins, a few other small children escaped parental supervision and ran around, dodging legs and ignoring warnings to behave themselves. Several people came in from the terrace and they were not wet, so I assumed the rain had let up for now.

"We should be friendly," Bernie said at last.

"Must we?"

"Yes, we must." She left me standing alone and went to the bar to ask for a fresh drink. I shook the melting ice in my own glass. I was supposedly here to assist Rose, but she clearly didn't need any assistance. At the moment she was laughing uproariously at something Reggie said, while Elizabeth looked on, smiling.

I'd had my doubts about coming on this trip. About closing the tearoom and leaving the B & B underutilized. Traveling across the ocean to a place I'd never been, in the company of an elderly woman, to visit people I didn't know and had nothing in common with. But now, I was glad I did.

The only thing that would make this evening better was if Simon was here with me. But I'd be seeing him soon. Yet about that I was also unsure. A long-distance relationship is difficult to maintain, even if it had only been a few weeks since he left. I found myself parsing every word and sentence in his phone calls and texts, looking for clues as to whether or not he'd moved on and was afraid to tell me. I hadn't confided my worries to Bernie. She, always the optimist, would tell me I was looking for problems where none existed. I watched Bernie join a circle of chatting guests and comfortably introduce herself.

"Get you another, love?" Jack, the bartender, asked me.

I passed him my glass of watery ice and a lone orange rind. "Thanks. Negroni, please." While he made my drink, I asked, "Have you worked here long?" He was in his early fifties, and he handled the bottles of liquor and mix with practice and skill. "Thirty years," he said. "Started out in the kitchen washing dishes and chopping vegetables, and one day Elizabeth suggested I think about going to bartending school. I hadn't so much as thought of doing that, but it turned out to be the best move I could have made."

"The staff here seem very fond of Elizabeth."

"We love her," he said simply. "Tough but fair. Always tough, driving us to do our best, and always fair when she knows we are. Course, she's less hands-on these days, and young Tony handles most of it." He passed me my drink and looked over my shoulder. "I'm glad I've put in my years. Things are going to change soon. And it won't be for the better, I can guarantee that."

"What do you mean?"

"Never mind me, love. You enjoy yourself. The rain

stopped, and we've mopped up out on the terrace and dried off the chairs. If you're wanting some air, it's nice out there of an evening."

"I'll have a look." Unlike Bernie, I'm never comfortable meeting new people. So many faces here I didn't know and would likely never see again after tomorrow. I stood alone, clutching my drink, feeling quite uncomfortable. I headed for the table where Elizabeth was holding court, with Rose and Reggie as her courtiers. I slipped up behind my grand-mother's chair and leaned over to whisper, "You okay here? Can I get you anything? Do you need the restroom? Are you ready to leave?"

"I'm perfectly fine, love," she said. "Haven't had such a good time in ages. Reg, this is my granddaughter, Lily."

"What?" the old man bellowed.

"My granddaughter, Lily," Rose bellowed back.

"Your daughter? Pretty girl. Looks just like you, Rose. Did I tell you I live in town now? Nice enough place but no room for the horses."

Rose smiled at me, and I left them. I wanted to call Simon, just to say hi. I'd texted him earlier to say we'd ar-rived and sent a selfie of the three of us grinning broadly at the entrance to the house, but I wanted to hear his voice. I crossed the room in the direction the bartender had indi-cated, pushed open the door, and stepped out. It was cool, and I was glad I had a jacket, but the air was as fresh as it always is at night after a rain, when you're far from the city. Fairy lights glimmered from the tops of the trees, and low lighting illuminated the footpaths. The ground was covered in flagstones, moss pushing beneath the cracks. The wall, lined with trimmed bushes, was made of old, weather-worn, darkened stone. A handful of people were sitting around small wrought-iron tables, wrapped against the cold, some of them smoking. Electric candles glowed from the center of each table. I walked to the end of the wall and peeked around a corner. Another terrace over-looked a sunken garden, formally laid out in a hip-high maze. A young couple stood in the center of the maze, arms around each other, staring into the eyes of their beloved. I stepped back. I wouldn't explore the grounds tonight, but if I got up bright and early, I should have time before reporting to the kitchen for duty.

"How much longer do you think she's going to last? She's a hundred years old for heaven's sake." The voice was a woman's, the accent less pronounced than that of most of the people I'd met in Yorkshire, coming from the other side of the wall.

"She'll last as long as she wants. To spite us all. I wouldn't put it past her." A man. Julien by the sounds of it. "We need to go to the courts."

I stayed where I was, frozen in place. Clearly, this was meant to be a private conversation, and clearly, I'd already heard more than I should.

"The courts will throw you out, with costs, along with any reputation we might still have as a united family, not to mention as a trustworthy company to do business with. She's obviously in full possession of her faculties."

"That can be . . . altered."

"Perhaps. By someone who serves her dinner and pours her wine, or who takes care of her medications and gives her a glass of water to take to bed at night. Not you. Not me. If you start fussing around, wanting to fluff her pil-lows, she'll be on her guard instantly."

"People can be paid to help with that sort of thing."

"Julien, don't you even think of going there. Granny's staff are amazingly loyal to her. They'll betray you in a heartbeat. Betray Father, too. Mother, most of all."

"Don't get your knickers in a knot, Jacqueline. I'm just throwing out some ideas," he said.

"Well, stop it," she replied.

I pushed myself further into the damp cold wall. Julien must be talking to his sister. She called his parents "Father" and "Mother." Not your father or your mother. Tony told me Jacqueline was the name of the mother of the twin girls. This must be her.

"All we can do is bide our time," she said. "No one lives forever, Julien, and then you and Father can do with the place as you like. And Mother will finally achieve her heart's dream: the right to wear the Frockmorton Sapphires. Now, I'm freezing out here, and I saw a bottle of Prosecco behind the bar with my name on it."

I heard the sound of her heels tapping on the stones, gradually fading.

A lit cigarette butt landed on the ground at my feet. I stared at it and was about to pretend I'd only just come from the garden maze, but Julien muttered a curse and also headed inside. The cigarette lay in a puddle, fizzled once, and went out.

Chapter 5

Over Bernie's protests, I set my alarm for seven a.m.

When it went off, I considered that might have been a mistake. With the time difference between Cape Cod and Halifax, my body thought it was the wee hours and wanted several more hours of blessed sleep. Never mind that the drinks party had gone on until late, and Rose was having such a wonderful time, I stayed even as my eyelids drooped, attempting to smother a series of ever larger yawns.

Bernie had also been having a great time, and once I started mixing I did, too. The other guests were an interesting combination of extended family, neighbors, people who'd grown up with Elizabeth's children or grandchildren, and former Thornecroft Castle staff. Rose particularly enjoyed regaling the kitchen helpers who'd followed her with stories of how things had been done "in my day."

"You put nuts into the Christmas cakes? Without checking if the guests were allergic?" a woman in her fifties said in horror.

"Never killed anyone," Rose said. "Far as I know."

"There was that man who choked on a chicken bone," another woman said. "Do you remember that, Elizabeth?"

"Oh, yes. That happened not long before Edward died, after your time I believe, Rose. We had the vicar and some of the local dignitaries to dinner. The man dropped dead on the spot. I believe it was his heart; he just happened to be eating chicken while arguing about the miner's union. And getting most agitated about it."

I hadn't been subject to any more of the family's bickering or heard anyone else plotting to take control from Elizabeth.

I remembered why I'd set the alarm, and I reluctantly threw off the bed covers. "Are you awake?" A line of light leaked under the door to the corridor, otherwise all was dark.

"No," Bernie replied.

"Fine. I'm going to shower and then head out to explore. Breakfast is at nine, and I said I'd be in the kitchen at ten."

"You're actually going to work?"

"I'm looking forward to seeing how they do things here." Out of curiosity, before we came on this trip, I checked the web site of Thornecroft Castle House and Hotel. Afternoon tea was a regular feature of the restaurant menu. At the eye-watering prices they charged, I expected they'd do an impressive job of it.

"I suppose I can sleep when we get home," Bernie mumbled. "You can switch on the light. Wake me up when you're out of the shower, and I'll come with you."

The night before, several people had told us the ruins of the castle, after which the house had been named, was a must-see. It was now owned and run by the National Trust, but the family and their guests were welcome to explore before opening hours.

While Bernie showered, I threw on jeans and a heavy sweater under a puffy vest. The sun was beginning to rise when we slipped out of our room. I told the young woman at the reception desk we'd been told we could see the castle, and she gave us directions. "It opens to the public at ten, but if anyone's there early, tell them you're guests of Lady Frockmorton and they won't charge you."

"Big day," Bernie said to the receptionist.

"It is. We do a lot of special events here—weddings, anniversary parties, and the like. But for Lady Frockmorton, we're going all out." She was young, so I didn't ask how long she'd been working here, but just thanked her for the directions.

Bernie and I stepped outside into a cool breeze and a slowly rising sun. The sky was clear, which boded well for the birthday party this afternoon. When we arrived yesterday, we'd been preoccupied with getting our things, and ourselves, inside and out of the rain, so I hadn't taken much time to admire the house. I did so now.

The main part of the building was three stories tall, with shorter wings stretching out on either side. Golden-brown brick, blackening with age, glowed in the sunshine. Small, deeply set mullioned windows, a steeply pitched slate roof dotted with clumps of moss, numerous chimney pots, low doorways. Shrubs were planted beneath the windows, vines climbed to the roof, and tubs of red flowers, still lush despite the dropping temperatures, lined the walkway from the parking lot to the house. Hanging baskets graced some of the smaller doorways. The newer part of the house, where our rooms were, stretched out from the back of the original building, not visible from the front.

"Matt says hi," Bernie said as we set out, heading for the footpath I'd been directed to. "I called him when you were in the shower."

"How's his book going?"

"Slowly, he says. The retired cop he went to York to meet with is being more evasive than he'd like. Matt's not paying for info, but he's beginning to suspect his source is expecting to be paid in pub lunches."

Last night, I'd taken a break from the party to escape to the quiet of my room and phoned Simon. I'd been more than pleased at the warmth in his voice when he answered.

Bernie and I walked about halfway down the driveway, in the direction of the main road. On the other side of the driveway lay a house, barn, and barnyard. The house was even older than Thornecroft, all blackened brick, narrow windows, chimney pots, climbing vines. A satellite dish mounted on the roof and plastic garbage bins by the door interfered with the feeling of stepping back in time. The barn might have been even older. Same dark brick, slate roof. No one was around, not even any animals in the churned-up, fenced yard.

As instructed, we cut off the driveway down a rough footpath, still muddy from yesterday's rain. Low drystone walls separated the path from the fields, and we hadn't gone more than a few yards when we heard the baa of sheep and saw several of the animals grazing on the lush green grass.

"They do have rather a lot of sheep here, don't they?" Bernie said. "They're everywhere. It's like if we let a herd of cows munch Simon's plants in front of the B and B."

We kept the stone wall to our right and a patch of bushes to our left, and in no more than a few minutes, we emerged into an expansive clearing, and Thornecroft Castle itself lay before us.

"Wow," Bernie said.

"Wow, indeed," I said.

The castle was now nothing but ruins. Lines of moss-covered stone, not much more than a foot high, marked where the walls had once stood. The entrance was across a grassy causeway over the wide depression circling the castle grounds. Likely it had once been the moat.

The view itself was worth the trip. The rising sun, green fields surrounded by stone walls or ancient trees, yet more grazing sheep. To the west, red-roofed houses and a church steeple.

From where we stood, we could see a small modern building, with wide windows, likely the ticket office and souvenir shop. One car was parked in front, and the gate over the moat was unlocked.

We walked across the causeway. The area surrounded by the moat was about four acres in size, crisscrossed by stone walls ranging from inches to waist high, with the occasional crumbling steps. The grass was trimmed, bushes cut back. The only structure still standing must have been the main part of the castle. Two stories in the middle, three stories on either side. The roof on one wing was intact, completely missing from the other.

"A real castle," Bernie said. "How cool is that? I don't see any turrets and ramparts and such, though. I wonder if they fell down."

"I suspect this place is newer than the King Arthur era you're thinking of," I said. "Last night, one of the former staff told me the original parts of the castle are fourteenth century, predating the first earl taking it over in 1671. The Crawford family was on the Royalist side during the Civil War, and some important battles were fought around here. After Charles II reclaimed the throne, the family was naturally in his favor, and they were granted the title and all the land hereabouts, while the previous owners made haste for France. Time passed, the family got richer, drafty old stone castles ceased to be attractive places to live, so a later earl built the house we're staying in. Elizabeth's husband sold the castle and its grounds to the National Trust."

"Imagine knowing what your family was doing in the English Civil War," Bernie said. "Do you know anything about your family history? I've never asked."

"Granddad's family was from Scotland, thus the Campbell name. I don't even know when they immigrated, and Rose doesn't know the name of any of her ancestors beyond her grandparents. She assumes they were born and raised in Yorkshire, and likely never traveled farther than the nearest market town, coal mine, or wool factory in all their lives. When Rose went to America to marry Granddad, it was a big deal. She told me she never expected to see anyone in her family again. People didn't travel back and forth regularly, even then, not if they didn't have a lot of money."

We had great fun exploring the crumbling old building and the grounds and taking pictures of each other posing on the walls. In the castle ruins itself, steep steps led through narrow archways to underground passages. A modern wooden staircase with sturdy handrails curled up to the second floor of the center wing, where we read about the history of the castle, its original owners, and the First Earl of Frockmorton.

We worked up a good appetite, then headed back to the house to meet Rose for breakfast. She texted to say she was up and would meet us in the dining room. We found her sipping a cup of tea and reading her book. Her phone rested on the table next to her. She closed the book and gave us a wide smile as we pulled chairs up to the white-tablecloth-clad table, laid with silver cutlery and tea things.

"Good morning," the young waitress said. "Tea?"

"Coffee, please," Bernie and I chorused.

"You look bright and perky this morning, Rose," I said. "Particularly for someone who's rarely out of bed before nine, never mind the five-hour time difference between here and home."

"At my age, love, time zones are of no relevance. I'm not going to waste a minute of my visit here wondering if I should be tired or not."

"Good attitude," Bernie said. "As for me, I'm going to have a nap this afternoon, before the tea. Fortunately, for me, my roommate is going to work, so I can have a nice sleep. You snore dreadfully, Lily."

"I do not," I said.

She plucked the breakfast menu out from between the salt and pepper shakers and consulted it as the waitress returned with a silver pitcher of coffee, separate jugs of cream and sugar.

Bernie said, "What's a black pudding?"

"If you have to ask, you don't want it," Rose said.

"Isn't pudding another word for dessert here? What dessert comes with breakfast?"

"It can have other meanings," Rose said. "Yorkshire pudding is an oven-baked batter served with roast beef."

"I want to try everything. I'll have the traditional Yorkshire breakfast."

"Muesli and yoghurt for me, please," I said.

"When in Yorkshire," Rose said. "I'll have the traditional breakfast also. Thank you."

"Toast for the table?" the waitress asked.

"Sure," Bernie said.

"How your grandfather loved his full English," Rose said with a happy sigh. "A complete fry up almost every Sunday morning over all the years of our married life. Although, as time passed, I had to reduce the amount of bacon I was giving him, and the amount of fat I was cooking it all in. I'm sure what they do here will be delightful, yet still modern and healthy."

"Did you enjoy yourself last night?" Bernie poured coffee for us both.

"Very much. Such great fun remembering the old days. Poor Reg isn't quite with it anymore, as I believe you young people say, but he was full of stories about the people we knew back then. So many things I've forgotten. It was nice to meet some of the staff members who came after me and learn how much things have changed over the years. Imagine, this house is a hotel and restaurant. When the family had dinner parties, we only had to prepare one menu, as elaborate as it might have been. Never mind dietary requirements. Not only children ate what they were given in my day, love. You came to a formal dinner or a ball at a house like this, you ate what they gave you."

"And you walked uphill to school," Bernie said, "both ways."

Rose winked at her.

"Have you seen Elizabeth's sapphires before?" I asked. "They sure were something."

"I have seen them, yes. When her husband was alive, Lady Frockmorton wore them on special occasions. I never came upstairs when they put on grand dinner parties, but she would always come down before guests began to arrive, to check how things were going and to express her thanks to Cook. Mrs. Beams, of course, was usually sleeping it off next to the fireplace, so I knew the thanks were directed at me. She's planning to sell them."

"What?" Bernie and I exclaimed.

"Elizabeth is going to sell the jewels?" I asked.

"She told Reg and me last night, in a brief lull between people coming to congratulate her. The family no longer circulates in the type of society in which ostentatious items of that sort are considered appropriate. Until last night, the jewels haven't been out for years—decades—and there are far better things to do with the money they would get from selling them. Your mother texted me yesterday to say her audition for that new Broadway musical went well. Did you know that?"

"What's that got to do with—?"

The waitress and her helper arranged dishes on the table. "Can I get you anything else? More tea, Mrs. Campbell?"

"Please."

I enviously eyed the two plates across the table from me, overflowing with breakfast offerings. Maybe I shouldn't have been so virtuous. Bernie and Rose had been served glistening plump sausages, one huge mushroom nestled in a bed of caramelized onions, two fried eggs with bright yellow yolks, baked beans. And a large round black thing.

Bernie poked at the large round black thing with her fork. "Is this anything like mushy peas?"

"That's a black pudding. Does it look anything like mushy peas?" Rose said.

"No. Just checking."

"As for the sapphires, she hasn't told the family about her plans yet, and it's not something I want the wait staff accidentally overhearing from me. Or anyone else." The tables next to us were unoccupied. By the fireplace, a group of four talked loudly among themselves. "She took the items out of the bank vault under the pretext of wearing them last night, but her true purpose is to show them to a representative from an auction house who will be arriving on Monday."

I thought of Annabelle, the current Countess of Frockmorton, the look on her face when she saw the jewels. "The family might not be happy to hear that."

"The family, so Elizabeth tells me, are not happy with many of the decisions she's had to make over the years.

And she does mean 'had to make.' Not all of them have been easy. The estate is struggling, despite the success of the hotel. The pandemic and subsequent lack of business was a blow they're still recovering from. Maintenance around the farm and in some of the houses they rent out is being delayed to the point that it will be more expensive when the work finally gets done. On top of all that, taxes will have to be paid upon her death. She wants to sell the sapphires while she can still control what to do with the proceeds."

As I scooped up muesli and yoghurt, I thought about the argument between the cousins Bernie and I overheard at the pub. "Despite any financial troubles they might be in, Elizabeth is putting on this big party. We're not paying to stay here, right?"

Rose nodded.

I held up my spoon as further evidence. "Nor are we paying for our food and drink. The booze sure flowed last night, and it wasn't the cheap stuff. I assume the staff are being paid this weekend as normal, and all the other expenses have to be met."

Bernie cut off a tiny bit of her black pudding. She popped it in her mouth and chewed thoughtfully. She didn't spit it out, but she didn't look all that enraptured, either. "It's okay," she said at last. "But not something I'm going to have again." She pushed the remainder to one side.

"It is an acquired taste," Rose said. "I'll have yours if you don't want it." Bernie passed it over. "Not many things I missed in the way of food when living in America, other than a proper cup of tea in a restaurant, but black pudding is one of them.

"As for Elizabeth, I suspect she had more to drink last night than she's accustomed to. I certainly did. My glass was scarcely empty before someone was offering me another. She talked to Reg and me as though she was thinking out loud. Perhaps a habit one gets into as one ages. People do tend to tune older people out."

"I never tune you out, Rose," Bernie said. "See, I'm listening intently to everything you're saying."

"And so you should. Edward died when Elizabeth not only had four small children to care for but the weight of the earldom itself. She inherited a lot of land, a big old house, and a precarious financial position. Edward was several years older than Elizabeth, and he had a good head for business. Which is sometimes exceedingly rare in the old families. Anyway, the companies his family controlled made a substantial amount of money during the war, but these grand estates have a way of chewing rapidly through any outside income one might earn. The Frockmorton family are not her family by birth, but Elizabeth took her responsibilities to Edward's legacy seriously. Takes it seriously. She's determined to leave the estate on a firm foundation when she dies. Which will, she acknowledges, likely be not too much longer, despite her continuing fine health."

"Doesn't her son and heir have anything to say about this?"

"Elizabeth owns the property and everything on it. As long as she is of sound mind and no one can prove otherwise, she can do with it as she likes. Entailed estates are no longer a thing, and the laws of ownership and inheritance apply to her precisely as to the rest of us. If memory serves, I recall your uncles having a few things to say when I sold the house in Grand Lake and used the proceeds to purchase Victoria-on-Sea. It was suggested at the time that I might prefer a small yet comfortable retirement community. By which, your uncles meant cheap."

At ten o'clock I reported for duty in the kitchen. Aside from the new wing of guest rooms, the house was decorated and furnished as it would have been in the glory days of the Frockmorton family. Fortunately, such did not apply to the kitchen, which was as modern and efficient as any I'd worked in in Manhattan. It was a lot nicer, not to mention a lot bigger, than the one at Tea by the Sea.

"We have one hundred and sixty guests coming for tea," Ian, the head chef told me as he passed me an apron. "Far, far more than we'd normally ever get at one time, so I'm mighty glad of the help. Thanks." Ian was a short, round man, nearly bald, with a mouthful of crooked teeth and a friendly smile, dressed in the traditional chef's uniform of checked pants and white jacket with offset buttons.

"Thank you for letting me join you," I said. "At my own place, I try as hard as possible to serve a traditional afternoon tea, but I'm always on the lookout for ways of improving."

"Traditional is what we do here," he said. "We've been baking extra for weeks, whenever we got a moment to spare. Scones are mostly done and in the freezers, as are many of the sweets. We need help this morning with the sandwiches and the sweets that don't freeze or need to be finished."

All around us, the kitchen was a flurry of well-organized chaos. Batter whipped, pastry rolled, biscuits cut, decorations piped. A large corkboard on the far wall listed the day's offerings. Along with the food, there would be several choices of tea, as well as sparkling wine. Staff not cooking or baking were laying out serving trays, while others checked that dishes and glasses were clean.

"I had tea yesterday with Lady Frockmorton," I said. "We were served a delicious chicken sandwich with a taste of curry. I particularly liked it, and I might want to serve it at my place."

"Coronation chicken," Ian said. "Always popular. Do you know why it's called that?"

"No, I don't."

"At the time of the late queen's coronation, a curried chicken salad recipe was created specifically to mark the occasion. The idea was that everyone in the country could partake of the same meal to bring them together on that one day. For the new king, the dish was a quiche. Not nearly as good, in my opinion. Coronation chicken is now often served as a sandwich ingredient. Varying amounts of curry power are used in different places, but I like it fairly powerful and Elizabeth agrees."

"Does Elizabeth still supervise the menus?"

"Not usually, although we talked over our ideas for her party. I've been here seven years, but I've been told she was more hands-on before that. She still likes to know what's happening for the Christmas events—we do several special occasion meals in the weeks up to New Year's Day—and makes good suggestions, but otherwise, age is catching up to her." He grinned. "Although she pretends it isn't. Tony's the manager now, and he believes in hiring the best people for the job and letting them do what they do.

"Enough chat. Let's get on with it—we've got a lot to do. If you like, the coronation chicken can be your first task. The chickens are cooked and in the fridge. Recipes are in that folder there. If you can't find anything, just ask. You two, get out of here!"

Katy and Zoe, the twins I'd seen yesterday, had run into the kitchen. Shrieking with laughter, ponytails flying, they dodged cooks carrying pots of water and wielding sharp knives. "Biscuits!" one of them yelled, as she headed for a tray of shortbread cooling on a rack. Little hands grabbed as many as they could get on the fly, and then the girls were gone, nothing but their laughter left hanging in the air in their wake.

"Those two," Ian grumbled. "I'm all for letting kids run wild, but not through a professional kitchen."

I happily got stuck in. It was nice to simply have a task to do and not be keeping an eye on how everyone else was getting on with their jobs, although I did pay attention to what was happening around me. One hundred and sixty people was a heck of a lot to feed all at once for a restaurant not accustomed to those numbers. But every course of afternoon tea is served at the same time, and everyone gets pretty much the same thing, other than tea selections and the occasional dietary request, so almost all the work can be done ahead of time.

Five plump cooked chickens were awaiting my attention. I deboned, sliced, and shredded them, and then, as per the recipe, added mayonnaise, mango chutney, some chopped sultanas, and spices.

"I can give you a hand if you're ready to assemble," a woman said to me. She was short and thin, with pink cheeks in a heart-shaped face, dark hair stuffed under her hairnet, overgrown eyebrows, brown eyes behind heavy black-rimmed eyeglasses, and a big smile. She was around forty, I guessed, and spoke with the local accent. A long white apron, similar to the one I'd been given, was wrapped around her tiny waist.

"Thanks. The sandwiches we had yesterday were all cut into rectangles. At my place we try for a variety of shapes. Circles, pinwheels, etcetera."

"I hope you don't serve bagels," she said.

"Perish the thought. Why do you ask?"

"My husband and I took the kids to Disney World a couple of years ago, and toured Florida after. We went to this place for afternoon tea, and they served salmon on bagels. Way too heavy. The tea was okay though, and I forgave the bagels because of that. Hard to get a well-made cuppa in America."

"It can be. But not at Tea by the Sea, my place."

"As for the shape of the sandwiches," she began laying

out slices of thin white bread in two long lines, "rectangles are faster and easier."

"My restaurant specializes in afternoon tea," I said, giving the chicken mixture a final toss to combine all the ingredients. "That's all we do in tourist season."

"My mum was telling me about it this morning. She cooked here for twenty years, until about five years ago. She talked to your granny last night."

"Family tradition? Working here, I mean?"

As we talked, we went up and down the row of bread assembly-line style. I buttered each slice lightly; my helper followed me to add a scoop of chicken salad and cover it with the top slice of bread. I then went back to the beginning, cut off crusts, and cut the sandwiches into neat rectangles. She placed the finished product onto trays and covered them with plastic wrap to keep fresh until serving time.

"No. I am, believe it or not, a pediatrician," she told me as we worked. "My surgery's in Woolshops, in Halifax. I'm helping out today because my mum told me to." She laughed. "I don't mind. Nice to have a day away from the kids. I worked here summers when I was in school, so I know my way around. They've hired some temporary staff from town to help out today. My mum would have loved nothing more but to come back and get stuck in, but her hip's acting up and she can't stand for any length of time or get around easily. I'm Alicia, by the way. Alicia Boyle."

"Lily Roberts."

"Everything under control here?" A woman asked in a high-pitched voice.

Ian was churning cake batter in a mixer. Over the roar of the small motor, I heard him say, "No!"

"What was that, Ian?" The new arrival asked.

He turned off the mixer and turned to her. The look on

his face was one of exasperation. "I said, everything is under control, Carmela. Would you expect anything less?" Carmela. This must be Julien's wife. I'd seen her at the drinks party last night, but we had not been introduced. She looked well maintained, I thought. Shoulder-length brown hair cut perfectly, traces of caramel highlights, nicely manicured nails, good skin and teeth. She wore a navy-blue dress cut slightly above her knees, with a thin white belt, and three-inch heels. "Only checking!" She laughed lightly. "Have you seen Tony. I've been looking for him everywhere."

"He's just about the only person who hasn't been through my kitchen this morning. If you're here to work, feel free to take over washing-up duties. Otherwise, get lost."

"Carry on!" Her heels tapped on the floor as she rapidly made her departure with a cheerful backward wave of her hand.

Alicia laughed. "Sometimes the family forgets it's not the eighteenth century any longer. When it comes to his domain, Ian is the lord and master here."

"Got that right," he growled, as the mixer roared back to life.

When we were finished and the little sandwiches looked absolutely perfect, Alicia popped them in the fridge and went on to help finish the Battenburg cakes. I've made Battenburg myself a few times in the tearoom. They look lovely, but they're fussy to create with their checkerboard pattern. I admired Ian for putting in the additional effort for so many guests. He was bent over a row of small raspberry tarts, wielding a piping bag, adding a drizzle of chocolate. I opened my mouth to ask what I could do next, and without even turning around he said. "Watercress sandwiches, please, Lily."

Like any good head chef, Ian has eyes in the back of his head.

I found huge bunches of watercress in the industrial-size fridge and was giving them a good rinse when Ian groaned, threw up his hands, and turned around. "Is this a stop on a tour no one saw fit to tell me about?"

"Don't be so dramatic," the new arrival said. "I can come into the kitchen if I want. Just checking everything is okay."

All morning, a steady stream of family members and special guests had paraded through the kitchen. All of them checking that "everything is okay." The newest arrival was Annabelle, Countess of Frockmorton.

Her position in the family clearly didn't impress Ian. "Well, I've had enough of it. Get out. All you lot are doing is getting in the way."

Annabelle's lips tightened. "I'll remind you who's paying your wages."

"Not you," Ian said. He lowered his voice and added, "Not yet."

Annabelle looked around for something to complain about and settled on me. "I hope we didn't pay to bring in an American sous chef. What do Americans know about serving a proper tea anyway?"

"She's not a sous chef," Ian said. "She's a pastry chef. A highly qualified and experienced one. She's been kind enough to offer to help out when she could otherwise be enjoying all the delights Yorkshire has to offer."

I smiled and held up a bunch of watercress as evidence. Annabelle eyed me.

"Seems to me," Ian said, "she's saving your business money. Now, if you're finished here, get out of my kitchen."

Several of the waiters and kitchen helpers had stopped work to watch the burgeoning argument. Others continued working, but it was obvious by the tilt of their heads and the way they'd stopped chatting among themselves they were taking in every word.

Annabelle wasn't prepared to leave without getting in one last shot. "That watercress is limp. Can't you find anything fresher?"

The watercress looked fine to me.

"Feel free to hit the shops yourself," Ian said. "But don't bring the bill to me. I have what I need, all recorded and accounted for." He turned back to his workbench.

"Carry on, everyone." Annabelle sailed out of the kitchen, head high, heels pounding a furious rhythm on the floor.

I'd scarcely finished drying the watercress when the kitchen door swung open again. A young woman passing by with a bowl of hardboiled eggs to be shelled and made into egg sandwich mixture, yelped and jumped out of the way.

"Everything okay in here?" Emma asked.

"Out!" Ian yelled. "I've had enough. Out, out, out."

Emma lifted her hands. She backed slowly away.

"One more person comes in here under the pretext of 'just checking' and I quit."

I noticed two of the kitchen helpers exchange winks. Good chefs have the reputation of being temperamental, the head chef at the Michelin-starred restaurant I'd worked at in Manhattan came instantly to mind. But clearly, Ian's staff didn't live in fear of him. He had, I thought, the right to be getting seriously annoyed. This party was a big event, and everyone wanted everything to go off smoothly.

Chapter 6

"Did you have fun?" Bernie asked.

"It was great."

"You're weird, Lily Roberts."

"Baking, as you well know, is my happy place. Not usually with so many other people around, but generally, they all worked well together. Not that I baked. I mostly made sandwiches, and then I helped set the tables."

"Get any ideas?"

"I'm definitely putting coronation chicken sandwiches on my menu. I snuck one when the chef wasn't looking, and I do like them. I think my customers will, too. I didn't help much with the desserts, but some looked interesting and were new to me, so we'll see what they taste like, and if necessary, I can try to wheedle the recipe out of Ian."

Bernie and I were in our room getting ready for the birthday tea. While I'd been in the kitchen, a truck pulled up outside and buckets of flowers delivered. I'd helped arrange the blooms and greenery in small vases to adorn each table. No rain was in the forecast, so tables and chairs had been set up throughout the gardens and terraces.

Blankets and throws were placed over the backs of chairs, and stand heaters switched on. At Tea by the Sea, I have a gorgeous patio area overlooking the gardens of the B & B, but not long after Labor Day, we take down the sun umbrellas, fold up the chairs, and stack the tables behind the building to await the arrival of spring.

The English must be hardier than us. Comes from living in old damp stone buildings, perhaps.

The table for the birthday girl and her family was set with Elizabeth's personal set of Wedgwood Renaissance Gold. The rest of the tables got nice (but nothing terribly special) white plates and cups with a thin gold trim. The teapots were silver, as were the three-tiered stands that would hold the food. Every place had a pressed white-linen napkin, silver cutlery, a silver tea strainer, water glasses, and a crystal champagne flute. Children and non-imbibing attendees would be served juice rather than sparkling wine to toast Lady Frockmorton.

"What did you do while I was slaving away?" I asked Bernie.

"I slept. A lovely, long, luxurious nap. Sorry, just teasing. I had a short snooze, and then I worked out some plot problems for the book."

"You are not relocating it to England, I hope."

"No. I decided going back and reworking it to give them reason to go to England would be too much. Maybe in the next book."

"Ready?" I asked.

"Ready," she replied.

As this was a formal tea party for a hundredth birthday, Bernie and I had decided it was appropriate to put on our best clothes. She wore a tea gown reminiscent of the Roaring Twenties, and I was in a scoop-necked beige linen dress with three-quarter-length sleeves and lace trim at the bodice. We both had feathered fascinators on our heads, and we carried pashminas, in case the patio heaters weren't up to the task.

I might have known that as much as my friend and I thought we were going all out, my grandmother would do us one better. The blouse under her emerald green suit had a high, fluffy pink collar. Enormous green and pink beads hung around her neck, and matching bangles jangled at her wrists. The outfit was topped by a sweeping green hat with pink flowers attached to the brim. Her eyeglasses had enormous round green frames.

"Wow!" Bernie said.

"I've never seen that outfit before. When did you get it?" I asked.

"I might have told a little white lie last week when I mentioned that Marian was picking me up for bridge." Rose gave me a wicked grin. "Instead, we went to Province-town, shopping."

"As always, Rose," Bernie said, "you are the belle of the ball."

"I hope not. I wouldn't want to overshadow Elizabeth."

We were not overdressed, and we didn't overshadow anyone, not in the least. The children were in suits and ties, for the boys, and party dresses, for the girls. Even the few teenagers present were done up nicely, and some of the older couples looked as though they were heading to Buckingham Palace to have tea with the king and queen.

Robert and Annabelle stood at the doors to the terrace, greeting guests. They were with a woman I hadn't seen last night. Judging by her age, I thought it might be Elizabeth's daughter, Katherine, the mother of Tony and Susannah. Robert was in a business suit of excellent cloth and cut, and Annabelle wore a floor-length black gown with fur at the collar and cuffs. The other woman was in a business suit. Lissie had taken up a spot on the low stone wall, basking in the weak sun, occasionally allowing guests to scratch between her ears.

As we waited in the reception line, I spotted Tony whispering instructions to a waiter putting the finishing touches on the head table. Susannah and Emma moved through the crowd, smiling and exchanging hugs and air-kisses. Julien did the same, while Jacqueline kept an eye on her daughters. The twins looked adorable in matching blue dresses and high white socks with gold-buckled shiny black shoes. Blue velvet ribbons held back their yellow hair. Elizabeth hadn't yet arrived.

A sign by the door to the terrace mentioned that the bar would be open all afternoon and guests were welcome to take advantage of it. More than a few appeared to have done so, as guests mingled holding glasses and beer mugs.

"Rose, how wonderful you were able to make it," Robert said when we reached the front of the receiving line. "We're absolutely delighted to have you. I hope you don't mind my saying you provide a touch of history of the sort my mother is so fond of."

"I don't mind in the least," Rose said. "I'm only glad I was able to reach sufficient age to be considered historical."

Everyone laughed lightly.

"Let me introduce my sister, Katherine Waterfield," Robert said. "Katherine arrived early this morning. Katherine, Mrs. Campbell, formerly of Halifax. Her granddaughter, Lily and, uh—"

"Bernadette Murphy," Bernie said quickly.

"Lily was kind enough to help in the kitchen this morning," Annabelle said.

"I'm sure that was appreciated," Katherine said. "Tony, the hotel manager, is my son."

"When we get a chance, you must tell me all about your career as a pastry chef," Annabelle said.

"I'd be happy to."

"A family tradition, is it? Working in kitchens?" Annabelle smiled at Rose.

Rose returned the smile. "An honest day's work for an honest day's pay, as my father always said. Better than some."

We moved on.

"Ooo-kay," Bernie said. "That line is going straight into my book. My gosh what a—"

"Never mind her," Rose said. "As the importance of the landed aristocracy fades into insignificance, some of them try to hold on to their self-opinion for all they're worth. Occasionally that consists of reminding others they used to be known as their 'betters.'"

"Happens in America, too," Bernie said. "You wouldn't believe the attitude of some of the scions of wealthy families I've encountered in my job. They found themselves in quite the pickle because they couldn't believe they'd squandered all the money they inherited. Or flat out cheated to get. Quite often the situation was entirely my fault, because I failed to treat them with the respect they naturally deserved." Bernie was a forensic accountant, and she'd worked for a top Manhattan criminal-law firm before quitting to come to Cape Cod to write her book. She chuckled happily. "When their file left my desk and went up the ladder to one of the lawyers, they learned the meaning of lack of respect fast enough."

"Good afternoon, ladies," Josh, the farrier, greeted us. "Mrs. Campbell, may I say you look simply stunning."

Rose colored ever so slightly. "You may."

"Granddad would enjoy the pleasure of your company." Josh gestured behind him. Reggie was seated at a table near the blackened stone wall. He gave us a toothless grin and a wave.

"I'll join him, then," Rose said.

"Can I get you something from the bar?"

"No, thank you, love. A small glass of champagne, later, will suffice."

"Welcome, Mrs. Campbell." Julien joined our little group. He held a glass of what looked like whiskey in his hand. "May I say you look quite striking this afternoon."

"You certainly may." Rose gave him a girlish smile.

Julien looked at Josh. Josh looked at Julien. They did not smile, and they did not greet each other. Instead, Julien said, "Make yourself useful, will you, Hansen, and help Mrs. Campbell to a seat."

"Wouldn't have thought of doing that all on my own, Your Lordship. As ever, thanks so much for your help. Anything else needs doing, let me know, seeing as to how your hands are full." Josh pointedly looked at Julien's whiskey glass, and then he held out his arm, and Rose slipped hers through it. He led her across the flagstone floor without another glance at Julien.

"I hope you enjoy yourselves," Julien said tightly, not looking at us. He walked away.

"Not the best of friends, those two, I'd guess," Bernie said. "Never mind them. A trip to the bar sounds good to me. Lily?"

"Sure. A glass of white wine, please."

She slipped away.

"My brother tells me you helped out in the kitchen earlier." Seeing I was momentarily on my own, Susannah approached me. "Singing for your supper?"

"More like wanting to see how it's done in a place like this."

"What did you think? And that's a serious question, by the way. Tony's the manager of the hotel, and this weekend I'm his spy."

"I was impressed. An efficient operation, with a head chef who's in control but not domineering." I didn't say anything about him ordering her relatives out of "his" kitchen.

"That's what we like to hear. Ian is good, and we were lucky to get him. Did you meet our mum, Katherine? She wasn't able to get away until this morning."

"I did. Does your mother have much to do with the running of the hotel?"

"Not a single thing. And that suits her perfectly, same as it suits me. I might have said I'm Tony's spy, but only I know that." She laughed.

The gardens were filling up quickly as more guests arrived. Robert left his place on the receiving line and disappeared. Bernie came back with my wine, handed it to me, and began looking around for people to talk to. Before she could move, Robert returned, his mother on his arm.

Elizabeth looked lovely, every inch the Dowager Countess in an ankle-length rose-colored dress with matching overcoat that fell past her knees. Her hat was the color of the dress, highlighted by a wide gray-lace band. She was not wearing the Frockmorton Sapphires today, just a string of small pearls around her neck, with matching ones in her ears.

Guests stood and applauded as Robert escorted his mother across the terrace. Julien followed, with his wife, Carmela, next to him. They might have been walking together, but they were keeping their distance and not looking at each other. The procession was preceded by Jacqueline's twins, looking extremely proud at their importance. Elizabeth greeted guests and spoke to them briefly, but in acknowledgment of her age, she was taken directly to the head table, where she took her seat.

Robert turned to the onlookers. "Ladies and gentlemen, welcome guests, please find yourselves a place. Service will begin shortly."

I snagged a seat for Bernie and me at a table toward the

back of the garden, overlooking the maze, and nodded politely to my table companions as the tea was brought out.

Wait staff circled with the teapots, offering us a choice of green tea, English Breakfast, or Lapsang Souchong—or juice, for those who didn't want tea. I chose the Lapsang Souchong. Our table companions were a woman from York whose late mother had been a close friend of Elizabeth, her husband, and a collection of distant relatives of the family.

We made pleasant small talk as the tea was poured and the three-tiered stands were brought out. "Be sure and try the coronation chicken sandwiches, I made them myself," I said proudly, sounding like a kindergarten student displaying her artwork.

I tried one and regretted telling everyone I'd made them. The sandwiches were okay, but not as good as the one I'd had the day before, or even the one I'd sampled after making them. This one was slightly too dry, perhaps. Had I added too much of something and not blended the mixture sufficiently? I struggled to identify what made this one different, but I couldn't place it immediately, and the conversation at my table went on. I couldn't help but notice that the woman from York put her chicken sandwich aside after talking only one small bite.

Scones are always my favorite part of afternoon tea, and these were wonderful, light and flaky. I thought I might ask Ian for his recipe and see how it compares to mine. The strawberry jam was lovely, and the clotted cream, thick and perfect. As for the desserts, I particularly liked the chocolate tart made with the slightest hint of coffee. It fit in perfectly as part of a dessert selection, and was so chocolatey and rich a tiny slice would suit all but the most fanatic of chocolate lovers.

Eventually, the tea was drunk and the food consumed. The staff continually circled with teapots and brought out more food, if asked. I kept half an eye on Rose, but she seemed to be enjoying herself, chatting with Reggie and the other elderly people at her table. When everyone seemed to have had enough, the staff quickly and efficiently whisked away the used cutlery and dishes, and what little remained of the food. Others, meanwhile, including my new friend, Alicia, began circulating with bottles of top-shelf champagne. People who were seated in the far-flung reaches of the terrace or around corners got to their feet and stood at the edges of the main area, ready to join in the toast.

When everyone's glass was full, Robert got to his feet. He raised his own glass. "To my mother, Elizabeth, the Dowager Countess of Frockmorton, on the occasion of her one hundredth birthday."

"Elizabeth, Lady Frockmorton," the toasts rang out.

Elizabeth beamed with delight, giving me a glimpse of the great beauty she had once been. She lifted her glass in acknowledgment and touched it to her lips. "I hope you'll pardon me, if I do not stand. These days the spirit is willing, but the knees and hips are not. To paraphrase Bilbo Baggins: *First of all, to tell you that I am immensely fond of you all, and that one hundred years is too short a time to live among such excellent and admirable Yorkshiremen and women.*"

The distant relatives at our table exchanged confused looks.

"Always loved *Lord of the Rings,* Elizabeth and my mother did," my table companion explained. "My mum didn't make to ninety, for all she was hoping to celebrate her eleventy-first. I have hopes Elizabeth will make it."

"I thank you all, from the bottom of my heart, for coming today," Elizabeth continued. "The years have not always been easy for me, but I hope—" She broke off in midsentence and turned to look at her eldest grandchild, seated at the far end of the head table.

Julien had let out a choked cry. He started to stand. His eyes were wide and full of fear, his left hand clutched his throat, and his right hand flailed in the air. Next to him, his sister, Jacqueline, leapt to her feet. Julien stared at her. He tried to talk but nothing came out. He clutched at the edges of the tablecloth as his legs gave way. China and glassware tumbled to the ground, and Julien slowly followed. Jacqueline screamed.

Everyone was on their feet now, some yelling for help, some asking others what was going on. I heard a mumbled prayer among the sounds of glass breaking, as champagne flutes were mindlessly discarded. One of the distant relatives at my table already had her phone out and was moving. My own first thought was to seek out my grandmother. My eyes found her, still in her chair, looking as shocked as everyone else. She saw me, and gave me a nod saying she was okay. She put her hand on Reggie's arm and spoke to him.

The woman I'd met in the kitchen earlier, Alicia, arrived at a run. "I'm a doctor. Let me through."

The distant relative reached the head table and told Alicia. "I'm a paramedic."

"I'm glad you're here," Alicia said.

"Has anyone called 999?" someone yelled. "We need an ambulance here, and fast."

All around me, phones were taken out and emergency calls placed.

Alicia and the medic crouched behind the table, examining Julien. Susannah had taken her grandmother's arm and was leading a shaking Elizabeth away.

"We need to let these people do what they do." Tony spoke in a loud firm voice, a man in control, issuing rapid orders. But he couldn't help taking a peek behind him, at what was happening on the far side of the table. When he turned back, his face was pale. "Bar's open, and we'll be serving tea and coffee in the restaurant shortly. Please ladies and gentlemen, go inside. The party is over. Irene, meet the ambulance out front and show them here. No need for them to go through the building."

The waitress dashed away.

"I'll get Rose," I said to Bernie. "Meet you inside."

"Got it."

Most people were sensibly leaving the gardens, but a handful of the curious—or maybe the ghoulish—remained, and I pushed my way through them. By the time I reached Rose's table, Josh had arrived with his grandfather's walker and was helping the old man to stand. "Never could hold their liquor, some of them," Reggie said.

"I don't think that's the problem, Granddad."

"Always a problem with the men in that family."

In the hullabaloo, Rose's cane had fallen to the floor. I scooped it up and handed it to her, and then I assisted her to stand. "Heart attack, do you think?" she said to me.

"Most likely," I replied.

I couldn't help throwing a glance over my shoulder as we walked away. I couldn't see what was happening on the ground, nothing but the backs of the two women as they bent over Julien, doing what they could for him. That was a good sign, I thought—I hoped. Julien's parents, Robert and Annabelle, stood a few feet away, their eyes wide and frightened. I couldn't help but noticing that Carmela, Julien's wife, stood apart from the rest of the family. Even as her husband lay on the ground in medical distress, no one's instinct was to comfort her, and she did not seek their support.

"Does this man have any medical history we need to know about?" the medic called. "Medications? History of heart problems? Allergies?"

"I—I—" Robert said.

"Nuts," Annabelle said. "My son is severely allergic to tree nuts."

"Were nuts in any of the food served here?" Alicia asked.

"I wouldn't think so," Annabelle replied. "They don't do that these days, do they?"

No one answered.

As we entered the house, the sounds of sirens could be heard in the distance, coming our way.

Chapter 7

"I've had enough tea," Elizabeth said. "I scarcely had any of my champagne, but it's left a foul taste in my mouth. A G&T. Heavy on the gin, please, Susannah."

"Mrs. Campbell?"

"The same," Rose said.

"Mr. Hansen?"

"A pint would be welcome, love," Reggie said.

"Anyone else?"

Josh, Bernie, and I declined, and Susannah slipped away.

Susannah had been standing by the door when we came inside the hotel. She said, "My grandmother's taken a seat in one of the small dining rooms. She asks if Mrs. Campbell would care to join her."

"I would," Rose said. "I'm sure your cousin will be fine, love, but it was rather distressing for a moment there."

Bernie and I had followed Rose, simply because we had nowhere else to be.

After Susannah left to get the drinks, the rest of the family began drifting in. No one brought any news other than that the ambulance had arrived and the paramedics were checking Julien out prior to taking him to the hospital.

A waiter came in with the drinks Susannah ordered, followed by Katherine Waterfield. "Do you want to go to your room and lie down, Mum?" she said to Elizabeth.

"Not yet, Katherine, thank you. Rose, have you met my youngest? Katherine is Tony and Susannah's mother. She only arrived this morning."

"We did meet earlier, yes." Rose said with a fond smile. "As well as a long time ago. I'm sure you don't remember me. Kathy, they called you as a child, and as I recall you had a terrible weakness for chocolate-covered biscuits."

"Rose was employed here many years ago," Elizabeth said.

Katherine broke into a huge grin. "I don't remember you, I'm sorry—but I remember those biscuits. Mum had to finally order the kitchen not to make them anymore, as she was afraid I'd put on weight."

Elizabeth's orders must have had their desired effect. Katherine was slim to the point of wiry. Her thick gray hair was tied into a braid thrown over one shoulder, her deeply tanned face clear of makeup, no attempt made to disguise the network of fine lines caused, no doubt, by the amount of sun she seemed to get. She wore a colorful dress under a denim jacket. Plain ballet flats were on her feet. "Let us know when you're ready to go to your room, Mum, and someone will help you. I'm going to see if they need anything outside."

After she'd left no one said anything for a long time. The three elderly people sipped their drinks. In the lobby, the antique grandfather clock ticked the time away. People passed in the hallway, speaking in low voices.

Tony came in. He'd discarded his tie, undone the top button of his shirt. "Julien's been taken to hospital. Aunt

Annabelle went with him in the ambulance, and Uncle Robert has gone to his rooms to await news."

"Carmela?"

"Don't know," Tony said abruptly. "I didn't see what she got up to. I thanked Alicia for her assistance and suggested she go home, but she's gone back to the kitchen to help with cleanup. I asked Ian if he's able to go ahead with dinner, and he's agreeable, if you are, Granny."

"Guests have to be fed, darling. See to it."

The restaurant was closed to the public that night, but would reopen the next day. That night's dinner was not officially part of the birthday celebrations, but guests staying at Thornecroft Castle or nearby, had been invited to join the family at eight.

More expense, I could almost hear Julien say. Poor Julien. I didn't know him well, and what I had seen of him I hadn't particularly liked, but I wished him well.

"Finish that beer, Granddad. Time to go," Josh said.

"I'm not ready to go," Reggie replied. "I think I'll have another." He downed what was left in his glass and held it out for a refill.

"Not on. I told them you'd be back by five. It's almost that now."

"Oh, yes. Back to jail." Josh brought the walker to his grandfather's chair and helped him to his feet. "Don't get old, Rose," Reggie said. "They'll think you're incompetent and stick you in a home for the addled old people. Rob you blind while they're at it."

Josh winked at me. He'd shown nothing but affection for his grandfather, and the bond between them was obviously close.

"I'll try to remember that sage advice," Rose said dryly.

When they'd left, I said, "We shouldn't keep you any longer, Elizabeth. You must be tired."

She sighed. "Not addled, as Reg so politely put it, but yes, I do tire easily. Did you enjoy the tea, Rose? Until the end, at least."

"It was lovely. And I do know of which I speak when it comes to a proper afternoon tea." She smiled at me.

"I'll get Susannah," Bernie said.

"No need," Elizabeth said. "You two beautiful young things can escort me. Would you like to see the Frockmorton Sapphires? Up close, I mean. You can try them on if you like."

"Gosh, yes," Bernie said. "I mean—if that's okay."

"I am inviting you. Good jewels need to be seen. That is their entire purpose in this world. Mine have been locked up in a bank vault for far too long, which is why I've decided to sell them. Did Rose tell you that is my intent?"

"Yes," I said.

"Good thing Julien had his heart attack today. Get it over with, before he finds out they won't be coming to him. Or to his mother, as much as she wants to get her sticky hands on them."

I ignored that surprisingly catty comment and asked, "Do we need to call a cab or an Uber? Or do you have your own driver?"

"No need. I live here, now."

I took hold of Elizabeth's arm and helped her to her walker. Bernie and Rose followed. We walked down the hallway, up the two steps, and into the lobby. Rather than going straight, to the corridor that led to our rooms, Elizabeth turned left, and we passed through a set of doors into another, older wing of the house. As the doors shut behind us, the buzz of conversation coming from the bar fell away. "When I converted this house into a hotel, the children and I moved to the Dower House," Elizabeth said. "Edward's mother was living there at the time, and not at all pleased at having a headstrong widowed daughter-in-law and a pack of teenagers moving in with her. But she was, above all else, a practical woman, and she accepted the situation. She died a few years later. When my children grew up and moved away, I didn't need to live in that large, drafty, creaky old house any longer. We rent the Dowager House out now, and I have a small suite of my own here. And here we are." Elizabeth unzipped her small purse and fumbled around inside. She came up with a room key and handed it to me.

I fitted the key into the lock and opened the door.

I don't know what I expected from the private rooms of a dowager countess, but this wasn't it. Although I should have realized that Elizabeth was nothing if not practical and would be unlikely to furnish her living space with valuable antiques and paintings, lush velveteen drapes, and oriental carpets. The furniture was much the same as in Bernie's and my room. Mass produced. Functional. A 52-inch flat screen TV hung on one wall, opposite a damask-covered wingback chair, the fabric of the arms torn and the stuffing poking out. A small side table was placed next to the chair. A couch and a coffee table provided seating for guests. At the moment the coffee table was almost buried under an avalanche of envelopes. "Birthday greetings," Elizabeth said. "I've scarcely had time to open most of them."

The kitchen contained not much more than a small fridge, space for a toaster and kettle, and a table for two. More greeting cards covered that table. A small alcove off the sitting room held a desk with a computer, turned off. The art on the walls was mostly photographs of Yorkshire scenes, green hills, small twisting streets, sheep. More sheep.

"My second son, Thomas, that's Emma's father, lives in Canada now," Elizabeth explained. "He was unable to make it to my party as he, the fool, broke his leg a week ago playing tennis. His son worked here for a few summers, and those are his photographs."

"They're very good," Rose said. "Is he a professional?"

"No. He's an accountant, of all things. Lives in Germany now. He was too busy at work to come for this weekend, but he FaceTimed me last night, to wish me a happy birthday. The sapphires are in my room. Don't hesitate. Come along."

Elizabeth's bedroom was spacious and comfortable. King-size bed, red silk covering, mountains of plump pillows. Long drapes matching the bed coverings, held back by golden ropes to show the sunken garden. I peeked out of the mullioned leaded window to see a few people sitting at the tables with drinks in front of them. A chaise longue under the windows was positioned to catch the evening sun in summer. In late October, at almost five o'clock, the sun had already dipped behind the trees and outbuildings. A hardcover book rested on the night table, too far away for me to read the cover.

A huge gilt-framed mirror, showing its age, hung over a large oak dressing table, a small stool pulled up to it. The surface of the table was covered with jewelry boxes—cardboard, not wood—handkerchiefs, scarves, pots of face cream, tubes of hand cream, pill bottles and dispensers, and two photographs. One showed young Elizabeth smiling next to a handsome man, likely Edward, taken shortly after their wedding, and another taken a few years ago. Elizabeth surrounded by her family on the Thornecroft Castle terrace.

One small old jewelry box lay in the center of the jumble.

Rose took a seat on the chaise longue, and Elizabeth settled on the stool. She reached for the old box and opened it.

Bernie and I leaned over. I held my breath in anticipation.

The box was empty.

Chapter 8

Elizabeth stared into the box.

Bernie and I exchanged glances. Did either of us dare ask this elderly lady if she was sure she'd put them in there?

"Are you sure you put them away last night?" Rose asked.

Elizabeth turned around, her face drawn and pale. "I'm sure. I will readily admit some things escape me these days, but I would never lose track of the Frockmorton Sapphires. I distinctly remember putting them into the box, because I reflected as to how that would be the last time anyone in the Crawford family would wear them. The fourth earl would not be pleased. But, by all accounts, he was a brute and a scoundrel, so who cares what he thinks." She reached for the phone on the dresser, lifted the receiver and pressed 0. "This is Elizabeth, Beth. I'm in my personal suite. I'm going to have to ask you to call the police, please. I fear I've been robbed. What do you mean, they're on their way? I've only just discovered they're missing. Very well."

Elizabeth hung up and spoke to Bernie and me. "My receptionist tells me the police have been called regarding Julien. No doubt some minor form needing to be filled out. I don't move as fast as I once did. Will you please go and find out what's happening, and let me know if there's any news as to how he's doing? Tell Tony I need to speak to him as soon as possible."

I glanced at Rose.

"Go, love. Elizabeth and I are perfectly fine here. Unlikely the thief is hiding behind the drapes. I see no toes sticking out."

Bernie and I hurried back to the main wing of the house. "If the cops have been called because of Julien, that means he didn't have heart attack," Bernie said.

"Let's not speculate, until we know more," I said.

"Like that's ever stopped us before."

We reached the reception area as two police cars, painted in a bright checkered pattern of yellow and blue, pulled up to the front of the house, followed by a plain car. The driver didn't worry about searching for a parking spot. Two people got out. The woman wore black trousers and a blue leather jacket, the man was dressed the same, but his jacket was black. They were both in their early forties, and I recognized the no-nonsense expression on their faces. They were not late-arriving party guests, and they were not here to check in.

The detectives came into the hotel, followed by one uniformed officer, while the other remained with the cars.

Tony was waiting for them, and he stepped forward, hand outstretched. "I'm Tony Waterfield, hotel manager."

"DI Ravenwood, and this is DS Capretti." The man spoke but both detectives shook Tony's hand.

Bernie and I stood quietly in the shadows next to a bookcase in the comfortably furnished sitting room tucked next to reception.

"My cousin was taken to hospital a short while ago," Tony said. "Has something happened?"

"I'm sorry to have to tell you," Ravenwood said, "but Mr. Julien Crawford—"

"Viscount Darnby," Tony said.

"Whatever," DS Capretti said. She was short and stout, with dark hair, dark eyes, and olive skin hinting at her Italian heritage. In contrast, her partner was tall and lean, with deep-set hazel eyes, hair a mass of ginger curls, and a face full of freckles.

"Your cousin died a short while ago," Ravenwood continued.

Tony dipped his head. The woman behind the reception desk stifled a sob. Bernie and I exchanged glances.

"We have some questions," Ravenwood said.

"What sort of questions?" Susannah climbed the two stairs from the restaurant and bar area.

"These people are here about Julien," Tony said. "But I don't know why. There can't be any doubt about what happened. He had a heart attack. In front of more than a hundred people."

"That remains to be seen. You are?" Ravenwood asked Susannah.

"My sister," Tony said. "Susannah Reilly."

Jacqueline and Emma were next to arrive. "Someone said the police are here."

"Uncle Robert has gone to the hospital." Emma's eyes were red, and she clutched a cotton handkerchief in her hand. "He got word that Julien died. I can't believe it."

"He wasn't exactly known for healthy living," Susannah said.

"That was uncalled for," Jacqueline snapped. "My brother is—was—fifty-one."

Susannah lowered her head and mumbled something indecipherable.

"Has someone told Granny?" Emma asked.

"No," Tony said, "Not yet. Far as I know."

DS Capretti looked around the room, taking everything in. The cousins, snapping at each other, the weeping receptionist, the sounds of laughter coming from the bar, light conversation from the dining rooms. The comfortable furnishings, the patina of old money and gracious hospitality. A young couple holding hands came down the hall, nodded to Tony, paid no attention to the police detectives, and walked out the main door. A uniformed waitress passed by outside, giving the police officer by the car a curious glance.

The detective also noticed us. "Help you?" Her intense stare focused on Bernie and me. Her Yorkshire accent was very strong.

"Thanks, yes." Bernie stepped confidently forward. I sort of slunk along behind. "Bernadette Murphy. I'm a guest here. Lady Frockmorton would like to speak to you about another matter."

"American, are you?" Capretti said, not entirely approvingly.

"As I said, we're guests of Lady Frockmorton."

"That's right," Susannah said. "Her grandmother is . . . something."

"You can tell Lady Frockmorton we'll get to her in due course." Ravenwood turned back to Tony. "First, I want to see the scene where Julien Crawford took ill, and then we'll need to speak to your guests and staff."

"I don't see any need to disturb everyone," Jacqueline said. "Not tonight. Can't your questions wait until tomorrow? The news is spreading, and people are very upset." She flinched as a sudden burst of male laughter came from the bar.

"People are here for a party, we've been told," Ravenwood said. "They'll be on their way home soon, but aside from that, I will ask questions when and to whom I see fit."

"But Julien had a heart attack," Susannah said. "In front of a hundred and sixty some guests. No mystery about it." Her eyes widened. "Is there?"

The detectives said nothing. The phone on the desk rang, but the receptionist made no move to pick it up. It rang again. Tony whipped his head around and snapped, "For heaven's sake, Beth, answer that. We still have a business to run here and a house full of guests."

She flushed and picked up the receiver, silencing it mid-ring.

"I realize you have matters to attend to," Bernie said, "but Lady Frockmorton wants to report a theft."

"As you so astutely noticed, madam," Ravenwood said, "we have other matters to attend to. Her Ladyship can wait."

"Considering today is her hundredth birthday, maybe she can't wait all that long," Bernie said. "Her necklace and earrings have been stolen."

"Old ladies are losing stuff all the time," Ravenwood said, with a tired sigh. "Tell her to look under the bed, and if she still can't find them, phone the station and make a report."

"Stolen?" Susannah said. "You don't mean—?"

Tony stared at Bernie. "What necklace?"

Bernie glanced at me. I didn't know why it was suddenly up to me to speak up, but I did so. "She took us and my grandmother to her room to see the Frockmorton Sapphires. They're gone."

Tony swore. Beth, the receptionist sucked in a breath. The three other women looked more shocked at my words than they had at news of the death of their brother and cousin.

"Like I said—" Ravenwood began.

Interest flicked behind Capretti's dark eyes as she took in the look on the faces around her. "Sapphires? Sapphires that have a name? Would you say these are items of some value?"

"Millions of pounds," Tony said.

"Tens of millions, likely," Jacqueline said.

That finally got Ravenwood's interest. "Do you think this has something to do with the death of Mr. Crawford. I mean, Viscount—whatever."

Everyone stared at me. "I don't know," I said. "All I know is Lady Frockmorton wore them last night, put them in her jewelry box upon retiring, and didn't open the box again until she wanted to show them to us." My voice trailed off. "So she says, anyway."

"Meaning," Capretti said, "that at the time of this birthday tea, when Mr. Crawford took ill, the jewels were unaccounted for?"

"Yes," Bernie and I chorused.

Jacqueline dropped into a chair with an audible moan.

"Surely she's just misplaced them," Emma said. "With all the excitement, she got confused."

"Granny doesn't get confused," Tony said. His face had gone even paler.

"DS Capretti," Ravenwood said. "You go with these people and check it out. I'll see about the other matter. Take a uniform with you and call for more backup. We might have to secure the lady's rooms."

"Wait here," Capretti said to us, before slipping outside.

"I'm going to check on Granny." Susannah headed to the private wing at a considerable pace. Jacqueline leapt out of the chair and followed.

"Mr. Waterfield, if I may have your attention once

again," Ravenwood said. "Are dinner preparations under-way in your restaurant?"

Tony almost visibly shook himself off in an attempt to pull himself together. "Yeah—I mean, yes. We have a hotel full of guests."

"Put a stop to that, please. A forensics team will be here shortly, and they need access to the kitchen."

Bernie and I exchanged glances once again. We knew what that meant. My kitchen at Tea by the Sea had once been closed for a police investigation. The police must believe it was possible Julien had been poisoned. Accidentally or otherwise.

"For what possible reason?" Tony asked.

At that moment two white vans pulled up out front, followed by another yellow-and-blue police car. Capretti crossed the forecourt to speak to them. People had begun to notice the official activity. Windows opened and heads popped out. Guests wandered in from the garden, glasses in hand. Staff hesitated in doorways.

"Emma," Tony said, "can you speak to Ian? Let him know what's happening, and tell him to stop dinner prep."

"Sure."

"Thank you," Ravenwood said, as Emma hurried away.

"Detective Inspector, before this goes any further, I must ask why you're here." I wondered if Tony was genuinely not understanding that the police were conducting themselves as though they believed Julien's death to be suspicious, or if he simply didn't want to admit it to himself. Even a hint that a diner had been killed by something prepared in the restaurant could destroy the hotel's reputation permanently.

Seeing that Capretti was distracted by the arrival of the forensics team, Bernie gave me a jerk of the head and edged slowly back into the shadows. I followed.

"The doctor who treated Mr. Crawford on arrival at the hospital," Ravenwood said, "found clear indications that the man suffered an allergic reaction. His mother told the paramedics he was severely allergic to tree nuts."

"That's right," Tony said. "It was no secret. My chef would never have used nuts."

"An autopsy has been ordered, and tests will be conducted. In the meantime, I've opened an investigation. Even if"—the detective paused to give his words dramatic emphasis—"it's determined the nuts were added to the food inadvertently, I'd think you'll want to know that. Wouldn't you?"

"Well, yes. But that's impossible."

"Which is what we're here to find out."

Capretti came into the hotel, followed by a uniformed officer and two people in plain clothes, lugging bags of equipment. "I've sent the other team round the back with one of the waiters who can describe the layout and show them where the deceased was sitting at this tea. We're securing the garden area."

Ravenwood nodded. "Find out about those jewels. You people come with me. I want the kitchen secured and searched."

Tony groaned.

Quite the crowd had gathered on the small staircase. "What's happening?" a man called.

"Someone said Julien died. Do you think he was murdered?" another asked.

People gasped at the word "murder." A young woman lifted her phone and snapped a picture of the police. Ravenwood ignored her and turned to address his audience. "Ladies and gentlemen, I'll ask you to go about your own business, please. You will all be interviewed in due course, but if you have anything you think we'd like to be apprised of, please speak to one of my officers. Thank you."

Everyone stared at him.

"By 'go about your own business,' I mean now," he said.

A few people slipped away. I couldn't blame others for being curious. After all, Bernie and I were attempting to remain concealed behind a bookshelf. Although, I told myself, I was needed to take DS Capretti to the scene of the missing sapphires.

"I want the names and contact info of everyone at this party," Ravenwood said to Tony. "I assume you can get me that."

"I can," Tony said, and the two men moved out of earshot.

"If you don't mind, ladies," DS Capretti said to us.

Chapter 9

"This room wasn't like this ten minutes ago," I said.

When we returned to Elizabeth's rooms, we found Jacqueline and Susannah searching for the Frockmorton Sapphires. Couch cushions were tossed in a heap, the snowstorm of envelopes scattered across the carpet, books and magazines piled on chairs, furniture askew. Even the edge of a rug pulled up.

Elizabeth sat in front of her computer, and Rose was perched uncomfortably on the edge of the couch, where only one cushion remained in place. Lissie the cat lay on the desk in front of Elizabeth, sprawled across the computer keyboard.

Jacqueline and Susannah looked up as we came in. Jacqueline held a vase in one hand and a bouquet of birthday flowers in the other. Susannah was on the floor, feeling around under the couch, while Rose tried to keep her feet out of the younger woman's way.

"I assume you are with the police, young lady," Elizabeth said. "You have that look about you. I am Elizabeth, Dowager Countess of Frockmorton. We don't stand on ceremony here. You may call me Elizabeth."

Capretti blinked. "DS Sophia Capretti."

"Let me assure you, Detective Sergeant, I did not confuse the Frockmorton Sapphires with a bunch of flowers. Nor did I conceal them beneath the rug for safekeeping and forget where I put them. Do you remember the time, Rose, when Cook said the brandy for the Christmas cake had been stolen?"

"I do. What she meant was she'd drunk most of it and then panicked when she realized how much was gone and added water to the bottle hoping no one would notice."

"You, of course, did notice. Unlike our late cook," Elizabeth said to DS Capretti, "I did not drink my jewels."

Capretti blinked again. I had the feeling she was not often at a loss for words.

Jacqueline put down the vase and dropped the flowers in. Susannah struggled to her feet with a hand to her back and a muffled groan. "We just want to be sure, Granny."

"Can you tell me more about these jewels?" Capretti said to the two younger women. "You said they were quite valuable."

"You may speak directly to me, Detective Sergeant," Elizabeth said. "I am the owner of the Frockmorton Sapphires and the last person who saw them. Save for the thief, of course."

"Okay," Capretti said. "Tell me. But first, who are you?" she asked Rose.

"Mrs. Rose Campbell, of North Augusta, Massachusetts, late of Grand Lake, Iowa, and even later of Halifax, Yorkshire. Is late the correct word, Elizabeth? I don't wish to imply I'm dead. Or shortly to be so."

"It is correct in the sense of living arrangements," Elizabeth said.

I thought DS Capretti showed enormous self-restraint in not rolling her eyes. My grandmother has had more than a few runs-in with the police in North Augusta, and that never ends well. Not for Detective Chuck Williams at any rate. She didn't care to be ignored, nor to be considered incompetent simply because of her age. It would appear Elizabeth was the same. They would not make it easy for DS Capretti.

"I was acquainted with Elizabeth and her family many years ago," Rose said, "and thus, I had the honor of being invited to her birthday party. My granddaughter and her friend, who I see you've met, came with me."

"I can do more than tell you about the Frockmorton Sapphires," Elizabeth said. "I can show you. She nudged Lissie to one side and reached for the cell phone on the computer table. The cat jumped down. She crossed the floor and sniffed at the detective's shoes.

DS Capretti, I guessed, was a cat person. She appeared to be exercising enormous self-restraint in not immediately dropping to her haunches to exchange greetings.

Jacqueline on the other hand, was not a cat person. She took a step forward. "I'll put that animal in another room. It's getting in the way."

"Don't be ridiculous," Elizabeth said. "Leave her alone."

Jacqueline's lips tightened, but she didn't move any further.

The door opened and Emma came in. "We've had to cancel dinner, Granny. What should I—?"

"Not now," Jacqueline snapped at her.

Emma blinked and threw a poisonous look at her cousin. Then she looked around the room, taking in the mess and confusion.

"One moment, please, dear," Elizabeth said. She found what she was looking for and passed the phone to Capretti. "The Frockmorton Sapphires. That photograph was taken only yesterday, as I was readying myself for drinks in the bar."

"They're very beautiful," Capretti said. "Real gems?"

"Yes, real. Some of the stones are hundreds of years old. Of course, all stones of all types are millions of years old, but I mean in their current cut."

"Do you have an estimate of the value?"

"When my husband died in 1965, they were valued at ten million pounds."

Capretti couldn't help sucking in a breath. I might have, too. I glanced at Bernie. She formed her mouth into a round O. The cousins watched their grandmother.

"You're sure the ones in this picture, the ones you wore last night, are the originals?" Capretti asked.

"When my husband died, I put them into a safe at the bank. And there they remained, awaiting one last appearance. In this family, at any rate."

"What does that mean?" Jacqueline said. "My mother's asked you if she could wear them on occasion, and you always said they'll come to her. Eventually."

"I changed my mind," Elizabeth said calmly. "I decided to sell them while it is still in my power to do so. So foolish, ten million pounds, likely a good bit more these days, wrapped up in silly baubles."

Sudden fury filled Jacqueline's eyes. She shouted at her grandmother, "The Frockmorton Sapphires belong to the family. You have no right to sell them."

"They belong to me, my dear, and I have every right to do with them what I like. My late husband, the tenth earl, entrusted the fate of the family to me, and I will say in all modestly I have not done badly by any of you."

"You can't—"

"Moot point," DS Capretti said. "At the moment the sapphires are not to be found, are they?" She held up Elizabeth's phone. "I'm going to send myself this picture. I have to tell you, Lady—uh, Elizabeth, although we will open an investigation, the death that happened here earlier today will take priority."

"Death?" Rose said. "You mean you're not here about the theft, but about—"

"I'll fill you in later," I said quickly.

The blood drained from Elizabeth's face. "Julien?"

"My apologies," the detective said. "I wasn't aware you hadn't been informed by your granddaughters. At this time, we're regarding Mr. Crawford's death as suspicious."

"I'm so sorry, Granny," Susannah said. "Jacqueline started making such a to-do about searching for the necklace and earrings, I didn't get a chance to tell you." She stepped forward and took her grandmother's hands in hers. "I'm so sorry," she repeated.

"Don't be so quick to point the finger at me," Jacqueline said. "You wasted no time before starting the search."

"Out of curiosity only. Why would I care what happened to the jewels? They're not going to come to me, are they?"

Emma let out a sharp laugh. "Actually, they'll come to me. Julien was Robert's only son. That means after Uncle Robert dies, the earldom goes to my dad and I'm his only daughter. Hey, I'm going to be a Lady."

"This is not the time," Rose said, "to indulge in a blame game."

"Or for counting your inheritance," Elizabeth said.

Lissie, altered by the change in Elizabeth's voice, leapt onto her lap. Elizabeth pulled her hands away from Susannah and began stroking the cat.

"My condolences," Capretti said. "I am sorry about the loss of your grandson. But I have to get back to the subject at hand. When did you see the necklace last?"

Elizabeth buried her hands in Lissie's soft white fur. She closed her eyes and took a deep breath. Gathering herself. Tears for her grandson would come later. We all waited until she opened her eyes, and said, "Last night. We had a drinks party in the bar for my guests. I returned to my room around ten and put the necklace away into my jewelry box. Most of the pieces my husband bought for me were sold off long ago, but I kept the box. Sentiment, I suppose. I then prepared for bed. I slept soundly and well."

"Were you alone when you took off the jewelry? Where was your maid?"

"My finances don't stretch to a lady's maid these days. My son Robert walked me to my door and bid me a good night there." Her voice broke. "I'm sorry, but I'd like to lie down. This business seems rather insignificant now, doesn't it?"

"You did call us to report the theft," Capretti said.

"Perhaps we can help," I said. "My grandmother, my friend, and I were with Lady Frockmorton when she discovered the jewelry missing. I should be able to answer some of your questions."

Rose stood up. "An excellent idea, love. We'll leave you, Elizabeth. Please have the desk call my room if you need anything tonight."

"Thank you, Rose. I suspect I have a long, restless night head of me."

Elizabeth nudged the cat, who took the hint and jumped down. Emma helped her grandmother to her feet and led her to her bedroom, and Susannah followed. Jacqueline couldn't help peeking into another vase.

Elizabeth turned and looked at Rose. Her stricken face betrayed every one of her hundred years.

Rose was also feeling tired and wanted to go to her room. I suggested we talk later about dinner plans, but she demurred. "It's been a long, emotional day, and I had more than enough to eat at the tea. We can meet at breakfast in the morning."

"If there is a breakfast," I said, as we watched Rose walk slowly away.

Bernie and I told DS Capretti and the uniformed officer with her, who had never been introduced to us, what we knew of the missing jewels. She asked if it was possible, despite her insistence such had not happened, Elizabeth had misplaced them, and we insisted that Lady Frockmorton was in full possession of her faculties. Yes, I admitted, anyone can misplace anything and often does, no matter their age. But Susannah and Jacqueline had searched her rooms. If Elizabeth had, for some reason, taken off the jewels elsewhere in the hotel and forgotten them, surely they would have been found and handed in. "She told us," Bernie said, "she specifically remembers putting them in the box, because doing so caused her to think about their history and their importance to the family."

"I find that easy to believe," I said. "She was about to sell them, and she knows doing so will cause dissension in the family."

"As we saw by Jacqueline's reaction," Bernie said.

"Do you know if she keeps the door to her room locked during the day?" Capretti asked.

"It was locked when we got there," Bernie said. "Elizabeth used a key to unlock it. The key was in her purse."

"Thanks," Capretti said.

"What happens now?" Bernie asked.

"I'll have an officer check the outside of her windows for signs of a break-in. I'll file a report. And then I will investigate a suspicious death. When are you planning on leaving?"

"Tomorrow for us," Bernie said. "Rose is going to stay on for a few more days, and Lily will come back for her. That was the plan anyway. I don't know what's going to happen now."

"Don't leave before you've been interviewed," the detective said. Almost to herself she added, "A death at a hotel, at a big party no less, is always a nightmare. Guests, staff, tradespeople, passersby, all sorts of people no one knows, and no one can say if they are allowed to be where they are or not. All to be questioned. All with their own questions and demands for answers. All with their own interpretation of what happened."

"The very opposite of a locked room mystery," Bernie said.

"If you're a fan of detective shows on telly, I do not want your opinion on what I should do next."

"Always happy to help," Bernie said.

The detective walked down the hallway, and the uniformed officer followed her. Capretti's phone rang and she answered. "Leaving now. Is that so? She's right here." She put away the phone and turned back. "Lily Roberts?"

"That's me."

"You've been moved up the interview list. DI wants to speak to you. Now."

"Me? Now?"

"You. Come with us."

The receptionist told us where to find DI Ravenwood, and we walked through the door beside the front desk to emerge into the service corridor I'd used earlier today to get to the kitchen. Bright lights, beige paint on the walls, no pictures, tiled flooring, closed doors leading off the hallway. A uniformed officer stood outside the kitchen, and crime-scene tape was draped across the entrance. I couldn't help sneaking a peek, and saw people in white suits, hair-covering hats, booties over their shoes, one going through bags of flour, tubs of sugar, containers of spices, while another dusted surfaces with a small brush. Checking fingerprints in a commercial kitchen must be a nightmare.

The police had taken over one of the business offices as an incident room. Another officer guarded the door, and inside, DI Ravenwood sat behind the desk. Ian, the head chef, was coming out, as I was shown in. He threw me a look I couldn't decipher as Capretti hustled me into the room.

The Yorkshire police seemed to have been able to pull a major investigation together in remarkably little time. I wondered if they were always this efficient, or if it happened to be a slow time of the year.

I hadn't done anything wrong, but there's something about being the subject of a police interview that makes any innocent person nervous. I wiped my palms on the hips of my beautiful dress and lowered myself into the chair facing the desk. I took a guess that this was Tony's office. It was a good size, with two visitors' chairs. Drapes were pulled over the window, but the sound of a car engine outside indicated it looked out over the parking lot. Pictures covering the walls showed famous and important people visiting the hotel. Even I recognized an internationally known baker, a famous chef, and a couple of actors. Many of them posed with Elizabeth, some of the photos going back decades, judging by her changing age and the clothes and hairstyles of the period. The surface of the desk was almost completely clear, nothing but a pad of paper, a pen, a large computer monitor and keyboard, an open laptop, a cell phone. For a moment, I thought the state of his desk indicated Tony had a tidy mind. Until I noticed the stack of papers on the floor and more documents haphazardly piled on a credenza. Ravenwood had simply shoved everything he didn't need off the surface.

"There is something to the missing jewels," Capretti said to her colleague as we came in. "According to the owner, Elizabeth Crawford, Lady Frockmorton, they're worth upwards of ten million pounds, and at the moment, I have no reason to believe she misplaced them."

"Is her room secure?"

"No more secure than any hotel room on the ground floor. The jewels were in an unlocked jewelry box on her dressing table, not kept in a safe. She claims to have put them away last night, and when she opened the box a short while ago, they weren't there."

"Okay." Ravenwood glanced at me. I tried to smile. "We'll talk about that later. The two incidents might be related, and we'll assume so until proven otherwise. Speak to the staff and what guests you can locate, and ask if anyone knows anything, about both the jewels and the man's death."

Capretti left without another word.

I continued smiling.

Ravenwood did not smile back. He got straight to the point. "You worked in the kitchen this morning, I've been told."

"I did."

"Why? Aren't you a guest here?" He indicated my pretty party dress, shoes with heels, dangling silver earrings and matching necklace.

"I own a restaurant and tearoom in North Augusta, Massachusetts, where I live. I'm a pastry chef. I like to bake, I like to watch restaurant kitchens working, but mostly I hoped to learn some new things."

"Did you?"

"Did I what?"

"Learn new things."

"Not really. Afternoon tea is afternoon tea just about anywhere in the world you go. The food and presentation is traditional. That's what people expect."

"Did you bake?"

"No. I made sandwiches, and I helped arrange flowers and set the tables."

"Make any sandwiches in particular?"

I studied his face. He was digging for something. I

thought back over my morning. So much had happened in the hours since. "I made the watercress sandwiches, and the coronation chicken. That was something new for me. I guess I did learn something as I'm thinking of putting them on the menu at home."

"Coronation chicken," he said. "So called because the dish was created for the late queen's coronation. I've been told it's flavored with curry power, as a nod to the glory of the empire, as it was in the queen's early days."

"Yes. Curry powder and mayonnaise. Some mango chutney."

"While you were working, I assume you were also watching, as you said you were interested in how they do things here. Did you see anyone adding any ingredients you thought were unusual, or anyone attempting keep their movements unnoticed?"

"No. I mean, it was all new to me. The people, the layout. Even though the food is, as I said, much the same, every pastry chef has their own way of doing the most basic things. My shortbread, for example, is a lot better than what Ian's staff made." Why on earth I mentioned that, I do not know.

Something flickered behind his eyes. "Was something wrong with it?"

"I don't mean that. I only meant I like my recipe better. A matter of personal preference, I suppose."

"Did anyone come into the kitchen who did not belong?"

I relaxed fractionally at the direction this interview was taking. The inspector was simply asking for my observations, as the outsider I am. He wasn't going to accuse me of anything. Unless he'd suddenly whip around, like Columbo, and say, "One more thing." I know what Columbo does, because that's one of Rose's favorite TV programs.

"I can't say who belonged and who didn't, but I can say a lot of people came in who had no intention of getting their hands dirty. Family members, party guests, all wanting to check on how it was going or, for old-time staff, take a walk down memory lane. Bored kids of all ages hoping to grab a snack. Adults hoping to grab a snack. The two little twins ran in and grabbed cookies, what you English call biscuits, barely avoiding colliding with someone. Finally, Ian's patience snapped, and he yelled at Annabelle and ordered her out."

"Annabelle. That would be Annabelle Crawford, the current Countess of Frockmorton, Julien's mother?"

"Yes."

A wayward ginger curl fell over his forehead. I wondered if it had been deliberately arranged to give him an innocent, boyish expression. Or was his hair the bane of his existence? Bernie hated her thick red locks when she was a child; now she loves them. Although she pretends not to.

He said nothing for a long time. Outside a car drove by. A woman laughed. A man shouted. In the far distance sheep bleated.

"While you were in the kitchen, did you see any nuts being used? I don't mean peanuts but tree nuts. Walnuts, almonds—"

"I know what tree nuts are," I said. "I know they're different than peanuts. I own and cook in a restaurant, and we have to be so careful these days. I am. Very careful."

"Easy to get confused, in a strange and busy kitchen, I'd imagine. Might you have accidentally added ground nuts, or maybe some nut powder to the coronation chicken mixture?"

"What?" My mind raced as I tried to remember every step of preparing the sandwiches. I'd followed the recipe Ian had shown me exactly. I'd made no additions or changes. Had I reached for a container of nuts or nut flour by mistake? "Definitely not. There wasn't any flour in the mixture and no nuts in the recipe."

"Would you say Ian Carver is careful?"

"I can't say. He seems efficient and well organized to me. But I only saw him working for a couple of hours."

"Thank you, Ms. Roberts. How long do you intend to stay here?"

"I'm meeting a friend tomorrow for a few days touring the area, and then I'll be back to get my grandmother. That's the plan anyway. I don't know if things will change."

"Leave your phone number with the constable at the door. I'll be in touch if I need anything more."

I started to stand.

"One more thing," he said.

I dropped back down.

"As an outsider, what would you say relationships are like in this family? Specifically, between the late Julien Crawford and the rest of them?"

I would say, but only to myself, that the extended family had their differences. I remembered the argument Bernie and I overheard between Julien, Tony, Susannah, and Emma at the pub. Was that only last night? I remembered Julien and his sister Jacqueline arguing in the garden about trying to wrest control of the business and the estate from Elizabeth. I remembered the cousins saying Annabelle couldn't wait to get her hands on the Frockmorton Sapphires. If Elizabeth had died, I'd tell the inspector all that, in detail. But she hadn't, and so I debated how much to say. If anyone in my family died under mysterious circumstances, the relationships between my mother and her brothers wouldn't look good under police scrutiny.

"I did catch some overtones of tensions between various family members," I said. "Largely to do with the running of the family business and inheritance issues when Elizabeth dies. But we did only arrive yesterday, and we haven't spent much time with any of them, other than causal party chitchat."

"What sort of tensions?"

"You're better off asking them," I said. "As a total stranger, I don't want to make something out of nothing. In my experience, all families have their disagreements, and this one had a lot to deal with this weekend."

"I'll do that," he said. "Thank you for your time."

I found Bernie sitting at the little desk in our room, typing away madly on her iPad. She'd changed out of her party clothes into jeans and a loose sweater. "I'm glad to see you're not under arrest," she said as her fingers flew.

I dropped onto the bed. "Not under arrest, but not entirely in the clear. He had questions about the sandwiches I made."

"Fair enough, if the allergen was added to the food. He'll be asking the same of everyone."

"What are you working on?"

"I'm introducing a subplot into the book about Rose's grandmother's jewels that were stolen when she was a child suddenly appearing again."

"You don't need any more subplots. You need to concentrate on the main plot."

"Subplots illustrate character and provide red herrings to distract the astute reader." She stopped typing and turned around. "Are you bothered by it?"

"By subplots? Sometimes. If they get in the way of the main story."

"Which is quite obviously not what I'm asking, Lily."

"I'm bothered that a man died, yes. I'm sorry for his family. But on a personal level, not really. I know Julien wasn't poisoned by anything I made. They do seem to be strongly implying he was killed by nuts in something he ate, as you just pointed out. If nuts got into the food accidentally, that's bad, very bad, for Ian and for the hotel. If they were put in by someone acting deliberately, that's a whole new thing."

"Yup," Bernie said.

"I haven't heard anyone suggesting Elizabeth had any food allergies, have you?"

"No. You're thinking she might have been the target?"

"We know some members of the family aren't happy with the way she controls the money and the businesses. We know they weren't happy she was planning to sell the sapphires. I thought it possible the nuts or whatever could have been intended for her, but that doesn't seem likely."

"The family didn't know she was going to sell the jewels, though. Not until she told Jacqueline and Susannah a short while ago."

"She told Rose. She might have told someone else. People overhear things."

"True. As for the jewels, my money says someone saw them last night being worn by an old lady and knew this place isn't exactly a secure facility. So they slipped into her room while Elizabeth was at breakfast or at the tea and helped themselves. A hotel room isn't a bank vault. Easy enough to break into."

"How do you know that?"

Bernie winked at me. "I know plenty of things, Lily. I also know this entire situation has nothing to do with us. I called Matt earlier and told him what's going on. He'll be here around noon tomorrow to pick me up. I'm excited about seeing York. Did you speak to Simon today?"

"A text this morning telling him about my time in the kitchen, but nothing since. I don't quite know what to say: *Bernie and I have tripped over another murder?*"

At that moment my phone buzzed with a text from

Simon. I wondered if he'd picked up telepathic signals that we were talking about him.

The text read: **News says Julien Crawford, Viscount Darnby, took ill at Thornecroft Castle and has died. Isn't that Frockmorton heir?**

I replied: **Sadly yes. Police investigating.**

Simon: Not accidental or natural causes then?

Me: Still to be determined.

Simon: You okay? Want to talk?

Me: Perfectly okay. Situation is sad, but not distressing. Fill you in tomorrow

Simon: ♥

Bernie had turned her attention back to her iPad. "Checking social media and online news. Word is out about Julien but no cause of death given yet. Police investigating. I don't see anything about the sapphires. Never mind that. I'm starving. What about you?"

"Not hungry."

"I don't much care. You can watch me eat. Let's go to that pub again—it's the closest."

Chapter 10

Breakfast the following morning was cereal and pastries laid out on a long solid oak buffet table. "Sorry," the waitress said. "The police haven't let us back into the kitchen yet, so Ian and Tony made a run into town first thing. We do have coffee and tea, though, as made in the staff room, and someone brought a toaster from home, so we can do you toast."

I didn't mind. I chose an almond croissant so delicious I helped myself to a second one. Bernie had yogurt and granola, and Rose settled on two slices of toast.

Bernie and I had gone to the pub for dinner, but we hadn't stayed long. The mood was downbeat, not only from the hotel guests we recognized but others as well. The Frockmorton family had lived in these parts for generations and had always been intimately connected with the community. Even today, when legions of servants didn't live in small cold attic rooms, make the long trudge in from their own homes every day, or visit the estate office once a month tugging their forelocks to report on agricultural output, the family's hotel, farms, and rental properties employed and housed a good number of local people. From the scraps of conversation I overheard, it was clear Elizabeth was highly regarded, perhaps even loved, although the same could not necessarily be said for some of her descendants. Most people didn't even know Julien, but they grieved for him, because he was Elizabeth's grandson. I overheard a man comment that Julien could be "two-faced," but he was quickly shushed on the grounds that one does not speak ill of the dead.

I wondered what "two-faced" meant, but I didn't ask.

When we got back to the hotel, tired and subdued, we found the place being, essentially, tossed. Staff, watched by police officers, were searching the public areas. Tony stood in the doorway of the largest of the banquet rooms, usually used, we'd been told, for wedding receptions.

I wanted to simply to go my room and settle down with my book, but the ever-curious Bernie took a sharp detour and approached Tony. "What's going on?"

"They're searching for Granny's jewels on the grounds that she might have taken them off and absentmindedly dropped them behind a sofa cushion. I told Capretti that did not happen, but she insists on a search."

"Seems fair to me," Bernie said. "Before they pour time and resources into a nationwide hunt, they have to be sure such a thing didn't, in fact, happen."

"I suppose," he said. "Good thing we don't have any paying guests at the moment. It's easier for me to make excuses and apologies for the disruption when everyone's here by our invitation."

"Were they insured, do you know?" Bernie asked casually. That is to say, she spoke causally, but I know her well enough to know she was asking a very specific question. That forensic accountant mind would immediately start looking at all the financial angles.

"Can't really say. Probably. I don't know when they were last evaluated. They've been out of sight for a lot of years."

At that moment, a young woman approached us. She held out a ten-pound note. "Found this beneath a cushion."

"We should do this more often," Tony said with a tired sigh. "We're coming up with so many strange things, we might eventually have enough for a charity auction. Put it with the rest."

We wished him good night and headed for our beds.

Now, we were finishing up our breakfasts with Rose. Bernie and I still had to pack and prepare for our departure. Matt was coming to get Bernie, and I planned to go to where Simon was living, not far from Halifax. I was not looking forward to the drive. Fortunately, no rain was in the forecast, and the sky outside the breakfast room windows was clear and blue. Simon had offered to pick me up, but his only means of transportation was a motorcycle, and he admitted the weather in Yorkshire in late October couldn't be counted on to be dry. I was glad I'd turned the idea down. I had slowly, and reluctantly, grown moderately comfortable—meaning not always on the verge of outright panic—on the back of Simon's bike on the flat, quiet backroads of the Outer Cape. Going through those awful Yorkshire roundabouts, turning sharp narrow corners, brushing up against ancient stone walls, or hurling down the M1 did not appeal to me in the least.

As we left the breakfast room, the constable who'd accompanied DS Capretti to Elizabeth's rooms yesterday approached us. "Ms. Roberts. I was told you were in here. DI Ravenwood would like a word."

"Why? Has something happened?"

"I don't know. I'll take you to him."

I glanced at Bernie. "You've got lots of time before we

have to check out," she said. The hotel was again accepting paying guests starting today. "If you're delayed, I'll call Simon."

"Stop by and let me know when you're leaving, love," Rose said. "Have you seen Lady Frockmorton this morning?" she asked the constable.

"No, ma'am. I haven't."

"I'll give her a call to see how she's doing. I'll suggest we meet for tea later, perhaps."

The young police officer escorted me to Tony's office, her face impassive and unsmiling. I didn't bother attempting to make polite conversation. We passed the still sealed-off and guarded kitchen. I'd gone for a short walk before breakfast, down the driveway to the road and back, and had seen police tape warning people away from the patios and terraces. Two marked police cars had been parked outside next to a plain white van.

DI Ravenwood was standing at the window when I was shown into the office. The drapes were pulled back, and I could see the parking lot and, beyond that, to sheep-dotted green fields, hedgerows, and stone walls. DS Capretti stood against a wall, framed by a TV baker on one side and the then Duchess of Cornwall on the other. Both detectives had changed their clothes. He'd had time to shave, and she'd washed and brushed her hair. Ravenwood turned when the door opened and I came in. "Ms. Roberts." Capretti said nothing.

"Good morning, detectives," I said. "Is everything all right?"

"Depends on what you mean by all right," Ravenwood said. "Have a seat."

I did so. He got straight to the point. "Yesterday, when questioned, you told me you made two types of sandwiches. Can you remind me what type they were?"

He didn't, I suspected, need any reminder at all. And that made me very nervous. "Watercress and coronation chicken."

"Why those in particular?"

"No reason other than Ian told me to."

"How did you know what do to?"

"Aside from the fact that I'm not only a professional chef, but the owner of a tearoom, he showed me his recipes. Even something apparently as simple as a watercress sandwich needs to be prepared as the chef wants, when the chef isn't doing it himself."

"Did you make all the watercress and chicken sandwiches?"

"I think so. I didn't see anyone else making them, and I used the pre-cooked chickens in the fridge. Why are you asking me all this?" I looked at Capretti. Her dark eyes watched me.

Ravenwood ignored my question. "Did anyone assist you with this sandwich preparation?"

I opened my mouth to say no, and then I shut it again. Ravenwood stared at me. "Ms. Roberts?"

"Not with preparing the filling, no, but I had help assembling the sandwiches. It's faster to do it assembly-line style. Work up and down the row rather than one at a time."

"Who assisted you?"

"Alicia. I don't remember her last name. She's a doctor and was helping out because her mother worked here at one time. It was her, Alicia, along with a paramedic, who tried to help Julien before the ambulance arrived."

"Doctor Alicia Boyle." Capretti spoke for the first time. "We've had run-ins with her and her father before."

I didn't have time to ask what a "run-in" meant.

"Were you and Dr. Boyle together the entire time you were making the sandwiches?"

"Yes. Please, I have to ask what's the purpose of all these questions. Am I being . . . accused of something?"

The two detectives exchanged glances. Ravenwood nodded, ever so slightly.

"Forensic results are preliminary at this time," Capretti said, "but because we were able to direct them to look for something in particular we got a fast report. Traces of powdered almonds were found in the remains of some of the coronation chicken sandwiches."

I'd been expecting something like this by the direction the questions were taking, so her words didn't come as a total shock, but it did set me aback. A chef's worst nightmare. To serve a customer something they were allergic to and in quantities sufficient to kill or seriously decapacitate them. "I—don't know what to say," I said.

"Most of the food prepared for the party had been consumed," Capretti continued, "but not all. There were leftovers, and in some cases, people took a bite or two and left the rest. Giving us an adequate test sample of almost everything. Of all the food served yesterday, it was immediately noticeable to us that a good number of the chicken sandwiches were sampled but not finished. We had to ask why that might be."

Now I remembered. I hadn't particularly liked my coronation chicken sandwich, either. I'd enjoyed the one I'd had at our tea with Elizabeth on arrival much more. I'd been embarrassed at the quality of the one I'd been served at the party, and blamed myself for not mixing the ingredients properly. I'd thought no more about it. There were so many other wonderful things to taste and enjoy.

"How many of those sandwiches would you estimate you made?"

"Three hundred and twenty. One hundred and sixty guests. Two for each."

"Did you make them all at once? All from the same containers of ingredients, or did you open a new jar of something?"

I thought back. "All at once, yes. I did the chicken ones first, and when they were finished, I started on the watercress. I had one big, commercial-size jar of mayonnaise, one of mango chutney, one bag of curry powder, a container of cinnamon, and a bag of sultanas. I measured everything according to the recipe I was given. Did they all have the nut powder in them? All the sandwiches you tested, I mean?"

"No, not all," she said. "The lab hasn't finished analyzing them all yet, but we have a good enough sample to determine that the nut power was added to some. What happened to the sandwiches after you finished them?"

"They were covered in plastic wrap and put in the fridge until serving time."

"Who put them in the fridge?"

"Alicia. Dr. Boyle. I have to ask: do you think Julien was the intended victim?"

The detectives exchanged looks. Ravenwood nodded, and Capretti said, "It's high on our list of possibilities. We immediately dismissed any suggestion of food accidentally going bad or bad ingredients having been purchased, as no one else, even the very elderly people present, appears to have taken the slightest bit ill. The hospital has no reports of anyone showing up last night or this morning with food poisoning. Not anyone who'd eaten here at any rate."

"Why would Julien eat the sandwich? People with allergies that extreme can usually detect the slightest quantities of danger."

Capretti cocked an eyebrow. "Why, indeed?"

"I've had coronation chicken several times lately," Ravenwood said. "With all the fuss surrounding the recent coronation, it suddenly became popular again. The curry flavor varies quite a bit depending on who's making it and how much of a heavy hand they have with the spices."

"Ian," I said slowly. "Has a heavy hand."

"It didn't help," Ravenwood said, "that Julien Craw-ford had several glasses of whiskey before the party began and wine during. We've been given to understand such was not unusual for him. His senses would have been dulled."

"I'm sorry I can't be of more help," I said. "I made the sandwich filling. Dr. Boyle and I assembled them. We covered the sandwiches in plastic wrap and put them into the fridge until it was time for the tea. I left the kitchen not long after, so I didn't help arrange or serve them." I stood up. "If I think of anything else, I'll let you know."

"Sit down." Capretti's tone changed. No longer chatting about possibilities, tossing around ideas, asking for my observations.

I sat.

"I've seen Ian Carver's recipe," she said. "It does not contain nuts of any sort or nut flour. Did you, Ms. Roberts, perhaps reach for an unfamiliar tin or package in an unfamiliar kitchen?"

"I most certainly did not. Let me remind you, once again, that I am a professional cook. Whether in America or in England, a jar of mayonnaise says "mayonnaise" on it. And it's white, not pale brown. A length of chives looks like chives, not ground almonds. I measured curry powder from a tin marked "curry powder." Maybe the almonds were in that. You should check."

"Thank you so much for your advice," she said. "Let me assure you, we have had it analyzed, not only the curry powder but the other ingredients mentioned in the recipe. Not a trace of almonds was found. Which makes us believe the ingredient was added as an extra feature. Did you think you could improve on the standard recipe? Try something different?"

It took me a moment to realize she was actually accusing me of adding the ground almonds that killed Julien Crawford, Viscount Darnby. I opened my mouth. I closed it.

Both detectives watched me.

"No," I said at last.

Ravenwood leaned forward. He smiled at me. The smile was warm, reaching his eyes. "Playing a joke on them all maybe? I mean, coronation chicken? What a pompous name. A dish celebrating the empire to boot. You Americans took yourself out of our empire a long time ago, but you don't seem to be able to forget it. You love our monarchy and all its trappings, but at the same time you can't help mocking it."

"I have no opinion on the monarchy at all. The King seems nice, though." I tried to make a joke of the accusations, but as soon as the words were out, I realized it might have been a mistake. Were Ravenwood and Capretti staunch Republicans, wanting to see the end of the monarchy and the hereditary aristocracy? "I am a professional chef. I've cooked in Michelin starred restaurants—"

"As you never tire of telling us," Capretti said.

"I keep telling you, because you don't seem to be listening. We do not make jokes with our food. Never, never, ever."

"Did you not know Julien Crawford was allergic?"

My head was starting to spin. Should I ask for a lawyer? Did they have to provide me with one if I did? Could I have one phone call, or would I just disappear into the depths of the British legal system? "I didn't know that, and there was absolutely no reason I should. It's not the sort of thing people discuss with people they don't know." Although, they did discuss it with people cooking and serving their food, all the time.

"You mentioned people were in and out of the kitchen

all morning," Ravenwood said. "Does that include Reginald Hansen?"

"Who? You mean Reggie? No. He didn't come in. At least not when I was there. I would have noticed him as he doesn't get around too well."

"What about his grandson, Josh?" Capretti asked.

"I don't know. I don't think so, but I wasn't paying attention to everything, all the time, and like I said, I left to get ready for the party before things were laid out. Why are you specifically asking about them?"

"Tell me about the Frockmorton Sapphires," Capretti said.

I shook my head in an attempt to adjust to the abrupt change of topic. Although, maybe it wasn't such a change of topic at all. "I told you yesterday what happened. Lady Frockmorton wanted to show them to my grandmother, my friend, and me, and she discovered they were not where she'd last seen them."

"You saw them at the drinks party."

"Yes, I did. Lots of people saw them at the drinks party. As I believe Lady Frockmorton said, the only purpose rare jewels have is to be seen."

"Did you like them?" she asked me.

"To be honest, no. I thought they were overly ostentatious and even a touch vulgar. Such was the style when they were made, right? When the excessive display of wealth was the entire point."

"Like them or not, admire them or not, they're worth a great deal of money."

"I don't know anything about valuable jewels."

"Your grandmother worked in this house in her youth. When the sapphires would have been brought out for dinners and parties. To be, as you said, seen."

I glanced at Ravenwood. He leaned on the edge of the

desk, letting his partner talk, saying nothing, simply watching me.

"My grandmother worked in this house more than sixty years ago. She was a kitchen maid. She wouldn't have had a reason to ever see them." Okay that was a lie, but I was getting very, very uncomfortable at this line of questioning.

"A kitchen maid. Does your grandmother carry much resentment about that time of her life? Working in the kitchens here? A servant?"

"That's ridiculous. My grandmother moved to America when she married my grandfather. She's scarcely given the place a thought since." Another lie. Rose talked constantly about her days at Thornecroft Castle, the Lord and Lady, the children, the guests, the parties, the drunken cook, all the work involved in putting on a formal dinner party or a midnight buffet for assembled guests returning from a ball at an even bigger and grander stately home.

She never talked about wanting to pinch the family jewels though.

"Did you, or your grandmother, think the jewels would be a nice souvenir of your visit?" Capretti asked. "A pretty bauble to take home."

I stood up one more time. "No. No. And No. I did not, inadvertently or otherwise, add ground almonds to the chicken. I did not steal anything, and the very idea that my grandmother hid some seething resentments from us all her life is preposterous."

"Elderly people sometimes take a fancy to pretty items and forget they're not entitled to them."

"That's a shockingly ageist comment, and also untrue. But I can reply that elderly people, such as my grandmother, are not exactly light and nimble on their feet. Her days of breaking and entering are long over."

"Your grandmother has a police record?" Capretti asked.

"I was making a joke. Sorry."

"You yourself, Ms. Roberts don't have a record, but you are not unknown to the police in your state."

"What?"

"We've been in touch with the authorities there. The police have been called to your tearoom and your grandmother's bed-and-breakfast establishment on several occasions."

"Yes, but we never *did* anything!" If they spoke to Detective Williams, who knows what he might have had to say about us. "Now, if you have specific questions as to what I observed in the kitchen, I'm happy to answer them. Otherwise, I'll be on my way."

"Not so—" Capretti began, but Ravenwood lifted one hand, silencing her. He said, "You earlier told me you plan on leaving here today, but Mrs. Campbell is staying on. Is that still your intention?"

"Yes, I'm meeting a friend for a few days."

"You'll be returning to get Mrs. Campbell?"

"Yes."

"Very well. You may go, Ms. Roberts. I have your phone number."

He didn't also say "I have your grandmother," but the threat was implied.

When I left the interview room, trying to control the shake in my hands and my wobbly legs, Ian Carver was waiting to be next under the bright lights. He didn't look like a man without a care in the world. I gave him a frown and a shrug, which he returned, and he was admitted.

I threw myself onto the bed in our room. "This isn't good," I said to Bernie.

Her own bed was a tornado of clothes, toiletries, shoes,

and computer equipment, as she contemplated how to stuff it all into her backpack. "You were such a long time I was about to call and ask if you'd gone for a walk."

I briefly told her what had been said. "I got the feeling they were on the verge of accusing me of deliberately adding the almonds to the chicken."

"You didn't even know the man. You had no reason to kill him."

"I might have done it, they implied, through neglect or as a joke. They might be thinking I did it as a distraction from Rose's theft of the sapphires."

Bernie's mouth hung open. "They think Rose stole the sapphires?"

"I don't know what they're thinking, Bernie. They were coming at me from all directions. They've spoken to the North Augusta police, who told them we've been mixed up in situations before."

"When I next see that Chuck Williams, I might poison his sandwich myself."

"You think it was Williams they talked to?"

"Of course it was. Even if he didn't want them to think you're a serial killer, he can always be manipulated into saying whatever anyone wants him to. You need to tell them to talk to Amy Redmond. She'll set them straight. I seem to have managed to successfully get everything I brought into this pack to come here, and although I have bought nothing at all since, I can't fit it all back in."

"You'll manage." I sat on the bed and watched Bernie struggle.

"Matt's been delayed," she said. "Something about a contact he's been trying to arrange a meeting with suddenly deciding today would be great. I called the front desk and asked if it would be okay if we checked out late, and she said I could have until three. If he's not here by then, I'll wait in the lobby or the bar. You?"

"I hope to leave at one. I'm meeting Simon when he gets off work at three. He says it will take about twenty minutes to get to Garfield Hall. I'm thinking of allowing two hours. If the GPS directs me down that side street again, the one that crosses the multi-lane road at an angle, I might be sitting there for ages."

Bernie chuckled. "As Lady Macbeth would say, 'Screw your courage to the sticking place.' What do you suppose that means, anyway?"

"I do not know, and I don't think Lady Macbeth ever had to drive in Yorkshire."

"Do you suppose I could leave my party dress and shoes with you to bring back for me? That would save me some room."

"If you must, although that will leave me absolutely no room for souvenirs."

"Souvenirs are vastly overrated. I—" She was silenced by a loud rapping on the door.

I was closest, so I answered to see the unsmiling face of the unnamed constable. "I'm looking for Ms. Bernadette Murphy."

"Here," Bernie said.

"DI Ravenwood would like a word."

"Happy to be of help. You've saved me from having to keep fighting with that backpack. See to it, will you, Lily."

"As if."

I wasn't invited to accompany them, so I waited a few seconds and then followed. A couple were at the front door, suitcases on the floor. The woman held both of Carmela's hands in hers and was looking deep into her eyes. Carmela wasn't dressed in black, but in a dark gray dress with white trim.

"Our condolences again on the death of your husband. Such an unspeakable tragedy," the departing man said. Carmela mumbled something.

"If you need anything, darling, do be sure and give us a ring."

"I will."

"Let us know the funeral arrangements when you have them."

"I will."

The woman released her hands, and they left. Carmela turned and caught me watching. I gave her a guilty smile. I'd followed Bernie and her escort without thinking about what I was going to do. The constable would stand at the entrance to the interview room, and it was unlikely she'd let me lean up against the door so I could hear what was being said inside. Not that such was necessary. Bernie would tell me everything as soon as she could.

"Can I help you?" Carmela asked in a tone that indicated she had no intention of doing anything of the sort. She clutched a lace-trimmed handkerchief in her right hand, but her eyes and face showed no sign of recent tears.

"No thanks. I'm leaving soon. Just saying my good-byes."

"Goodbye. Have a safe trip," she said by rote as she walked away.

"Can I help you, Ms. Roberts?" the receptionist asked.

"Uh—I, uh . . . Do you know if the restaurant's going to be able to open for dinner tonight?"

"I haven't been told so." At that moment the door marked STAFF ONLY opened, and Ian came out.

"This lady's wondering about dinner," she asked.

He blinked a few times. "Sorry, Lily. It doesn't look like it. What a mess. If anyone else asks, Beth, say, 'Not as far as we know.' "

"Everything okay?" I asked him in a low voice. "I assume the police told you they found traces of almonds in some of the chicken sandwiches."

He jerked his head toward the front doors, indicating he wanted to move out of earshot of Beth. We went outside.

"Let's walk," Ian said. The police cars and van were still there. Crime-scene tape fluttered in the light breeze. He headed down the driveway, toward the small footpath leading to the castle ruins Bernie and I had taken yesterday. On the other side of the stone wall, a couple of sheep watched us pass. The rest were too occupied in munching on the grass to pay any attention to us.

"Yeah," Ian said at last. "They had a lot of questions as to why I invited you to work in my kitchen."

"I hope—"

He lifted a hand. "Ravenwood was dancing around accusing you of adding the almond powder as either a joke or an attempt to sabotage the event, but his heart wasn't truly in it. You have no reason to want to do so. Your reputation as a pastry chef is a good one, although they told me you've had a couple of run-ins with the police back home."

"I wouldn't say run-ins. My grandmother owns a bed-and-breakfast. People bring their problems on vacation with them, and sometimes those problems burst into the open. You must know that. You work in a hotel."

"Oh, yeah. I do. My participation is strictly behind-the-scenes, but I hear things. They then turned their focus on me. Questions about my relationship with Julien. I told them I had no relationship with him whatsoever."

I sensed there was more to that comment than he was letting on, but I said nothing. The sun was out, and I was comfortable in my vest and sweater. The drystone wall ended, and vegetation crowded the path. A bird called from the trees, and another answered.

"The implication then became that I run a sloppy kitchen. Even a whisper of such a thing could ruin me. Me and the hotel."

"Have you worked here long?"

"Seven years. I'm from York, moved to London for culinary school, and worked in London after that. My wife's from Yorkshire also, and when her mother took ill, she wanted to come home. Seemed a good idea to me. I was ready for a slower-paced life. Better for our kids, too, we thought."

We walked in silence for a while. The castle ruins came into view ahead. A few people were skirting the remains of the moat heading toward the entrance while others crawled across the crumbling stone walls and foundations, many posing for pictures against the dramatic background of what remained of the crumbling old castle.

"The complication," I said at last, "seems to be the missing or stolen jewels. Did they ask you about them?"

"In that, I am completely clueless. I have no reason to go anywhere near Elizabeth's private rooms, and I never have. I don't even know exactly where they are. When we have business to discuss, she comes to my office, and we chat over a cup of tea and a biscuit. This is Elizabeth's family home as well as a hotel, but she treats the business strictly as a business. We don't even do much of that anymore. She's pretty much handed total control to Tony."

"How's Tony to work for?"

"Fine. Competent. Capable. Dedicated to the family and the hotel. More than some of the others in that family, but never mind that. That's their business."

"The police implied I poisoned the food to give my grandmother cover to steal the jewels."

He gave me a weak smile. "Some people watch too much telly. I don't suppose any of these police involvements you've had involved running a network of international jewel thieves."

"Nope."

We reached the road leading to the gift shop and ticket

office. On one side, the castle ruins stood outlined against the sky, on the other the sharp green hills, crisscrossed by low stone walls, and dotted with sheep, rolled away before us.

"It's beautiful here," I said.

"We like it," he replied. "Do you know, I've never been inside the castle itself."

"My friend and I explored it yesterday. It's so amazing."

We turned around and headed back the way we'd come.

"I told the police people were in and out of the kitchen all the time while we were getting ready," I said. "Just about anyone could have fiddled with the chicken sandwiches under the guise of looking for something in the fridge. Although it'd be hard to keep what they were doing hidden, I suppose. They'd have to be able to move quickly and discreetly."

"I said the same. But no one was in the kitchen for a brief while. Once everything was ready, I went outside for a smoke. Guests had begun arriving, so the waiters were working the bar, and the kitchen staff were finalizing the table settings or having a break of their own."

"DS Capretti said something about Alicia Boyle—Dr. Boyle. She helped me assemble the chicken sandwiches and put the trays in the fridge while I started on the watercress."

"Alicia Boyle has a certain reputation with the police, but not for anything criminal. She's heavily involved in social protests, mainly around cutbacks to the NHS and the reduction of children's services in Yorkshire. She participated in a sit-in in the MPs office a month or so ago. As I recall, about a year ago she embarrassed the chief constable by confronting him at a charity event, accusing the police of not taking seriously enough the disappearance of a teenage girl. The chief constable doesn't like to be embarrassed, and it's likely he passed his wrath on down to his subordinates. She's also known as a staunch and vociferous republican."

"She wants to see the end of the monarchy?"

"And the elimination of all remnants of the aristocracy. Inherited titles, to Alicia, are the scourge of a modern society."

"But she worked here, in the kitchen. Voluntarily. That seems odd."

"Plenty of people have conflicting views about the aristocracy. Many of the old families, like the Crawfords, work as hard these days as anyone else. They put their houses up as hotels or tourist attractions. Anything to make a quid or two. Local people know them as employers or colleagues, not overlords or factory or coal mine owners. This little hotel contributes a lot to the local economy. Good jobs, most of all. From what I've overheard, Elizabeth planned to sell the jewels to reinvest the proceeds in the hotel and her other businesses. That's a big win for the community."

"Did they ever find the teenage girl Alicia was concerned about?"

"She turned up a couple of days later, having run off with a boyfriend her parents considered unsuitable, before changing her mind and sheepishly returning home. Alicia, far as I know, never apologized to the chief constable. She might be theoretically opposed to the aristocracy, and not afraid to let everyone know it, but she knows Elizabeth treated her mother well when she worked here, and she showed her thanks by helping out yesterday."

"The other person they specifically asked me about was Reg Hansen, and his grandson Josh. Any reason for that you know of?"

"No. They asked me that, too. Josh helps out with the horses sometimes, but I don't know if he had any relationship with Julien. As for Reggie, I'd say his days of creeping about unnoticed are long past."

We reached the hotel steps and stopped at the portico. Only one marked police car remained, and the white van was gone.

"Do you have any idea as to what might have happened?" I asked.

Ian shook his head. "Someone offed Julien all right. Someone who knew about his allergies, and someone who had access to the food in the kitchen. Unfortunately, this weekend, that's just about everyone in the house."

"Someone," I said, "who wasn't overly bothered if another guest was also allergic to tree nuts and would also eat the sandwiches."

"The police spoke for a long time to the waiter who served the head table. As it always is at afternoon tea, the food was provided for the group, not on individual plates. The waiter says he simply picked up one assembly at random and took it out at the same time everyone else was being served. The food for the head table wasn't marked or set aside. No way of telling in advance what plates they would get. As for the jewels, I'm not even going to speculate. I can't see someone killing Julien as cover for the theft, but I don't know how the mind works of a person who'd not only kill someone as a distraction, but not worry about getting an innocent person at the same time."

"A scary thought," I said.

As if she'd been summoned by our conversation, Alicia Boyle came out of the hotel. The look on her face indicated she was not happy. At that moment I felt sorry for the chief constable.

"Ian. Lily. This is a coincidence, although maybe not. I've just been talking about you."

"And us about you," Ian said. "Can I take a guess you've been chatting with the officers of the law?"

" 'Chatting' might not be the right word. More like 'being interrogated.' I wasn't surprised to hear Julien died from an allergic reaction. That was obvious to me at the time. I was, however, surprised to hear the police believe the substance was added to the chicken sandwiches you made, Lily."

"We made," I said.

She smiled at me. The smile didn't do anything to relax the fury in her eyes. "Yes, we. And that is the crux of the matter. I've encountered Ravenwood before. He's looking for someone to accuse. Anyone will do. Anyone, that is, other than a member of the Dowager Countess's sainted family. Now, if you'll excuse me, I've wasted enough time on this nonsense. I have ward rounds to do."

"We're wondering if—" Ian began.

"I am not," Alicia said. "I've done my duty by showing up here as ordered, and that's the end of it." She marched away.

"I fear," Ian said, "it's not the end of it. Even if Dr. Alicia Boyle wants it to be."

Chapter 11

It was now almost noon, and I needed to get packed and be on my way. I decided to go to Rose's room first, to check if she needed anything before I left.

Bernie had arrived ahead of me. She rested on the double bed, head propped up on pillows, feet up, ankles crossed. Rose had taken the chair under the window. The weak sun flooded in, and Lissie the cat was curled up on my grandmother's lap.

"Can't say I'm surprised," I said, "to see you with a cat."

"She followed me when I left Elizabeth's rooms. Naturally, I couldn't turn her away when we reached my door."

"Naturally. How did your chat with the police go, Bernie?"

"Not as well as I might have liked," she said. "I'll fill you in in a minute, but Rose and I have been talking."

"I've no doubt about that," I said. Those two were as alike as two currants in a raisin scone, and I never knew, but always feared, what they'd get up to when they put their heads together.

"My news, first," Rose said. "I called on Elizabeth earlier in her rooms. She's grieving her grandson's death, obviously, but at the same time worried about this situation. Word is getting around that Julien was killed by food or drink served to him at this hotel, and the police are actively investigating. Newspaper people have been pestering the guests and staff, and have subsequently been escorted from the premises. Staff are forbidden to speak to reporters under threat of instant dismissal. The hotel has had some room cancelations, and even more for the restaurant. Not only that, but the restaurant remains closed under police orders, and they won't tell Tony or Elizabeth when it can reopen."

"Does she have any theories?" I asked. "About Julien's death or the disappearance of the jewels?"

"No. Nothing she's confided in me, at any rate. She canceled her appointment with the prospective selling agents and instead instructed Katherine to deal with the insurance company."

"Why Katherine? Not that I suppose it matters much who does it."

"She can't ask Robert or Annabelle, love. They have their son's arrangements to make and their own grief to deal with. Tony's swamped with unexpected hotel business. As for Carmela, it was obvious to me that Elizabeth isn't, for lack of a better term, overly fond of her grandson's widow. Although she would never come right out and say so. Trouble in the marriage, Elizabeth suggested, but she offered no more information on that."

"As for my news, I was not happy with the direction the police questions took," Bernie said. "They're not finished looking at you, Lily."

I bristled. "I told them plenty of other people had the chance to doctor those sandwiches and far more motive."

"I told them that, too, although they asked how I knew, and I had to say I only knew because you told me what went on in the kitchen. They had questions about the police cases you've been involved in at Tea by the Sea and Victoria-on-Sea."

"We've been involved in. As I recall, in some of those cases, I was only involved because you and Rose"—I threw a stern glance at my grandmother, and both she and Lissie smiled at me—"dragged me into it."

"Whatever. They know about the time that guy died from drinking the poisoned tea."

"Poisoned by the herbal tea he provided himself!"

"And then the man who drank whiskey laced with digitalis in his room in Victoria-on-Sea."

"Digitalis put in his drink by an enemy who followed him!"

"I know all that. The North Augusta police know all that. Ravenwood and Capretti know that, too. But those sorts of stories don't help allay their suspicions."

"You have to admit, love, we have had more than our share of misfortune at our places of business," Rose said.

"I admit nothing of the sort. However, I will admit the situation doesn't look good for the hotel. Ian, the head chef, and I went for a walk just now. Obviously, as the person in ultimate charge of all the food served at the tea, he's also under suspicion. More than that, if they don't find the person responsible, and if rumors spread that he was somehow careless, his reputation will be toast."

"He'll be lucky to get a job as a dinner lady," Rose said.

"What's a dinner lady?" Bernie asked.

"School lunch cook."

"Not exactly fine dining."

"No."

Lissie looked at us, one after the other. I looked at Bernie. Bernie looked at me. Rose watched us both.

Someone rapped on the door. I recognized that knock. As I hadn't yet sat down, I answered. And there she was, again, the unnamed police constable. "Mrs. Rose Campbell?" she asked.

"Here," Rose called.

"DI Ravenwood would like a word, if you don't mind."

"And if I do mind?"

The slightest smile might have touched the edges of her mouth. Then again, it could have been a trick from the hallway light above her. "He'd like a word, anyway."

"If I must." Rose gave Lissie a nudge. She didn't move. Rose gave her a stronger nudge, which had the same effect. "I seem to be trapped here."

Bernie swung her legs off the bed and stood up. She picked up the cat.

Rose got to her feet, reached for her cane, threw her bag over her shoulder, and hobbled slowly across the room. She was laying on the feeble-old-woman act—and a mite too thick, at that. "If I am not back in half an hour, love, call my lawyers."

Bernie and I left the room with Rose and the young policewoman. Bernie put the cat down, and then she took Rose's arm and led her slowly, slowly, down the hallway, cane tapping, while the constable twitched with impatience. I didn't think it was wise for Rose to play games with the police, but I could hardly say so in front of our escort. Lissie leapt onto a deep window casement.

"We'll call you if we or Mrs. Campbell need anything further from you," the policewoman said when we reached the staff door.

Bernie and I got the hint and didn't try to follow.

When the door had shut behind them, we went into the small sitting room and dropped into the deep cushions.

"I hope Rose doesn't try to needle DI Ravenwood the way she does Chuck Williams," I said. "He seems on the humorless side to me."

"No one could be more humorless than Williams," Bernie said. "But I do get your point. Hopefully, there will be no cracks about how she always wanted to own priceless jewels."

Then we spoke at the same moment. "Look, Lily, I—" Bernie said.

"I'm thinking—" I said.

We looked at each other.

"You go first," Bernie said.

"I'm thinking of not leaving. Aside from anything else going on here, Rose's friend is in distress, and Rose will naturally try to do what she can to be of assistance. There is, we can't forget, a killer and a jewel thief in this hotel."

"Who might, or might not, be one and the same. They, singular or plural, might not be in this hotel any longer, but long gone. However, I do get your point. I'm not comfortable leaving Rose in case there are further developments."

"Simon will be disappointed. He's looking forward to showing me the highlights of Yorkshire. And I'm looking forward to seeing them. And him."

"Same with Matt."

Our minds were made up for us when Beth the receptionist put down the phone and called to us. "Ms. Roberts, Ms. Murphy, I'm glad you're still here. Don't worry too much about checkout time. We've had, I'm sorry to say, yet another cancelation, and this one was for a twin room."

"Could we keep our room for a couple more days?" I asked.

"That should be okay."

"Any chance of booking another room?" Bernie said.

"Several have come free, and I'm dreading there will be more this afternoon."

"Let's do it," Bernie said to me.

"Okay," I replied.

Chapter 12

I called Simon while Bernie contacted Matt.

I was so happy to hear his deep voice and his beautiful London accent. "What's up, Lily? Are you delayed?"

"More than delayed. I want to suggest a change in plans. The police are still investigating the death and the theft that happened here."

"What theft?"

I remembered that detail hadn't been in the news yet. "An additional complication. We, meaning Bernie and me, would prefer not to leave Rose here while things are so uncertain."

"I understand. I was looking forward to showing you Garfield Hall, and I told the owners I was having a special guest. That can wait. Do you want me to come to you?"

"I do. If you can."

"I've booked the days off and I'm ready. I'll be there in about half an hour."

"I was hoping you'd say that. We took the liberty of booking an extra room. Bernie's talking to Matt, too."

"Be just like old times. Cheers, Lily."

*   *   *

Nothing dramatic happened during Rose's interview with the police, and she was not marched out in handcuffs for getting smart with an officer of the law or for making a joke that was not appreciated. She told Bernie and me they had the same standard questions for her as they asked everyone: did she notice anyone acting suspiciously? Did she observe anyone hovering too close to Julien or his food? Had she herself gone into the kitchen at any time? What was her relationship with Julien Crawford, Viscount Darnby?—to which she replied, "None." As for the Frock-morton Sapphires, when DS Capretti asked if Rose would object to a search of her room, she told them to have at it. They replied that that wouldn't be necessary, "at this time."

"I'm surprised they didn't search our room," I said. "If you had pinched them, you could have given them to us to take care of."

"Even they must know they have no more reason to believe we did it than anyone else who was in the hotel yesterday," Bernie said. "Difficult business, searching every guest room in a hotel. If someone refuses, they have to get a warrant. In America, anyway, I don't know if it's the same here. That would give the miscreant time to bury the jewels in a plant pot or something. Plenty of people were here Friday night and Saturday afternoon who aren't staying in the hotel, so they had the opportunity to walk out the door with the them before the loss was noticed. Even if they're staying in the house, the same applies. You and I went for a walk before breakfast in the morning, Lily. Plenty of good hiding places in those old stone walls at the castle or in the pits of the cellar."

I was waiting for Simon in the forecourt of Thornecroft Castle House and Hotel as his bike roared down the driveway. He pulled it to a stop and took off his helmet. His sandy hair was tousled from the helmet and longer than it had been last time I saw him. Beneath his leather jacket, his shoulders were still broad and his arms thick with muscle, as befitted a man who worked in gardens all day. His tan had faded slightly since his return to England, but his blue eyes still twinkled with good humor. And, I hoped , affection.

I ran into his arms, and we smothered each other in kisses. Finally, we separated, and he said, "Where can I park?"

I pointed to the bend in the driveway. He drove away, and I trotted after him.

He tucked his helmet under his arm and adjusted the backpack on his back. "It's beyond brilliant to see you in person." He slipped an arm around my shoulders. "Zoom just doesn't cut it sometimes."

"Likewise," I said.

He studied the imposing building in front of us. "So this is the Thornecroft Castle I've heard so much about."

"Would you like a quick look around before we go inside? Matt'll be here about four."

"Sure."

The police tape had been taken down, I was pleased to see, so I led the way to the sunken garden and we wandered through the maze. "Nicely done," he said in professional admiration.

"How's your job going?"

"Good. Great, actually. Nice owners, not too stuck up, and fully aware their home is their business now. Good staff. Keen village volunteers to help out. Tell me what's been going on."

I did so, and he didn't interrupt. When I was finished, he said, "I wouldn't waste much time worrying that you're going to be accused, Lily. You had absolutely no motive, and although you had means and opportunity, it sounds like the same can be said for a substantial number of other people."

"I know, Simon. I know. It's just—I don't think I can simply go away and enjoy myself while this cloud hangs over the hotel, and over Ian, in particular. Not to mention that Rose is worried about Elizabeth. You know Rose will try to do what she can to help."

"I do," he said. "What do you know about this Ian, the chef?"

"Nothing, other than what he told me and what I've observed."

"Then don't take everything he says at face value. Let's leave it for now. We can talk it all over when Matt arrives and decide what, if anything, we want to do. Let's get me checked in."

Matt got to the hotel shortly before four o'clock. The restaurant was still closed, but the police had permitted the bar to open, and we arranged to meet there when Matt was settled.

The place was empty when we came in. Most of the birthday party guests had headed home on Sunday evening or first thing Monday, and new reservations were being canceled in droves. With the restaurant not open, no one was dropping in for a predinner drink.

We found a table on the far side of the room from the bar itself, close to the huge old fireplace, where a wood fire was cheerfully burning. The bartender must have heard us come in, and he slipped out from the back room. In proper English fashion, Simon and Matt went to the bar to get the drinks, while Bernie, Rose, and I made ourselves comfortable.

"Nice of your young men to change their plans," Rose said. "Your grandfather, as I recall, was due to go on to York to visit with friends when we had our first meeting."

Meaning when she'd knocked him flat, not looking where she was going as she came out of a butcher's shop in Holgate. "His plans were interrupted when he was taken to hospital. I visited him there, so dreadfully embarrassed about what happened. By the time he was released, I'd had to return to Halifax, to this very house, in fact. Instead of continuing on to York as intended, Eric changed his plans and came to Halifax. To see me."

I'd heard that story more than once, as had Bernie. The details changed sometimes, between one telling and another: Holgate butcher; Halifax teashop. But none of that mattered, because the love and joy on Rose's face when she told us always had us smiling. Love truly is infectious, even over miles and decades.

Matt put a G&T in front of Rose and a martini for Bernie. Simon awkwardly carried two mugs of beer and my wine. They sat down; we lifted our glasses, said, "Cheers," and clinked.

"Barkeep's worried about his job," Matt said, after he'd enjoyed his first welcome sip. "This place is far enough out of town that not many people drop casually into the bar—not if they're not having dinner here. No one knows what's happening. The cops haven't said when the restaurant can open. Guests are canceling, even some that have nonrefundable rates."

"It's understandable to be concerned," Bernie said, "but I hope you told him these things pass. It's only been one day. Even if they don't arrest someone, new cases come up, police attention moves on. It'll all blow over. As we know, right, Lily?"

I grumbled.

"Maybe not so fast," Simon said. "This isn't an ordinary murder. Rather, it's the stuff the tabloids live for. The Viscount Darnby, son of the eleventh Earl of Frockmorton, poisoned at a well-known Yorkshire landmark, at a hundredth birthday party for the well-respected and much-loved Dowager Countess."

"The press is on it," Matt said. "Some are camped out at the gates, and a security guard's been posted. I had to identify myself before they'd let me through."

"Their attention will wander away soon enough," Bernie said. "Without fresh meat to feed on."

"How soon," Rose said, "is the question."

"There is another complication," I said. "The theft of the Frockmorton Sapphires."

"I was wondering when you'd get around to that," Simon said.

Matt's eyebrows rose. "Theft?"

"I'm surprised it hasn't been in the papers," Bernie said. "Everyone who'd been in the hotel yesterday afternoon or this morning knows about it. The public rooms were searched and people asked if they'd seen them."

"The impression I got," Rose said, "from chatting with various people over these past days, is that the staff are loyal to the family. To Elizabeth, at any rate. Don't forget all the guests were family members or lifelong friends. Not the sort to spread gossip."

I wasn't so sure about that, but I said nothing.

"You need to tell me everything," Matt said. "Bernie, you start."

"Let Lily. She's the one the police have accused."

He stared at me. "You've been accused?"

"No, I have not." With much interruption and clarification from Rose and Bernie, I told the story, from us overhearing the cousins squabbling in the pub, to me eavesdropping on Julien and Jacqueline plotting against Elizabeth, to working in the kitchen, to Julien collapsing at the tea, to Elizabeth finding, in our presence, that the Frockmorton Sapphires were missing, and the arrival of the police and the direction of their questions. By the time I finished, my glass was empty.

Matt got up to get us another round and Bernie joined him.

"I guess the main question, other than whodunit," Matt said when they returned, "is, are the murder and the theft related?"

"Hard to say," Bernie said. "It could be a coincidence. The sapphires haven't been out of the bank vault for fifty years, and for all anyone knew, they'd go back the following day not to be seen again for the next fifty years. If someone had in mind to take them, this weekend was their only chance."

"I'm inclined to think thief and killer are one and the same person," I said. "Elizabeth told Rose she intended to sell the jewels."

"So, they weren't being returned to the vault," Matt said. "Even more reason to get them snatched now. Did everyone in the family know of her intent?"

"The opposite," I said. "She hadn't told them."

"She was concerned," Rose said, "about causing dissent in the family—so she would present them with a done deed, so to speak. Even in her youth, when Elizabeth made up her mind, it was made up. No point wasting time discussing the matter."

"People were supposed to be coming here today, to meet with her, to make the arrangements," Rose said. "She would tell the family of her plans then."

"What sort of people?" Matt asked.

I looked at Rose and Bernie. We all shrugged. "Insurance company, representatives of the auction house, diamond experts, I assumed," I said. "They didn't come today because Elizabeth told them not to bother."

"She intended to use the proceeds to invest in the hotel and the family's other businesses, not to take herself on a round-the-world cruise," Bernie said, "but she knew some members of the family would not be happy about it. Did someone take the jewels to avoid them being sold? Did Julien either assist this person with that, or see them doing it, and thus this person decided Julien had to be gotten rid of?"

"No one in the family would ever be able to wear the jewels," Simon said. "Not publicly. They're on record with the police as having been stolen."

I thought of Annabelle, the current countess, the greedy look in her eyes when she saw the Frockmorton Sapphires and how her nieces had said she was desperate to get her hands on them. Had Annabelle stolen the necklace and earrings, not wanting them to be taken out of the family? That might be possible, but I couldn't accept that Annabelle killed her own son. People can do strange things, but that seemed too much of a stretch to me, and I told my friends so.

"Are we sure the jewels were stolen?" Matt asked. "Not"—he made quotation marks in the air with his fingers—"deliberately misplaced?"

"Elizabeth knows what she did with them," Rose said firmly. "Once you meet her, you'll see what I mean. She is in full possession of her faculties."

"Which," Matt said, "is precisely my point. From what Lily told us, Julien wanted to see Elizabeth legally declared unable to manage her affairs and control given to him and his sister, bypassing his father. Did she know that? Did she take steps to ensure that didn't happen? And, for some reason, decide the jewels had to disappear until that unpleasantness was cleared up?"

"Impossible," Rose said. "Elizabeth is forthright, never underhanded."

"You haven't seen or been in contact with this woman for sixty years, Rose," Simon said. "Even then, you were boss and servant, right? Not confidantes."

"I am an excellent judge of character." Rose huffed.

"Everyone believes they're an excellent judge of character," Matt said. He lifted one hand. "Hear me out. The book I'm researching now is about seniors who kill. Think about it. If one has a, shall we say, murderous disposition, that doesn't always go away with age."

"That may be true," Simon said, "but the physical ability does."

"If we assume, and it's most likely what happened," I said, "that someone—so far unknown—slipped into the kitchen, either in the mad rush of getting everything ready or when the kitchen was empty for a few minutes before service began, the most unlikely person is Elizabeth. She cannot move quickly and nimbly, and she of all people, would be noticed. Staff would ask if she needed anything. Guests would approach her to offer their congratulations on her birthday."

"Good point, love," Rose said. "I'm fifteen years younger than Elizabeth, and I can no longer nip around corners as well as I once did."

"Hidden access?" Simon asked.

"What do you mean?" Bernie said.

"Many of these big old houses have doors and corridors that have been locked up and left unused for years. Some have built-in hiding places, although this house is too modern to have needed to accommodate a priest hole. The place where I'm working, Garfield Hall, has a concealed staircase put in by one of the early lords of the manor so he could creep up to the female servants' floor without anyone knowing."

"Except the female servants, I suppose," Bernie said. "But I doubt their opinion mattered much."

"The staircase is now a popular spot for tourists to take selfies," Simon said with a grin.

Rose and I avoided meeting each other's eyes. Victoria-on-Sea had its own secret room. A small space accessible from the linen closet next to the drawing room. We hadn't put the secret room in ourselves; it was there when Rose bought the house, but we enjoyed knowing about it. I'd concealed myself on more than one occasion, listening to the police interview a suspect in our drawing room.

"I take your point about age and infirmity," Matt said. "Although some elderly people"—he smiled at Rose and raised his glass, and she blushed—"are fitter than others. And some can get around far better than they pretend. Sometimes, they're in the position to order a hit on someone. Is that a possibility here?"

"That Elizabeth ordered a hit on her grandson?" I asked. "Strange things happen, but I'd say no."

"Does it matter that Julien wanted to take Elizabeth to court? If she could arrange a contract killer, she's more than capable of running this hotel."

"She doesn't run it," Bernie said. "Her grandson, Tony, does."

"Tony's the manager," I said, "but as long as Elizabeth's the owner, she does have the final say."

"What about the chef, Ian?" Matt asked me. "He told you he went out for a smoke when everyone else took their break, but that might not be true."

"If you're asking me if Ian put the nut powder in the sandwiches, I'd say absolutely not. No chef would do something like that. Even if they were not charged with it, a situation like this can permanently ruin their reputation. Ian is already worried about the fallout if the police don't find the killer. The restaurant is closed for a police investigation. Everyone in the food business who talks about that will mention the name of the head chef in the same breath."

"The problem here," Simon said, "is just about anyone had access to the food. Am I right?"

"Totally. When we were working, people were constantly coming in and out of the kitchen. Sticking their heads in the fridge, hoping for a chance to sample the goods, kids running through. Two little girls made a grab for cookies on the cooling rack and just about knocked a sous chef flying when they rushed out with their prizes. It would have been substantially more chaotic than usual. Paying guests rarely wander into the kitchen asking if they can help, but nonpaying guests sometimes feel obliged to. With all the relatives in the house, many of them possibly having some sort of interest in the family business, and lifetime friends thinking they had the run of the place—yeah, a recipe for chaos."

Matt leaned back, cradling his glass in both hands. Simon took my hand under the table and gave it a squeeze.

"Let's back up for a moment," Matt said. "You made several hundred of the chicken sandwiches, right, Lily?"

"Right."

"Did the cops find the nut powder in them all? All they tested, at any rate."

"No. Ravenwood specifically told me they hadn't finished analyzing them yet, all they still had on hand anyway, but some of them didn't appear to have been tampered with."

"Which must mean the nut powder was not added to one of the sandwich ingredients, otherwise they should all have traces of it?"

I shrugged. "I guess that depends on how well the unwanted ingredient was stirred in. If it was."

"Might also indicate the killer only had time to tamper with a couple of trays," Simon said. "If the sandwiches were finished, arranged, wrapped, and in the fridge, the killer would have had to pull off the plastic wrap, lift the top piece of bread, sprinkle on the nut powder, replace the bread, and on to the next one. That takes time."

I thought about that for a while. "No guarantee, in that case, Julien would get one of the poisoned sandwiches."

"Or that someone else, also allergic, would not," Matt said. "Our killer was prepared to take a chance. Likely simply because the opportunity presented itself when the kitchen was either temporarily unoccupied, or everyone was concentrating on their own tasks. If this attempt had failed, would they have given up, or tried again?"

"No way of knowing," I said.

"Ready for another, Rose?" Bernie asked.

"No, thank you, love. Time to get back to remembering my daily limit."

Tony walked into the bar. He frowned and gave his head a shake when he saw how empty the room was. His sister, Susannah, and their cousins Jacqueline and Emma followed.

"Good evening," he said. "Hope you're enjoying the peace and quiet."

"We are," Bernie said. "Don't worry about it. Lily is in the hospitality business, too, and she's had experiences with police attention before. It's only temporary."

"I certainly hope so," Jacqueline said. "We can't go on like this. But will Granny—?"

"Not now," Susannah said.

Matt put down his empty glass and stood up. He leaned across the table, hand outstretched. "Matt Goodwill. I'm a friend of Lily and Rose."

"Hey, what about me?" Bernie said affectionately.

"Her, too," Matt said.

Simon also stood. "Simon McCracken. I spent the summer working at Rose's place, and now I'm the winter gardener at Garfield Hall."

Handshakes were exchanged all around.

TEA WITH JAM & DREAD   153

"Would you care to join us?" Matt said. "It's okay, if not. You need your family time."

"I need," Tony said, "a full hotel. Yeah, sure. It's not as though we can't find chairs." He and Susannah took a round of drink orders and went to the bar.

Jacqueline and Emma sat down, and introductions were made. All of the cousins, I thought, looked tired. Circles under their eyes, faces pale and drawn. The redness in her eyes and streaks in the makeup on Jacqueline's cheeks showed signs of recent tears.

"I detect traces of a Canadian accent," Matt said to Emma.

She smiled. Matt was good at helping people to relax. He could chat comfortably and easily, and he put people instantly at ease. I supposed he needed that skill when interviewing people for his true-crime books.

"You have a good ear," Emma said. "My dad's Elizabeth's second son, Thomas. He and my mom divorced when I was nine, and he moved to Canada not long after. I spent many of my summer holidays there. I worked so hard to get a Canadian accent, thinking that would impress my friends when I went back to school. Dad wasn't able make it this week. He broke his leg playing tennis. He's bragging that at least he made the save. Just like my dad," she added fondly.

"Elizabeth had four children, right?" Bernie asked. "We've met Robert and Katherine. Your dad's Thomas, what about the other?"

"Elizabeth and Edward's oldest daughter, Amanda, died in her early twenties," Rose said. "Elizabeth was talking about her last night. A skiing accident, I believe."

"That's right," Jacqueline said. "My father's Robert, the eldest son. Julien was my brother."

"I'm sorry for your loss," Matt and Simon said.

She dipped her head and said nothing.

Tony and Susannah returned, followed by a waitress with the drinks.

We made idle chitchat for a while, but there was no ignoring the elephant who'd plonked itself down at our table.

"The police," Tony said at last, "are being singularly uninformative. I need to get this place fully open again, and I can't get a straight answer out of them."

Susannah put her hand lightly on his arm. "Isn't that normal? They probably don't know what's going on, either."

"Bad enough we lost all weekend and most of last week," Jacqueline said. "On Granny's silly whim."

"Don't start with that again," Emma said sharply. "Granny does what Granny wants and there's no point in discussing it."

"And so she should," Rose muttered under her breath.

"We're here," Simon said. "Matt and I checked in earlier."

"Tell all your friends," Tony said.

I was keen to ask the cousins if they knew of any reason someone would kill Julien, but that did seem a rather inappropriate topic of casual conversation.

"I can't stop thinking there's some sort of mistake," Emma said. "It's all a silly joke, and Julien's going to pop his head around the corner and yell 'Surprise!' any minute now."

"Not that Julien, of all people, was known for his practical jokes," Jacqueline said. "We had our differences, and how. But he was my brother, and I did love him."

"How are your parents holding up?" Bernie asked.

"Stiff upper lip and all that, don't you know? Mustn't let the lower classes see standards slipping."

"Isn't that a bit harsh?" Susannah said.

"Is it?" Jacqueline shrugged. "Maybe it is. Mum's not

doing too well although she's trying to pretend, and Dad's as much help to her as he usually is. Meaning, none at all."

"Your brother's wife is here—Carmela, is it? Did they have any children?" Bernie asked.

"No, and just as well. Julien and Carmela were on the outs, heading to divorce court. She agreed to come this weekend to put on a show of happy families in front of Granny. As though anyone can pull the wool over Granny's eyes. She knows everything, but she doesn't, unlike some, talk about everything she knows. I doubt Carmela is all that upset at Julien's death. Makes everything so much easier, doesn't it, particularly as they don't have any children. Those two little blond tearaways you've seen running around and getting under and into everything are my twins."

"'Tearaways,'" Bernie said, "is a good word. They're so cute. How old are they?"

Jacqueline smiled for the first time. "Seven. Zoe and Katy."

"Will your father be taking control of the hotel when Elizabeth is no longer able?" Matt asked.

"Ownership and management are two different things," Tony said. "Uncle Robert's retired. His career was in banking, not hotels or property, and he's never shown much interest in how we do things around here."

"It was never said but always assumed," Jacqueline said, "when Granny's no longer able, control of the family businesses will bypass Dad and go directly to Julien. Now . . ."

"We have no idea what's going to happen," Emma said. "Granny's keeping the contents of her will very hush-hush."

"We didn't even know she was planning to sell the sapphires," Susannah said. "You could have knocked me over with a feather when I found that out."

"Those belong to the family, not to her. She never should have made a decision like that on her own," Jacqueline said.

"Legally," Rose said, "they do belong to her."

"You can be sure my brother would have put a stop to it. Had he but known," Jacqueline replied.

"Julien wouldn't have had a leg to stand on," Tony said, "legally speaking. As for control of the businesses, including this hotel, Julien made a lot of assumptions he shouldn't have."

"He could have delayed the sale of the sapphires for years, dragging it through the courts," Jacqueline said. "Delay it enough, and it would eventually become a moot point."

"If you want to put it like that," Rose said.

As Jacqueline spoke, I studied the other cousins. Emma and Susannah didn't seem concerned one way or the other about the prospective sale of the Frockmorton Sapphires. If, as she said earlier, Emma would be in line to inherit them, through her father, what use would a modern, not rich, woman have for them? She'd probably rather have a share of the money, if that was in the plan. Tony would have wanted to see them sold, particularly if Elizabeth planned to put some of the proceeds into the hotel, and I got the feeling that what Tony wanted, his sister, Susannah, usually agreed with.

"Julien always did insist on getting his own way," Tony said. "In that he was like Granny, without the charm or the consideration for others. I wonder what else he would have dragged through the courts, costing us time and money we can ill afford."

"My brother, may I remind you," Jacqueline snapped, "has died."

"And I'm sorry about that. Doesn't mean I have to approve of his actions when he was alive."

"Enough," Emma said. "We don't air our family laundry in front of other people."

"Stiff upper lip and all that," Tony said.

"If we were to speculate as to what happened," Susannah said, "I might think your mother took them, Jack."

Jacqueline turned on her cousin. "What does that mean?"

"Aunt Annabelle was almost drooling Friday night when she saw Granny with them. Everyone noticed. My mum says Annabelle's never been subtle about how much she wants to get her scrawny fingers on them. She's asked many times, more like begged, to be allowed to wear them, but Elizabeth always flatly refused. Mum told me there's been some big fights between her and Robert over the years. Annabelle is, after all, the current countess and she insisted she had rights to the jewels."

"What of it? Mum thought it was a waste to keep them locked up in a bank vault," Jacqueline said. "Julien and I agreed. Dad probably could have demanded Elizabeth hand them over, but he never had the backbone to stand up to Granny."

"When she eventually did take them out of the bank vault, look what happened." Emma snapped her fingers. "Gone."

Tony chuckled. "Good point."

Matt, Simon, Bernie, Rose, and I sat quietly, sipping our drinks and listening. It was as though the feuding cousins forgot we were there.

"Your grandmother," Rose said at last, "was well aware of dissent in the family about the jewels. And about other things. She hoped to avoid everyone fighting over them when she was no longer around."

"We aren't going to—" Emma began.

"Of course you will. You're arguing about them now, and Elizabeth is still alive. In some ways things were easier in the old days, as unfair as that was. On the death of the Dowager Countess, the current countess would take possession of all family and household valuables. Even before her death, if her son and heir wanted them. But Elizabeth's husband had the liberty to choose to leave everything to her, and thus Elizabeth can decide for herself. By my count, she has one daughter still living, two daughters-in-law, three granddaughters, and several great-granddaughters. Not to mention sons, sons-in-law, and grandsons. Perhaps, she simply wanted to avoid strife and preferred to sell the jewels while she was able and use the money for the benefit of all by investing it in her properties and businesses."

No one said anything for a long time. Finally, Jacqueline stood up. "Pardon me, it's been a long, tiring couple of days. I should check on my parents, see if they need anything."

"As I believe someone said earlier," Tony said, "it's all moot now. If the jewels aren't recovered, that is."

"Surely they're insured?" Emma said.

"They're insured. Whether or not to their full current value remains to be seen. In a way, the theft has done Granny a favor. Save her the bother of haggling over the price."

Jacqueline headed for the door. She passed a woman coming in and they exchanged the briefest, and coolest, of greetings.

"There you all are! I was beginning to think everyone had absconded without me." Carmela wore a thick blue turtle-neck under a black leather jacket studded with buttons and zippers and clips, shredded jeans, and ankle boots with two inch heels. Her hair was done and make up applied. Her husband died slightly more than twenty-four hours before, but she didn't appear to be sunken in grief. Then again, we all grieve in our own way. And from what I'd heard, their marriage was finished. She might even be relieved, as Jacqueline suggested, to find herself no longer subject to the trouble and expense of battling it out in court.

Had she taken steps to make that happen? I filed the idea away to consider later.

"The Widow Crawford," Susannah said. "Do take a seat."

"Don't mind if I do." Carmela settled in what had been Jacqueline's chair. She smiled at Matt and Simon and tossed her hair. "I don't believe we've met. I'm Carmela Crawford. Julien was my husband."

"Simon McCracken. My condolences."

"Matt Goodwill. I'm sorry for your loss."

"Thank you. I've never been one for keeping up appearances, and I'm not going to start now. I'm not going to pretend to be in deep mourning. I am sad, very sad, that poor Julien died so prematurely." She turned her smile on Tony. "We had our good times for sure, and at one time we were very much in love. Although I can scarcely remember when that might have been."

Tony twisted his glass in his hands and shifted uncomfortably.

Matt raised his eyebrows at Bernie. I avoided looking at Rose.

"I believe in total honesty," Carmela continued, "so I should explain that Julien and I were in the early stages of getting a divorce."

"That surprises me," Susannah said. "I would have thought you'd hang on to the marriage, no matter what, for the chance of someday being the Countess of Frockmorton."

"Aristocracy, dear, is vastly overrated these days. You're so lucky to be out of the direct line of succession."

"It would seem I'm now in it," Emma said. "You and

Julien didn't have any children, so after his father dies, my dad will be the new earl. I called Dad earlier. He said that and two dollars fifty will get him a double double at Tim Hortons."

"Whatever that might be." Carmela laid her hand lightly on Tony's arm and gave him a radiant smile. "Tony, love, would you mind dreadfully getting me a drink? I'll have a dirty martini."

Tony shrugged her hand away and pushed himself to his feet. "I have a hotel to run. See you all later." He raised his voice. "Jack, a dirty martini for Mrs. Crawford."

Carmela watched him go. The smile was still on her face but the edges had tightened, giving it a frozen appearance. Then she turned back to the group, and asked, "Any news about the sapphires?"

Chapter 13

"Feuding families," Matt said around a mouthful of steak pie. "I'd be out of work without them."

We had made our escape from the hotel bar and the squabbling cousins, when Rose received a text. She read it, put her phone away with a smile, and said good night. We then said we were off to dinner. Fortunately, none of the feuding cousins had asked to join us.

Rose's text had been from Elizabeth, asking if Rose would like to join her in her rooms for a light supper of toast and soup.

"Anything you want me to ask her?" Rose said to us.

"Why not come right out and ask if she hid the jewels, hoping for an insurance payout?" Matt asked.

"She's not going to tell if she did," I protested.

"She might," Matt said. "Seniors can get away with a lot if they play their cards right, as I've learned in my research, and sometimes that makes them overconfident."

"What was it you called me once, love?" Rose asked me. "'Madam Blanc,' after the detective in those Daniel Craig movies. Lovely man. Horrible accent. I will admit to an interest in the shenanigans of our hostess's family, but if Elizabeth confides any secrets in me, up to and including a confession to insurance fraud and murder, I will not tell you."

We'd all had a drink or two in the hotel bar, so we called an Uber to take us into Halifax. It was dark by the time we left, and the lights of the city spread out far below us, and more lights climbed the surrounding hills. The skies were clear and the rising quarter moon illuminated the fields, hedgerows, and stone walls sprinkled between the houses and villages.

We found a lovely old pub on the main street and settled comfortably close to the coal-burning fireplace.

I was having the lamb shanks, and Matt a steak pie. Simon and Bernie were digging into their fish and chips. Mugs of beer and glasses of wine rested on the table.

"If Rose finds out something from Elizabeth she wants to keep to herself out of some sense of loyalty, we'll never get it out of her," Bernie said. "Meaning, one of our main lines of inquiry is closed."

"We didn't hear from the police today," I said. "I would have thought they'd be back with follow-up questions."

"That we didn't see them," Bernie pointed out, "doesn't mean they weren't there. We didn't have a guard on the door at all times."

"True," I said. "I hope the fact that they didn't ask to talk to me again means I am no longer in the frame, as they put it. What do they say in England, Simon, when someone's a suspect?"

"Someone is a suspect," he said.

Matt laughed. "The common phrase, 'helping the police with their inquiries,' pretty much means the cops know that person did it and they're looking for evidence to prove it."

"I don't know what the coppers say," Simon said. "I don't watch a lot of telly, and until I started work at Victoria-on-

Sea, I'd never been involved in a police case. You lot are a bad influence on me." He gave me his gorgeous wicked grin. My heart turned over as I smiled in return.

I was due to go home in less than a week. Back to Tea by the Sea, back to making sandwiches and baking scones. Back to Victoria-on-Sea, back to preparing the B & B breakfasts. Simon would be going back to the grounds and greenhouses of Garfield Hall. Would he say something to me before I left? Something about wanting us to be together? If he didn't, should I?

"Not much I can do about determining who might have wanted to kill Julien Crawford," Matt said. "Although if I were investigating, I'd have a closer look at his wife."

"Why?" Bernie said. "It wasn't a secret known only to his wife and mother that Julien was allergic to nuts. I'll admit Carmela didn't seem all that broken up about his death, but they were divorcing."

"It's not so much the not-broken-up part," Matt said, "but she seemed to be almost—"

"Flirting with us," Simon said. "Me. Matt. Even Tony."

"We don't know if it was a false front or just her usual way of acting around men," Bernie said. "Tony and Julien were first cousins, but Carmela isn't a blood relative of Tony."

"True. But it didn't sit right with me, that's all," Matt said. "As for what I might be able to do, there could be something. My next book's going to be about seniors who kill—and I am not saying I think Elizabeth did it, by the way. One of the chapters is on this old guy operating in York some decades ago. He was considered a doddering old fool by his neighbors, meanwhile he was out at night slaughtering said neighbors."

"This relates to the Frockmortons how?" I asked.

"The Crawfords," Simon said. "The family name is Crawford. Frockmorton is the title."

"Okay," Bernie said, "How does this relate to the Craw-fords, if you're not accusing Elizabeth. Or, come to think of it, Rose. A couple of other elderly people were at the tea, including that old guy who told us he once entertained hopes of winning Rose's heart."

"Really?" Simon said. "Tell us more."

"No more to tell. She married Eric Campbell and moved to Iowa, and that was the end of his hopes."

"If we can return to the matter under discussion," Matt said. "My point isn't that the current matter is a case I want to use in my book, but I have a contact who might be able to be of some help." He put down his fork and took a long swallow of his beer. "My primary source in York is a retired police officer, one who worked on the aforemen-tioned case. He loves nothing more than to talk about his glory days, and along with other stories, he told me about a man who worked as a jewel fence well into his eighties, and I got the feeling that wasn't all that long ago. I can talk to the cop again, find out if the man is still alive, still active, and what contacts he might still have in that world. Before I go on, does anyone have a picture of the jewels?"

"I do." I pulled out my phone, found pictures I'd taken at the Friday night party, and handed Matt the phone. Simon leaned over to see them. "I took several shots of Elizabeth with Rose," I said. "As you can see Elizabeth is wearing them."

Matt used his fingers to zoom in. He studied the photo.

" 'Ostentatious' is the first word that comes to mind," Simon said.

"Which is why Elizabeth hasn't worn them for such a long time," Bernie said.

Matt handed back my phone. "Dealing in stolen jewels of the value and prominence of the Frockmorton Sap-phires is not a job for an amateur. If they were stolen by an amateur, perhaps on a sudden whim, the person responsible has bitten off far more than they can chew, and I'll venture a guess the sapphires will turn up in a couple of days, or the thief will be in jail. If, however, they were taken by someone who knew what they were doing, the word will be circulating far and wide among people who deal in that sort of thing. Intermediaries as well as prospective buyers. Famous jewels reported stolen can't simply be worn out in public. They have to be recut, remounted, sometimes combined with and into numerous other pieces. All of that requires a great deal of sophistication."

"Cool," Bernie said. "I've always fancied the life of an international jewel thief."

Matt grinned at her.

"You think this retired copper might be able to put you on to someone who knows the ins and outs?" Simon asked.

"Wouldn't the police already be doing that?" I added.

"They should be. Bear in mind my contact is retired. They might not think to talk to him. I'm not saying he can help us, but it wouldn't hurt to ask," Matt said. "We're not looking to recover the jewels, just get an idea of what might have happened to them. If I learn something, I'll pass it on to the police."

"If *we* learn something," Bernie said. "I'm coming with you."

"Do you have to go to York?" Simon asked. "Can't you email this guy or phone him?"

"I learned the hard way he wants face time. He's divorced, estranged from his children. Doesn't appear to have a lot of friends. He's lonely, and if I spend time listening to his stories and treating him to a few rounds at his local, he'll talk to me. Not otherwise. I can try to set something up for tomorrow."

"Great," I said. "As for the murder itself—to be honest, I don't know what I thought we could accomplish by calling you guys here. We know about tensions between people in the family. We know Julien and Jacqueline wanted to take control of the business from Elizabeth, but as has been pointed out, there's no reason to think they'd be successful in that. What else do we know? Nothing."

"We absolutely and positively know you didn't put nuts into the chicken mixture," Bernie said. "The police do not."

"There is that," I said.

"It wouldn't hurt for you two to have a talk to the coppers," Simon said. "Find out the general direction their investigation is taking."

"They're not going to kick back, pour us a cup of tea, and share information with us," I said.

"You somehow seem to get Amy Redmond to do precisely that."

"Only when it's to her advantage," I said.

"My point exactly."

"Simon does have a point," Matt said. "If a random serial killer was passing through the hotel kitchen that afternoon, and the police are hot on their tail, we're wasting our time here, and we can head off to enjoy the highlights of Yorkshire as planned."

"You think a serial killer did this?" I asked.

"No."

"Okay."

Bernie lifted her wine glass and her eyes twinkled. "We do have another line of investigation we can pursue."

"I was wondering when we'd get to that," Matt said. "Can you do it?"

"I can only try."

"Do what?" Simon asked.

"We're dealing with two issues here. Two we know of,

anyway, which may or may not be connected." Bernie held up her index finger. "One: the disappearance, possible theft, of valuable jewels. Two: the inheritance, or at least the control of, the family businesses. The Frockmorton—sorry, Crawford—family doesn't appear to be fabulously wealthy, as in the landowners of old, but they have money by normal standards. Particularly, if you consider the sale value of the sapphires. Elizabeth's eldest son, Robert, the current earl, apparently doesn't want to run the businesses after Elizabeth, for any reason, steps down. His son, the late Julien, was in line to take over. We know, from what Lily overheard, he wanted to do that. Immediately. Without waiting for the eventual death of his grandmother. I have to ask: What about the others in the family? Any of them hoping for either control or a cut if Julien was removed from the picture? I can do a deep dive into the financial affairs of the various family members."

"We're in England, remember?" I said. "You don't know anyone in England you can ask."

Bernie flexed her fingers, as though she were sitting down to a keyboard. Her college major was in accounting. Her minor was in computer science. As she'd proven at her previous job, she was a formidable adversary to anyone trying to hide evidence of financial crimes in the nether regions of the online world. And these days, everything is online. "First off, I'll simply look for what's available for anyone with the skills, legally speaking, to find. If I need more info, my previous employers do a fair amount of business in the UK and Europe. Financial crimes know few international boundaries. I can always persuade someone at the company to help me out."

"Do I want to know this?" Simon asked.

Bernie winked at him. "I haven't been caught yet. For

now, you can consider it a case of me satisfying my curiosity."

Matt stood up. "I'll call Dennis now and arrange to meet tomorrow afternoon in York. Bernie, you have computer stuff to start on, and Lily's going to chat to her police friends."

"As for me," Simon said, "I'm going to have another beer."

Chapter 14

When we got back to the hotel, I checked in with Rose while Bernie and Simon swapped rooms. Aside from wanting to be with Simon, I was glad I wouldn't have to share a room with Bernie tonight. If she started following a computer trail, she'd be at it all night, and she rarely refrained from commenting to herself, out loud, on how it was going.

I knocked on Rose's door, and she called, "It's open."

My grandmother was in bed, dressed in her nightgown, face scrubbed clean, hair askew, propped up on a pile of pillows, reading in the glow of the bedside lamp.

"You need to lock your door," I said. "The killer might still be here."

"If so, they have no reason to worry about me, love. Besides, I knew you'd be around soon, and I can't be disturbed." She pointed to the purring lump beneath the bedcovers. "I can't turn out the light while my visitor is still here, as I have no food or litter box for her."

"I wonder what Robert the Bruce will have to say about it when you return home smelling of another cat."

Rose closed her book. "Pleasant evening?"

"Yes, it was. Despite talk of murder and jewel theft. We have a plan for tomorrow, but I'm going to modify it slightly. Why don't you drop into the police station in the morning and try to find out how the investigation is going?"

"I suppose I can do that. What's the rest of this plan?"

I filled her in, and then I said, "How was Elizabeth?"

"She's doing as well as can be expected. I hope my company provides some small comfort to her. Two old ladies with nothing in common but that we've each seen a lot of things, and lost many things, over the course of our lives. The police haven't yet said when they will be releasing Julien's body, and that's always hard on the family. She knew, by the way, that Julien and Carmela are getting divorced. I'm only surprised they thought they could hide it from her. Not that it matters, but Elizabeth never cared for Carmela. Elizabeth called her a 'party girl,' silly and frivolous. She was disappointed her twin great-granddaughters, Jacqueline's girls, didn't come in to say good night, but their mother said they didn't seem to be feeling well. Overcome, no doubt, by all the recent excitement. It's clear how much joy they bring to Elizabeth's life. It must be nice," said my grandmother with a martyred sigh, "having great-grandchildren so close."

"I'll ignore that comment," I said, "on the grounds that you moved freely and willingly away from Iowa, where you do have great-grandchildren."

"Point taken." She rubbed the lump beneath her blanket. The lump stretched.

"Is Jacqueline married? I don't think I've seen sign of a husband and father to the twins."

"He's around somewhere, I believe."

"Hard to keep this family straight, sometimes. Do you need anything before I go?"

"I'm quite content, love. I was nervous about coming here. After so long. I'm glad I did."

"Despite what happened, I'm glad we did too. I'll say good night, then."

"Good night, love."

"Do you want me to take the cat out?"

"No, I'll do that. As you pointed out, I should lock the door."

We'd arranged to meet over breakfast. Simon and I were first to arrive, promptly at eight. I stifled a yawn as we sat down.

"Jet lag?" Simon said.

"I feel okay, but the time change has gotten to me. What is it at home now? Three a.m.?"

"About that."

"Good morning," the young waitress said. "I'm pleased to be able to tell you the kitchen has been reopened, so we can offer the full breakfast menu."

"That is good news," I said. "Are you fully open, as in lunch and dinner, too?"

"Far as I know. I only work breakfasts here, unless there's something special like the birthday party."

"I do the same. My grandmother owns a bed-and-breakfast on Cape Cod, and I'm the breakfast cook."

"Then I'll ask Ian to make sure you get something special this morning. Not," she hurried to add, "that all our meals aren't special."

"Understood," I said.

"Can I bring coffee or tea?"

"Tea for me," Simon said.

I asked for coffee and then said, "Would it be okay, do you think, if I pop in and say hi to Ian?" I indicated the empty, except for us, room. "As long as you're not busy."

"Shouldn't be a problem. You worked in the kitchen on Sunday, right?"

I put my napkin to one side, and said to Simon, "Be right back."

In the quiet, spotlessly clean kitchen, I found Ian flipping through a cooking magazine.

"Not too busy?" I asked.

He put the magazine down. "As you can see. We had a couple of people in earlier, but the hotel's still mostly empty. At least I can cook again, so once word gets around that the restaurant's open, we're hoping the reservations will pick up."

"Did the police find anything of interest in here?"

"Not that anyone's told me. Forensic tests take time, or so I've been told, but DI Ravenwood called me last night and reluctantly admitted that not a trace of nuts was found in anything they took away to be analyzed, other than the chicken sandwiches themselves. The great British public, and our favored visitors, are in no danger from anything I might cook."

He didn't look entirely happy at the news, so I asked, "But?"

"But. That means Julien's death wasn't an accident or the result of negligence. Someone quite deliberately added almond powder to the chicken, and that someone almost certainly knew Julien was deathly allergic."

"Do you have any suspicions?" I asked.

He studied my face. The waitress came in and said, "Two orders of the full breakfast, and one order of the same without the black pudding. All with fried eggs. That's the group at your table, Lily. Do you want anything?"

"Two poached eggs and toast, please."

She poured coffee into a silver pot while Ian turned up

the heat under some of the elements on the big range. He said nothing until the waitress left with the coffee things.

"Do I have my suspicions?" he said. "If I do, it doesn't mean anything. I'm just the cook here. I don't usually do breakfast, but in light of recent events, I thought I'd show my best side. The restaurant's doing okay. The hotel's doing okay—from what I can tell, at any rate—but the tourist business is a tough one. Things are going to change around here, for all some people pretend Elizabeth's going to live forever. She's already disinvesting herself of a lot of control. Handing more and more responsibility over to Tony."

"How's Tony to work for?"

"Fine. Better than some bosses I've had. It's no secret Julien was wanting a bigger role and no secret Elizabeth resisted that. She didn't think he was up to it. Funny how we're here in the twenty-first century, and some people in Britain still think they're entitled by birth order to be in charge."

"Same happens in America. We have what we call a 'failson.' A son who believes he's entitled to take over from their father by right of birth but proves to be not up to the task. Do you think Julien was not up to it?"

"I can't say. I never much liked the man, I will admit. He could switch back and forth between false charm and ham-handed attempts to act like one of the gang and, a minute later, lord of the manor addressing the common people. I heard he made some suggestions that didn't go down well with Tony, but Julien generally didn't pay a lot of attention to what goes on here in the kitchen, and that suited me fine." He cracked eggs into the hot frying pan.

"Do you have any idea what might have happened to the sapphires?"

"No, I don't. I'd never heard of them before this weekend, and I've never seen them. I wasn't in the bar Saturday night when Elizabeth wore them. My guess is some chancer—staff, family, guest, doesn't matter—took them on the spur of the moment."

"Does Elizabeth keep the door to her private rooms locked?"

"I'm just the cook here, Lily, so I couldn't say. But let me remind you this is a hotel. Maids, maintenance workers, all need access to the rooms. Even the private ones. Now, back to more important matters. How do you like your poached eggs?"

I like my poached eggs soft and these ones were done to perfection.

When I got back to the table, I found Bernie and Matt as well as Rose at the table. Voices came from the adjoining dining rooms, but no one else was seated in ours, so we could talk freely, stopping only when the waitress approached our table.

"I'm meeting Dennis, my retired police officer, at three this afternoon in York," Matt said.

"How long's the drive to York?" I asked

"Little over an hour, give or take, depending on traffic. Bernie and I'll leave in good time, in case traffic is worse than usual."

"I'd like to come," I said.

"Why?"

"For one thing, I've never been to York. For another, I want to hear what your contact has to say. He might talk more freely in front of Bernie and me. Two eager American women all keen to hear stories about how the English police do things. We can tell him we're big fans of the Rebus and the Banks novels and TV shows."

"It might work. He'll fall all over himself telling you what rubbish those police procedural programs are."

"On the other hand," Simon pointed out. "He's just as likely to get distracted on the details of what books and telly get wrong and forget about sticking to the main point."

"Are you actually going to eat another slice of that black pudding?" Bernie said to Matt.

He froze, laden fork half way to his mouth. "Why not?"

"Because it's horrible, that's why."

"I like it."

"An acquired taste," Simon said, munching happily on his serving. "Do you know what it's made of, Bernie?"

"Not exactly. Ground vegetables mixed with something like oatmeal I assumed. Whatever they could salvage from what would otherwise be thrown out."

"As I recall"—Rose sipped at her tea; all she was having for breakfast was milky cereal and toast—"Edward, the Earl of Frockmorton, Elizabeth's late husband, loved his black pudding. About the only thing Mrs. Beans could cook properly, even when she was in her cups, was black pudding, which she made herself from some secret recipe supposedly handed down by her grandmothers through the generations. Perhaps that's why they kept her on. Although there was that time, I caught her sneaking a package wrapped in butcher's paper out of her shopping bag."

"Can we stick to the matter at hand, please," I said.

"Butcher's paper?" Bernie said. "You mean it has meat in it?"

"The trip to York?" Simon said. "If Lily's going, I'm coming, too. Someone is needed to show her the sites."

"Isn't anyone going to ask me what I learned last night?" Bernie asked, thankfully moving on from the topic of what's in a black pudding. I happen to know that because at Victoria-on-Sea we offer a traditional full English breakfast. Sans the black pudding, as it doesn't generally suit American tastes. Suffice it to say it's sometimes called "blood pudding."

"Just getting the organizational details out of the way," Matt said.

"I have an organizational detail to provide," Rose said. "The good detectives are stopping by this morning, and I've arranged to chat with them at ten."

"Here?" I asked.

"I offered to come to the police station, but DS Capretti said she had plans to drop in."

"Why?" Simon asked as he scraped up the last of his black pudding.

"Why do I want to meet with them? To skillfully and subtly probe them for what they have learned about the murder, of course. We can conclude that if they were focusing their attentions outside of the family and party guests, she would probably not be interested in speaking with me."

"Even if that's the case regarding Julien's death, they're still searching for the jewels." I said.

"True."

"Ten o'clock is good," I said. "I'll join you for the talk with the police and still have time go to York." I mopped up the last of the runny egg yolk with a piece of toast.

"I'll keep what I learned to myself, shall I?" Bernie said.

Matt gave her a fond smile. "We're teasing you. You were at your computer for a long time, so I suspect you do have things to tell us."

She cradled her coffee cup and leaned back in her chair. She peered into the empty corners of the dining room as though searching for eavesdroppers. Light running footsteps sounded in the hallway; a woman yelled to a child to slow down, and they passed on. "Okay. All this is legit stuff. I searched for only what was searchable. Generally speaking, the Crawford family businesses are in okay shape. Not great, but not as bad as they could be. The pandemic did a number on the hotel, but no worse than anyone else, and the family was protected to a degree by their farm and rental incomes. Elizabeth has no vacation homes or expensive hobbies, and she hasn't traveled outside of the UK for many years. She lives here, in Thornecroft Castle House, year-round. Before I continue, news of the disappearance of the Frockmorton Sapphires is out there. Police have asked anyone who knows anything about that to contact them. You might want to ask the police if they're learned any more when you interview them, Rose."

"When Rose interviews *them*?" Matt said.

"That's the way it works at home. With Detective Williams, at any rate. To continue, I checked the gossip rags, and no one in the family has much of a presence there. Meaning they don't attend wild parties at the hottest night clubs or get photographed boarding oil princes' yachts."

"Elizabeth told Rose Carmela's a party girl," I said.

"That can mean different things to different people. You and I went to some fun Manhattan parties in our glory days. Wasn't worthy of getting our names in the papers, though."

"Fair enough," I said.

"For all that the Crawford family are historic and titled, they aren't all that special, these days," Bernie said. "I wonder if that rankles some of them? I suspect Elizabeth doesn't much care, but it's not her birth family, is it?"

"No," Rose said. "Elizabeth is, above all, practical. A title doesn't put food on the table or a roof over anyone's head. They make do, or not, like anyone else."

"I found two pieces of what might, or might not, be of interest. One, Julien quit his job earlier this month. He was living in London and was a real estate agent."

"He sold houses?" Simon said.

"Yes. At quite a high level, it would seem. The company he worked for dealt mostly in multi-million-pound row houses in the West End, as well as some new flats in prominent developments in Greenwich and the Isle of Dogs. I had to look Isle of Dogs up to learn that it's not the name of a canine rescue park. Some of those prices truly boggled my mind."

"Why did he quit?" I asked.

"I can't find that out. As a real estate agent, he was doing okay, judging by his record of sales. He must have had some mighty well-heeled clients."

"To get them, he would have flashed the word 'viscount' around," Simon said. "Titles don't put food on the table, as Rose pointed out, but they can still open a lot of doors."

"Seems a funny time to quit a lucrative job," Matt said, "with a divorce pending. Then again, that might be why. Is he planning to plead unemployment in front of the court? What does Carmela do for a living?"

"She owns a couple of women's clothing stores in London. They don't sell Paris or Milan designer labels, but still high-end stuff. The business seems to be doing okay, from what I could tell."

She stopped talking as the waitress arrived to clear away our plates and offer refills of tea and coffee.

That done, and the waitress departed, Bernie continued, "Generally, the members of the family are exactly as they appear, and rather boring, to be honest. Jacqueline's a stay-at-home mom to the twins. Her husband, one Alistair McLeod, is a dentist. Standard middle-class dental practice, no scandal, no financial ventures out of the ordinary. Susannah Reilly, the youngest of the cousins, sister of Tony, is a legal secretary. Her husband, Ray, I believe his name is, is a firefighter. They have two young children who they left in the care of his parents for this weekend."

"How the mighty have fallen," Simon said. "Imagine, the granddaughter of an earl marrying a dentist, never mind a firefighter."

The waitress returned with our fresh drinks. She chuckled as she put the pots on the table. "Sorry, but I couldn't help but overhearing. My older sister dated Tony for a while. That was years ago, but I always imagined his ancestors rolling over in their graves. Can I get you anything else?"

"No, thank you," Simon said. "This has all been grand."

She walked away. "Otherwise," Bernie said when the coast was clear, "only one interesting thing came to light. Emma is in serious financial trouble."

"Which one's she again?" Matt asked.

"One of the cousins. The one with the short dark hair. Daughter of Thomas, Elizabeth's second son, who lives in Canada now. He had some sort of accident and couldn't make it to the party."

"Emma just happened to mention her father is next in line to the title," I said. "Now that the current earl's only son has died without, as they say in the historical romances, issue."

"Male issue," Simon said. "Still matters. Julien didn't have kids, but Robert has a living daughter, and she has children. Jacqueline won't inherit the title, but if the family is going to pass on the properties through the eldest child, regardless of gender, she is now next in line after her father, Robert."

"I doubt that's Elizabeth's intention," Rose said. "To leave everything to one child's line in its entirely, I mean. But that's only a guess. She has not told me the contents of her will, and although Elizabeth appears to be thoroughly modern in her outlook, not to mention business savvy, the old ways sometimes die hard."

"Might be worth keeping in mind," Matt said. "Bernie, you were about to tell us about Emma?"

"And so I was. Emma's in serious financial trouble. Like

way, way underwater. It seems she has this boyfriend by the name of Nigel Hawthorn—"

"I remember," I said. "On Friday night, someone asked her if Nigel was coming, and she snapped that Nigel was permanently out of the picture. She didn't know what he was doing, and she didn't care."

"Keeping his head down, if he knows what's good for him," Bernie said. "It would appear Emma lent this Nigel a lot of money, which he used to invest in cryptocurrency. Not only did she give him what she had in the way of savings, she borrowed to give him more."

"Oops," Matt said.

"Oops, indeed. He lost almost all of it, if not all of it. I can't be entirely sure, but it doesn't look as though Nigel invested any of his own money. Just Emma's."

"You found this out legally?" Simon said.

Bernie winced. "Sometimes I get carried away when I start following a trail. Emma's a high school teacher in Oxford, so she's unlikely to have had a great deal of money to begin with. That's fact, but I'm going to speculate the family doesn't know. They didn't even know she'd broken up with him."

"I can't see how the death of Julien could benefit her financially in any way," Simon said. "Her father isn't going to inherit the title until his own brother dies, and that might not be for many years. Robert's what, around seventy-five? His health seems fine. Besides, as we keep saying, the title doesn't necessarily come with money."

"I'm thinking about the sapphires," I said. "Did Emma snatch the sapphires thinking she could sell them?"

"Did Julien somehow find out she'd done that?" Bernie said. "Did he demand a share of the proceeds?"

"Did he threaten to expose her?" Matt said.

"You lot have eagerly leapt to a great many conclusions," Rose said. "That the young woman is in financial trouble is one thing. But she is young, comparatively speaking, and she has a stable career. I'd say it's natural enough for her not to tell her extended family what happened, through sheer embarrassment at being tricked and cheated. I get the feeling the cousins are not close."

"Tony and Susannah are," I said. "They seem to be very fond of each other. Although they're brother and sister, not cousins. Otherwise, I agree with Rose about the rest of them."

"All good points, Rose," Matt said, "We're not pointing the finger at anyone. Just gathering data."

"Perhaps we should gather our data elsewhere," I said. "That waitress is politely keeping out of our way, but she looks anxious to clear this table."

Chapter 15

Rose decided it would be beneath her dignity to be interviewed by (or to interview, depending on your point of view) the police in her room, so she and I were in the lobby at ten o'clock. A somewhat shabby and dirty car drove up precisely on time and parked directly in front of the main doors. The engine was switched off, and DS Capretti got out and came into the hotel.

"Mrs. Campbell," she said without bothering with polite greetings. "You have information for me?" Her eyes flicked to me.

I smiled. "I'll stay with my grandmother, if that's okay."

"Fine with me."

"I wouldn't exactly say I have information to depart," Rose said. "Shall we take seats?"

"Why did you ask to speak with me then?"

"Naturally, my granddaughter is concerned at the direction of your questions earlier, and we're wanting to know if we can be of further help."

"Is your granddaughter under arrest?"

I blinked.

"No," Rose said.

"Then she has no reason to be concerned." Capretti turned to me. "Not at this time, anyway."

I didn't much care for the sound of that, but I said nothing.

"Have you had any reports of sightings of the sapphires?" Rose turned to lead the way toward the small sitting room, her cane proceeding her. Few people can fail to follow an elderly lady in search of a chair.

Few people except, apparently, DS Capretti, who stayed where she was, watching Rose walk slowly away. Finally, my grandmother realized we weren't following, stopped and turned around, a confused look on her face.

Capretti unexpectedly laughed. It was a nice laugh, deep and hearty and genuinely amused. "I figured you were only interested in digging into what we've learned, but I agreed to meet you here, Mrs. Campbell, because I was coming anyway. I need to speak to Lady Frockmorton. It was suggested at one time you might have considered yourself entitled to help yourself to the jewels, because of your long-ago service in this house. I confess I have trouble believing anyone would carry a grudge for more than sixty years. Otherwise, there wouldn't be a safe peer or politician in all the realm. It's my observation, although some of my superiors might not agree, that elderly ladies make excellent witnesses. They notice everything that's going on around them, largely because people don't pay much attention to them, so they're left to amuse themselves." She turned to me, and the smile she gave me was very real. "Obviously, that doesn't apply here. You're close to your granddaughter and her friend. I like that. My parents died when I was young, and I was raised by my granny and granddad."

"How are they doing?" Rose asked, reluctantly rejoining us.

"Well, I'm happy to say. They leave for several months

in Spain every year immediately after Christmas. You can come with me to talk to Lady F., if you like." She went up to the reception desk. "Lady Frockmorton is expecting me."

Elizabeth received us in the drawing room. Tea things were laid out, along with a plate of shortbread, even though it was just after breakfast. Elizabeth smiled to see Rose and me with the detective and asked the hovering waitress to bring two more cups. Lissie had been napping on the rug next to the fireplace. When we came in, she got slowly to her feet, yawned, and stretched every fiber in her body.

"No sign of your jewels yet, Lady Frockmorton?" Capretti inquired, once we were seated.

"I would have told you if they'd turned up. My cat seems to like you, Rose."

Lissie had jumped onto Rose's lap the moment my grandmother sat down, curled into a ball, and made herself comfortable.

"I like cats." Rose stroked the white fur.

"Another reason I know I can trust you." The two women smiled affectionately at each other.

Capretti cleared her throat. "If we can get back to the jewels. We've put the word out, and police forces here and on the continent are on the alert for any sign of them. Have you been in contact with your insurance company?"

"I have. My daughter, Katherine Waterfield, is handling the details. They will, of course, try to get out of paying on the grounds that I foolishly misplaced them. I assume you will set them straight."

"I don't know you didn't lose them. Although foolish is not a word I suspect is used to describe you very often, Lady Frockmorton."

Elizabeth dipped her head in acknowledgment. Capretti then asked Rose and me to once again go over what happened when Elizabeth brought us to see the sapphires and she realized they were missing. We had nothing new to tell her. She drank her highly sweetened tea and ate two pieces of shortbread.

"If that's all . . ." Elizabeth said.

"Not quite," Capretti turned to me. "Now that I'm here . . . I checked with the reservations clerk this morning, and she told me not only did you and your friend not check out yesterday, as planned, but you've been joined by friends and have taken another room. Any reason for that?"

"I don't want to leave my grandmother on her own."

"Do you have reason to think she's in danger?"

Elizabeth's eyes widened. Lissie's pink ears pricked up.

"No, I do not. I thought she'd need my emotional support, that's all."

Capretti turned her stare onto Rose. Rose tried to look emotionally frail. At that, she failed.

"I've been told by the police in your town that you two, and your redheaded friend, sometimes get involved in things that are none of your business. And you don't always know when to become uninvolved."

"That's . . . been known to happen," I admitted.

"Someone has to help that fool of a detective the North Augusta police have supposedly in charge," Rose said. "I refer to Detective Williams. Detective Redmond is at least somewhat capable."

"And that someone is you, madam?"

"Whyever not?" Rose stroked Lissie. The big blue eyes surrounded by white fur watched the detective.

"We're investigating the theft of the jewels, but the murder of Mr. Crawford is our priority at the moment. Ms. Roberts, you told us Dr. Alicia Boyle helped you with the chicken sandwiches. Is that correct?"

"Yes."

"Did you have eyes on her the entire time she was doing that?"

"I don't know. I can't really say. I suppose I might have turned away. I wasn't consciously watching her, not after I told her what to do. It was all pretty simple." A thought came to me, and the detective noticed.

"You've remembered something." she said.

"While we were putting the sandwiches together, a man came into the kitchen. Early seventies, maybe, balding, overweight. Yorkshire accent. He said he was diabetic and needed to eat. Ian told him in that case he should have brought himself something, as they were not yet serving tea and the restaurant was closed for lunch that day."

"Bert Kellogg," Capretti said, "husband of a school friend of Katherine Waterfield's. He told us about that."

"I might have turned to see what was going on. By that time, Ian was starting to get mildly irritated at the number of people passing through the kitchen. I probably took my attention away from Alicia and the sandwiches, but it couldn't have been more than a few seconds. A minute at most."

"Why are you asking about Dr. Boyle?" Elizabeth questioned.

"My colleagues and I have been inquiring about everyone who was in the kitchen or the gardens when the food was prepared or served on Sunday. She was there."

"As were a great many other people. Dr. Boyle is a respected medical professional and well-regarded member of the community. Surely you don't suspect her of deliberately killing my grandson."

"You didn't wonder why she, of all people, offered to do unpaid menial labor in the kitchen?"

"Her mother worked here for many years, and I was happy to have her and her daughter as my guests. I wasn't aware Alicia was helping in the kitchen."

"Lots of people were helping," I said. "I was. I wasn't being paid, either."

"I've not got a problem with that," Capretti said. "But Alicia Boyle has strong republican leanings and is never afraid to express them, nor her opposition to the entire concept of hereditary titles and inherited money. Seems odd to me, that's all. When something seems odd, I have to ask about it."

"She told me she volunteered because her mother would have liked to but was unable," I said.

"That's what she told us, too. I've been told you spent some time chatting to Josh Hansen, both at the drinks party and at the tea. Is that correct?"

"I wouldn't say some time, no, but we did talk. He was escorting his grandfather, and I was with my grandmother, so we had something in common. That's all."

"Did Josh Hansen come into the kitchen while you were there?"

"Not that I noticed," I said, "which, as I've explained, doesn't mean a heck of a lot."

"Why are you asking about young Josh?" Elizabeth said. "If he's politically active, unlike Alicia, he doesn't make a point of advertising it."

"I've been told he and Julien Crawford didn't get on too well."

"I loved my darling grandson very much, as I do all my children and grandchildren. Julien, like the rest of us, was human. None of us 'get on too well' with everyone. We don't kill because of it."

"Except, in this case, someone did kill Julien Crawford." The detective put her teacup on the table, grabbed two more pieces of shortbread, and stood up. "Thank you for your time. I'll be in touch."

* * *

"Basically, we didn't learn a thing," I said.

"Maybe there's nothing for us to learn," Simon said. "Remind me again why we're pursuing this?"

"At first, because Ian and I seemed to be under suspicion. Ian's name didn't come up earlier, and I'm pretty sure Capretti realizes I'm about the last person to have killed Julien. Other, I suppose, than Rose. Seeing as how we'd never even met any of the people involved until Saturday."

Bernie twisted around in her seat. We were all stuffed into a tiny car and heading down the M1 toward York. Matt was driving, and Simon and I were crammed into the back, where I was happy to be, as that meant I didn't have to see what was coming at us. "Don't assume she's forgotten you, Lily. Even if you didn't have a motive, or even know the guy, you might be the type to get a thrill out of endangering people. Maybe you only wanted to disrupt the party and things went further than you'd planned."

"Thank you so much for those words of reassurance."

"Bernie's right," Matt said. "We don't know what the police are thinking, and they are unlikely to tell us."

"In that case, as much as I don't want to make the suggestion, might it be better if Lily goes home?" Simon asked.

"No," I said. "I'm not leaving. Rose and Elizabeth are becoming quite close, and Rose won't want to leave with all this going on and upsetting her friend. And what about Alicia and Josh? It seems as though Capretti is focusing on them, if not Ian and me. I like them both."

Simon touched my hand. "Does the fact that you like them mean they're not killers?"

"Yes, it does." I tried to settle back and enjoy the ride. Everything was so interesting, the small villages, the stone and brick houses, cracking with age, the corner pubs, the narrow twisting streets, the drystone walls, the fields full of grazing sheep. But it was hard to get my mind off recent events at Thornecroft Castle.

York managed to achieve that, for a while, anyway.

Matt had to park a good distance away from our destination, but that didn't matter as traffic had been light and we were early, and I enjoyed treading the cobblestones of the winding, narrow streets, twisting and craning my neck to take in everything around me. The ancient city walls, parts of which were built in Roman times. The Tudor buildings of black and white timber. The strong solid walls of York Minster looming over the town center. Bernie had her phone out and was snapping pictures of everything.

To my delight, the pub in which Matt arranged to meet his retired police officer was one of the oldest in this old city, located in the area around the Shambles, a narrow, winding medieval street of three- and four-story buildings leaning precariously toward each other.

The pub was warm and welcoming, and at two o'clock on a Tuesday, largely empty. Four elderly men occupied the table closest to the smoldering coal fire. They were all well into their eighties, if not older, and also well into their drinks, judging by the number of empty glasses in front of them. They barely looked up as we came in. In a tourist town, strangers were not worth checking out. Matt's contact was not one of them. "Looks like Dennis isn't here yet," he said. "We're a couple of minutes early. Find seats, and I'll get the drinks. Any requests?"

I asked for white wine, and Bernie and Simon said they'd have beer. Simon went to help Matt ferry the glasses to the table while Bernie and I located a table big enough to seat five. The windows were small, the casements deep, and the lights low, casting the room into a state of permanent gloom. We settled into seats around a table heavily scarred and marked with numerous water rings and studied our surroundings with interest. The ceiling was low, the stone floor uncarpeted, the walls wood-paneled, dotted with paintings of storm-tossed seas and ships under full sail, some looking as though they were old enough to have been hung when the pub first opened.

"Isn't this cool?" I said. "Sir Francis Drake might walk through that door this very moment, flinging aside his cape, bellowing for a mug of their best ale, fresh from plundering the high seas in the name of his queen."

"We're not near the sea," Bernie said. "Was Drake from York?"

"I have no idea. I'm commenting on the atmosphere, not the historical accuracy of the patrons."

Bernie whipped out her phone. "Let me make some notes. This might be a nice place to inspire a description of a pub in my book."

"It's too old to be in Massachusetts in the mid-nineteenth century. Unless—don't you dare tell me you've decided to change the time period."

"I am keeping my options open."

I groaned.

The men joined us, bringing an extra mug of beer for Matt's contact. He'd ordered a soft drink for himself as he was driving. "A word to the wise. Make your drinks last if you don't want to get absolutely hammered. Dennis has a way of stretching out every word as long as possible while drinking as fast as possible. As long as I'm paying, at any rate. There he is now." Matt got to his feet and waved.

Dennis was pretty much as I expected. Muscle gone to fat long ago. Watery eyes, the swollen red nose of a serious drinker, scraggly gray hair in need of a trim, gray goatee also needing a trim, rumpled clothes. He didn't smell all that good, either. If he was recently retired from the police, he couldn't be much older than his mid-sixties, but he looked a decade and a half older. He waved halfheartedly to the group of men by the fireplace, and they nodded in return, and then he joined us.

Matt introduced us as his friends, and Dennis declared he was always glad to meet Americans, particularly such "lovely young ladies." Simon, he ignored.

"That tip you gave me on the couple from Leeds really panned out," Matt said, as Dennis started on his beer. "I'm going to be able to do a lot with that."

"Glad to hear it. Your mate here's going to mention my name in the acknowledgments," he told Bernie and me. "I can't wait to show the book to some of those young lads still on the job. They think I'm past it. That'll show 'em." He slapped the empty glass down on the table.

"Can I get you another?" Matt asked.

"Don't mind if I do," Dennis said.

"I'll get this one," Simon said.

"Your mate's not American." Dennis watched Simon go. "A copper?"

"A gardener."

"Takes all kinds, I suppose. Did I tell you about that woman up in Thirsk who—?"

"I'm super interested in jewel theft," Bernie said. "I bet you ran into some cases like that in your long career."

He winked at her. "I might have, miss. I might have."

"Is it as exciting as it is in the movies?"

He laughed, showing a mouthful of prominent, stained teeth. "Crime isn't glamorous, young lady, and neither is police work. Sheer drudgery, most of the time. I remember some stakeouts I was on in the early days. Man could grow old on a stakeout. Many did. Cheers." He accepted the fresh glass Simon offered.

"I heard a piece of interesting news yesterday," Matt said. "Some rare jewels stolen near Halifax. Did you hear about that?"

"I did." Dennis shook his head. "Some ancient old

biddy with a title lost them. Family must be in an uproar. Millions of pounds worth, they say."

"The police believe they were stolen," I said.

"Happens," he said. "Flash bling around like that and what do the toffs expect?"

"Have you heard anything that wasn't in the news, Dennis?" Matt asked. "Any of your friends from the old days talking about it?"

"Not many friends left from the old days," Dennis said. "They died. Moved away. But yeah, some of us still get together over a pint. Or two. You think this might be something you can use in your book? Did the old Duchess snatch them herself?"

"Countess of Frockmorton, and no, I'm not thinking that. Not necessarily, but I am interested. As Bernie said, the reading public believes jewel theft is glamorous. There might be a book in it, when I'm finished with the one you're helping me with."

Dennis drank his beer.

"You told me about an old guy who was a fence, specialized in jewels, working well into his late eighties. Is he still around? Still active?"

"Still around, yes. Not active, but involved." He winked at Bernie and me. "If you catch my meaning, ladies. Lines between the law and the criminals blur when you get to be my age and everyone else moves on. Alfred and his mates and I get together sometimes to talk about the old times."

"Do you think he'd talk to me?" Matt asked.

"Don't see why not." Dennis swiveled in his chair. "Hey, Alfred! Writer here wants to talk to you about the Frockmorton job."

Everyone in the pub turned to stare at us, not least the table of old men huddled close to the coal fire. One of the men leaned over and said something into his neighbor's ear. Dennis waved, and he stood up. Alfred, presumably, picked up the cane propped next to his chair and slowly made his way across the room. Matt and Simon leapt to their feet. Bernie and I smiled.

"You call me, Dennis?" Alfred sneered. "I don't talk to reporters, you know that."

"I'm not a reporter," Matt said. "I'm an author. I'm writing a book, and Dennis here has been very helpful. Strictly historical cases. I don't write about current events."

"What's in it for me?"

"What can I get you?" Simon asked.

"Pint o' Guinness. Couple packet of crisps wouldn't go amiss."

"Another for me," Dennis said.

"Coming right up," Simon said.

The old man settled himself into Simon's chair. And he was old. Early nineties maybe, with ill-fitting dentures, gnarled and liver-spotted hands, a face as deeply lined as a topographic map of Europe. But his eyes were still blue and sharp as he studied each of us in turn. "Murder at Thornecroft Castle," he said at last. "Son of the earl got bumped off. No concern of mine."

"I'm interested in the theft of the jewels that happened around the same time. For my book," Matt said, as Simon placed a foaming mug of black beer and two small packages of potato chips on the table. "Have you heard about that?"

"Cheers." Alfred took a deep drink and sighed happily. "The Frockmorton Sapphires. Yeah, I heard. Time was, I would have given a lot to have them pass through my hands. Never did get the chance. After the earl died, his wife locked them up tight."

"I'm guessing you keep your ear to the ground," Matt said. "You look like a man who likes to know what's going on. Even if you're not actively involved anymore."

Simon had pulled up another chair for himself. He, Bernie,

and I said nothing. This was Matt at work. Make conversation, flatter the subject ever so slightly, probe gently. And then, hopefully, the subject will start to talk.

Alfred tapped his right ear, which contained a hearing aid. "Hearing's not as sharp as it once was, but yeah, I still hear things. I can put people in touch with the right people, if you get my meaning. For a suitable fee, naturally."

"Naturally," Matt said.

"He means," Dennis said to Bernie and me, "he can't move the goods himself any more but he knows people who can, and he'll provide a referral service in exchange for being adequately compensated for his trouble."

Alfred tore open a bag of chips and tossed one in his mouth. "Some things change. Some things stay the same. Not so easy to get the goods to and from the continent anymore, seeing as how the border's back in place and that means goods are being searched. Some young people are keen to hear how we did things in the old days."

"That might make a great topic for a book," Matt said.

"You better hurry up with it, if you want me to help. I won't be around all that much longer."

Dennis laughed. I got the feeling he didn't laugh very much. I felt sorry for him. About all he had left was memories of his career and afternoons in the pub in the company of the sort of people he would have thrown in jail at one time—and anyone who offered to buy him a drink.

"I thank you for the beer, young laddie," Alfred said, "but I'll be honest with you. I've nothing to tell you. There's not been a peep about the Frockmorton Sapphires in the usual talk. And there would have been, if there was anything to it. Word gets around."

"What do you think that means?"

"The old lady misplaced them, and they'll turn up one day, probably under her bed. Or whoever took them had no need for local information, and they're already on their way out of the country."

"What about the death of Lady Frockmorton's grandson?" Matt asked. "Anyone talking about that?"

"Other than stirring up old gossip about the family, no. Course, the old stories were being remembered anyway, what with the old lady's one hundredth birthday coming up."

"Do you know her?" Bernie asked.

"Unfortunately, our paths never had reason to cross. If you're asking me, laddie, if whoever took the sapphires killed the grandson, I can't help you with that, either. Except to say that no professional would have complicated a job like that. Snatch the jewels and get out of there, and fast. Anything more is just asking for trouble."

Chapter 16

I'd say that was a wasted trip, except I greatly enjoyed seeing what little I had of York. It was only three thirty when we left the pub, but rain was threatening, and Matt said he'd prefer not to stay in York much longer, which would involve driving strange roads at night in the rain.

We didn't say much on the way back to Thornecroft Castle House. I had to admit, if only to myself, I'd been hoping Dennis or one of his drinking buddies would have told us where to find the Frockmorton Sapphires and we could proudly carry them back to their owner.

The skies began to clear as we approached Halifax.

"What now?" Bernie asked, as we turned into the road leading to the hotel.

"I have absolutely no idea," I said. "We're going in circles here. We have no hope of finding a professional jewel thief who doesn't want to be found, and we don't have any viable suspects for the murder. I'd like to spend more time exploring York, and we haven't even been to Halifax the city yet, except for dinner that one time."

"You mean, give up?" Bernie said.

"I wouldn't put it like that, but yes, that is what I mean."

"We can do those things," Simon said. "And stay at Thornecroft if you want to be near Rose. She might enjoy a day's excursion."

"What do you think, Matt?" Bernie asked.

"I've no suggestions," he said as he pulled into the hotel driveway. "Except that while you guys had a drink, I didn't, so I'm ready to hit the bar. The restaurant's open. Why don't we see if we can get a reservation for tonight, rather than go out?"

"Good idea," Simon said. "Seeing as about all I did in that pub was jump up and down fetching drinks, I'll join you in the bar. Lily?"

As we drove past the entrance, Emma came out of the hotel. She was dressed in a heavy sweater, jeans, and hiking shoes, heading for the footpath leading to the castle ruins.

"You guys go ahead. I feel like a walk. I'll text you when I'm back." I jumped out of the car as soon as it came to a halt. Not entirely to my surprise, Bernie did the same.

"Was that Emma?" she said.

"It was. I'm thinking she might need someone to confide in. Someone outside her family."

"I like the way you think, Lily Roberts. Exactly like me. For once."

Bernie and I headed for the footpath. Emma walked slowly, as though she didn't have a particular destination in mind. We didn't try to catch up with her, but followed at the same pace. We emerged from the trees to see her standing on the hill overlooking what had once been the moat, the castle ruins outlined by the sky. She stood quietly, not moving. Three cars were in the ticket office parking lot, and within the grounds of the castle itself, people clambered over the walls and took photos. Two children ran up from the belowground rooms, screaming in delight.

Emma turned at the sound of our footsteps. Her face

was lined and drawn, deep shadows beneath her eyes indicated she hadn't been sleeping well. "Hi," she said.

"Hello. Lovely day, isn't it?"

"It is." She pushed her thick black bangs to one side. They immediately fell back into place.

"Are you checking out the castle?" Bernie asked. "Pretty impressive. To our American eyes, at any rate."

"I love it," she said. "I love Yorkshire and everything about it, this view, in particular. I don't come here"—she swept her arm in front of her, indicating the ruins, the green grass, the distant hills—"nearly often enough." She took a long deep breath. The air was fresh and clean, with a touch of a chill in it. "Not that long ago, these valleys would have been filled with coal smoke all day and all night. I've heard sometimes the sky looked as though it was on fire. Nice to know things can improve, isn't it."

"It is," I said.

"My family, on my father's side, has lived here since the seventeenth century. We know their names and their dates. We have paintings of them, so we know what they looked like. What they wanted to be seen as, at any rate. We know some things about them, good and bad. The Fifth Countess, who would have been my great-grandmother three times over, hated her stepdaughter to the point she wouldn't stay in the same room if the girl came in. The situation was highly embarrassing at dinner parties. Imagine knowing that. Even in England, not many people can trace their family back more than a couple of generations. I know all that stuff doesn't really matter, but there's something about having a lineage like that that makes me truly believe I belong here. I'm rooted here, in a real way." She looked down as she ground her right foot into the dirt, as though wanting to leave her mark. The Canadian accent was almost imperceptible as she talked about her proud English heritage.

"I understand," Bernie said.

She lifted her head and looked at us. "Do you? Can you? Even my father doesn't understand. He left England when my parents' marriage ended and went to Canada. He married again, has a new family. He comes back now and again to see his mother, but he has no desire to ever live here again. He's possibly going to be the next earl, and he truly does not care."

"Will you get a title when that happens?"

"Yes. I'll be Lady Emma." She lifted her head and gave us a small smile. "That'll be fun, but it won't do anything to solve my problems. Maybe the opposite. I'll attract gold diggers who think, because I have a title, my family's rich." She snorted. "As if."

I could think of nothing to say. I could hardly come out and ask if she'd stolen the family jewels to pay the debts we knew about because Bernie is a computer hacker.

She turned back to the landscape. "Not that at my age I have to worry about gold diggers much longer."

"I suspect you do," Bernie said. "You're an attractive woman."

She gave us a genuine smile. "Thanks for that. Let's walk."

We set off alongside the moat. Emma walked slowly, and as we'd been invited to join her, Bernie and I matched her pace.

"Will you be staying here much longer?" Bernie asked casually. "Where do you live?"

"Oxford. I'm a teacher. I don't know what I'm going to do now. I've taken some extra time off work because of the death of Julien but—well, things are difficult right now, and to tell you the truth I might not have a home much longer."

"Why is that?" Bernie asked.

"I can't afford the rent on my flat. I recently broke up

with my boyfriend. He left me in rather unpleasant financial straits."

Bernie was grinning with satisfaction. I, on the other hand, was getting uncomfortable with this conversation. The woman was entitled to her privacy and her secrets. Although, as Detective Amy Redmond has told me, more than once, in a police murder investigation no one is entitled to their privacy.

Then again, Bernie and I are not with the police. "I'm sorry," I said. "You came up here to be alone and think things over. Time we were getting back anyway."

Bernie threw me a narrow eyed, tight-lipped look of sheer disapproval.

"It's okay," Emma said. "You guys seem nice. My boyfriend, he who shall never again be named, invested just about everything I have in a seriously bad idea. And then, once he'd lost it all, rather than hang around to pay me back, scarpered with another woman. Yeah, I'm bitter. It's not been easy keeping up a smiling front this weekend, I can tell you that. Granny's noticed—she notices everything, but aside from asking me where he-who-shall-not-be-named was this weekend, and making some passing comment to the fact that she never liked him, she said nothing. I'm going to have to call my dad. Tell him I need money. I can't afford the rent on my flat on my own, or even the payments on my car anymore."

"Will he give it to you?" Bernie asked, her voice soft and sympathetic.

"Yes. Probably. Along with demanding to know when I'm going to grow up, and what's wrong with me that I can't land a decent man. He'll then suggest I move to Toronto if I'm not able to look after myself like a proper adult should."

"You didn't want to ask your grandmother for a loan?"

Bernie asked. "She talks very fondly about you. About all her granddaughters."

"Granny's not exactly liquid. About all she'll be able to offer me is a job in the hotel. Everything she has is wrapped up in the house and a few rental properties. Some income from the farms. They say she was going to sell the sapphires because she needed the money to put into the hotel. Tony says the roof's in terrible condition, and there's signs of black mold in the attic." She gasped and turned to us. "Please don't tell anyone I said that. We don't need word getting around the house isn't safe."

"I love the hotel," Bernie said. "I'll be telling all my friends back home about how fabulous it is."

"Thanks. Once the necessary repairs are done, Tony has ideas about putting on a new wing. The hotel does a good business in weddings, but it can do only small or medium-size ones. He's talking about more banquet space, a bigger bar, maybe expand the lawn to where the sheep are kept, and put up a permanent banqueting tent. He's even talking about expanding the stables so he can offer horseback riding as an optional excursion for guests. All that might not happen now the sapphires are gone. What a mess."

Emma, I now firmly believed, did not steal the jewels. Unless she was a heck of a good actor. Then again, people have fooled me before. As Bernie would be the first to point out.

"I'm an accountant by profession," Bernie said. "It can sometimes take a long time for insurance companies to settle a big payout. Particularly if there are questions about what happened to the item. Do you have any ideas?"

"Not really. At a guess, one of the party guests broke into Granny's room and took them. Everyone saw them on Friday night. At one time, I would never have thought anyone who worked for the hotel, or had been close friends with Granny, would steal from her. But she's old, right? They might have thought, what use does she have anymore for precious jewels or even the money from the sale of them. Not to mention that a lot of hangers-on, virtual strangers, came to the party." She looked directly at us. "Like you two."

Bernie held up her open hands. "You can count us out. We're going home in a few days, and I wouldn't dare risk being searched at customs. Other than members of your family, I don't know a single person in England who I could ask to sell them for me even if I wanted."

"I wasn't accusing you," Emma said.

"I know that."

"Other than the sapphires, the only thing of real value my grandmother has to pass on to the family is the house. To realize that, Thornecroft Castle House would have to be sold. I don't know if I could bear that."

We stood in silence for a few minutes. A bird called from a tree. The visiting family left the castle and nodded politely to us as they headed back to the parking lot, the children running ahead, waving invisible swords at each other.

"It helps sometimes, doesn't it," Emma said at last, "to talk to strangers. People who have absolutely no vested interest in what one does or doesn't do. Thanks for listening. I have to make a difficult phone call to my dad, and I might as well do it now and get it over with."

Bernie and I walked back to the house with Emma. Her mind appeared to be made up, and we didn't say anything further about the matter.

"Do you like horses?" Emma said out of the blue.

"I love them," Bernie said. "Being from Manhattan, that's in theory only, but still. Someone told us the hotel keeps horses. Do you think it would be okay if we went to see them?"

"That's why I mentioned it. I was planning to pay them a visit myself this afternoon, but—well, if I get distracted, I might lose my nerve and not call Dad." She pointed toward the barn and outbuildings at the other side of the driveway. "Stables are around the back. All we have now are two old nags Granny's too sentimental to part with. Zoe and Katy want to ride, but everyone thinks the horses will have heart attacks if someone tries to sit on them. You're welcome to go and say hi. Sometimes, carrots or apples are to be found in a plastic tub by the door of the first stall on the left."

"I'd like that," Bernie said. "Lily, you up for it?"

"Sure."

I wished Emma good luck with her phone call, and Bernie and I set off toward the farm buildings. Sheep watched us approach, but one else was about. A thoroughly modern tractor was parked in front of the barn as was an old truck, wheels thick with mud.

We followed Emma's instructions and took the paved walkway leading around the barn. The stables soon came in sight. The building matched the exterior of the barn, red stone, blackening with age, steeply pitched slate roof. The building was long and low, just one story, with room for six spacious stalls, each with a small window set next to it. The stables, I assumed, dated from when the family needed horses for transportation as well as recreation. Two of the stall doors stood open. A brown horse nibbled on a patch grass, its rope trailing after it. The gray horse stood still, one rear foot off the ground. Josh Hansen was holding the foot, doing something to the shoe, watched over by another man, whom I took to be the farmer. I'd seen him at the tea, but we had not been introduced. Both men were in overalls and mud-encrusted boots. They turned at the sound of us approaching. The farmer was in his sixties, ruddy-faced, wind blown, heavily bearded.

"Hi," Bernie said. "Hope it's okay. We wanted to see the horses."

"Guests always welcome," the man said. "We're almost done here, and then you can pay a call. These two will like you better if you feed them apples. Shall I fetch some?"

"Yes, please," Bernie and I said.

The two horses didn't look like ancient nags put out to pasture to me. But then again, the only horses I've ever seen not on a screen are the ones taking carriages around Central Park.

The man headed for a stall to get the apples. Josh let go of the equine foot he'd been holding, gave the horse a solid thump on her hip, and said, "Hi." He tossed his tool on top of a pile of other unrecognizable instruments. It looked like a particularly long nail file. That, I guessed, was exactly what it was.

The freed horse twisted her long neck and nuzzled Josh's shoulder.

"You've been giving them a pedicure?" Bernie asked.

Josh reached down, took a small cloth out of the open bag, and rubbed it between his hands. "That's one way of putting it. Horses' feet and shoes need regular attention."

"You told us you were the blacksmith here. I forgot that," I said.

"Yup. Paid my regular visit to these two and am catching up with George, who looks after them." He stroked the horse's powerful neck.

"How often do they need to be seen to?" Bernie asked.

"About every six weeks."

"Can I touch one?" I asked.

Josh laughed. "Go ahead. They won't bite. This is Ginny, and that's her brother, Harry."

"Harry?" Bernie said.

He laughed. "Not named after the wayward prince. Those are names the family have given their horses for a very long time. I don't know the origins."

I cautiously stretched out one hand. A giant, heavily lashed, liquid brown eye watched me.

George arrived with a bowl full of wrinkled apples, and Bernie and I each took one. Josh showed us how to hold it so we wouldn't lose any fingers.

"Emma was telling us Tony's thinking of getting more horses so guests can ride," I said.

"Tony thinks of a lot of things," Josh said.

I turned away from Ginny at the sharpness of his tone.

"Sorry," he said. "I don't have any problems with Tony. He wants to make a success of the hotel, that's all."

"If they're going to be plopping overweight city people and their ill-tamed kiddies onto me horses, they can find another farmer," George growled.

Bernie and I fed apples to the horses and complemented them on their beauty and general goodness. When the snacks were finished, George said, "Sorry, ladies, but I have chores waiting and need to put these two away first." He took their bridles and led the horses to their stalls. "You can come and visit anytime. Top of the doors is open most of the day. Please don't open the stall doors if I'm not around."

"Thanks, we will," Bernie said. "I mean, we won't."

"I'm glad I ran into you," Josh said. "I've been wondering if everything's okay with your grandmother, after what happened at the tea."

"She's fine," I said. "We're obviously upset about it, but we didn't know Julien at all."

"Lucky you," he said.

Bernie cocked an eyebrow. "What does that mean?"

Josh began gathering up his equipment. "Nothing. Let's just say Julien, or Viscount Darnby, as he liked to be called, and I had our differences. See you in six weeks, George," he called.

George waved. Josh headed for his truck, and Bernie and I walked with him.

I couldn't help but wonder how great those differences were.

Rather than simply wonder, Bernie asked. "Any reason for that?"

"No reason other than he was an officious jerk. In his fantasies, it was the seventeenth century and the heir to the title expected the peasantry to step aside and bow to their betters."

"Were you one of the peasantry?" Bernie asked.

Josh looked at her. "My grandfather was a stable hand. He mucked about in mud and horse droppings all day. I'm an independent businessman with my own farrier company, but I'm paid for the work I do here, so I guess that means I am."

"The police have been asking about your movements the day Julien died," I said as we rounded the barn and Josh's truck came into view.

"Not surprised to hear that. They've spoken to me on more than one occasion." He threw his things into the back of the truck. "They have their job to do. George told me he had to tell them about the time he had to separate Julien and me before we really got into it."

"Why?"

"I found the good viscount trying to get Ginny to go somewhere she didn't want to go. Let's say he wasn't being gentle about it, and I yelled at him. A minor incident, really, but a lot of years of hostility bubbled to the surface. We've had our issues since we were kids. Elizabeth has always been very fond of my grandfather, a lot of which has to do with how well Granddad and her husband got on. Edward was quite the horseman in his day. When I was a child Elizabeth allowed me the run of the farm, and as I got older I could take the horses out for a ride whenever I wanted. Julien, even at seventeen, expected me to tug my forelock and beg for permission."

"Which you didn't do?"

"No. And being a teenager as well, I told him what I thought of him. As I said, a lot of years of hostility since."

"When did the recent incident you mentioned happen?" Bernie asked.

"Six months or so ago. But that wasn't the last time we had . . . a disagreement. A couple of weeks ago he came into my local. Never seen him in there before. If I had, I would have found another place to drink. He was slumming it, I thought. See how the lower classes live. He was already drunk when he arrived with a couple of his London mates, also three sheets to the wind. He had to show them how important he was in the area. Asked me if I was still shoveling horse manure for a living. I might have said at least it was good honest work, unlike some. Foolishly, I made a crack about his wife leaving him."

"You know about that?"

"Talk of the town, Lily. Everyone knows. If you want to play the lord of the manor, you have to expect the common people to gossip about you. Anyway, he insulted me in return, and I took a swing. Nothing came of it. One of my mates grabbed me, I missed, but Julien fell flat on his arse, and everyone laughed. He was asked to leave, and he did so, throwing insults behind him all the way. It was *my* local, remember, and Julien was the outsider. I considered not going to Elizabeth's birthday party, but Granddad wanted to, and he couldn't have gone by himself. My folks are up in Scotland, visiting my sister, so it was up to me to take him." He rubbed his jaw. "It went okay. Julien and I might have exchanged a couple of mild barbs in passing, but we kept our distance. Until . . ."

"Until?" I said.

"Julien died and I'm a suspect. Because of some silly teenage antagonism and a bar brawl that never went anywhere."

"Did you come into the kitchen at any point on Sunday?" Bernie asked.

He shook his head. "Nope. Police asked me that, more than once. But I didn't. No reason to. They also asked if I was aware Julien was allergic to nuts, and I hadn't been. I'd be about the last person he'd tell something like that to. Man like Julien would have considered an allergy to be a weakness."

"I'm sure you're not really a suspect," I said. "They're talking to everyone."

"Even Lily," Bernie added.

One eyebrow rose. "Why?"

"No reason," I said.

"I couldn't stand the man, never could. But I'm sorry he's dead, if only for the sake of his parents and Elizabeth. If I had killed him, you can be sure, I'd have been a lot more upfront about it than to poison his tea."

Chapter 17

Rose invited Elizabeth to join us for dinner, and Lady Frockmorton entertained the table with stories of the grand old days when her husband was alive and Thornecroft Castle was at the center of what passed as West Yorkshire society in the 1950s. "Even then—particularly then—we were having to make do as best we could and stretch every penny to the seams." She laughed. "I didn't even have a lady's maid. One of the housekeepers helped me dress for formal dinners. These days, I dress myself."

She looked lovely in a black pant suit dotted with sparkling silver sequins worn over a satin silver blouse. The blouse showed signs of wear around the collar, and I noticed a few rough stitches holding the buttons of her jacket in place. Her only jewelry was small gold circles clipped to her ear lobes and the plain gold band on her left hand. Conversation was light and casual, and Elizabeth seemed to be genuinely interested in hearing from Matt and Simon.

"If you ever want to write a book about the undersides of the once-great families of Yorkshire, I can put you in touch with people who know that sort of thing," she said to Matt.

"I remember Garfield Hall, back in the day," she told Simon. "Beautiful property and fabulous house. Edward and I went there only once, as I recall, to a ball. The father, or was it the grandfather, of the current earl was an incredible spendthrift. He entertained as his ancestors had done before him and just about drove the property into receivership. A common enough story. I'm glad to hear they're doing well again."

"Lily and I are planning to go to Halifax tomorrow," Simon said. "As tourists. I'm not from around here myself, and I've been working since getting here. Anything in particular we should see?"

"If you're interested in industrial history, no place better on earth." Elizabeth launched into a recitation of the glories of Halifax. I smiled at Simon, looking forward to the outing.

Simon urged me to try the sticky toffee pudding for dessert, and I just about found myself in heaven. Bernie, who'd refused dessert, reached across him, grabbed a spoon and dug in. "Oh, my goodness, that is good," she said as she scraped up caramel sauce. "I don't suppose you can find a way to put it on the menu at the tearoom, Lily?"

"Can't see that it would fit," I said. "Everything at tea is usually eaten with the fingers."

Elizabeth dabbed her lips with her napkin and laid it on the table. "The night is still young, but I am not. This has been delightful, but it's time for me to turn in."

No one had said a word during dinner about the death of her grandson or the disappearance of her jewels, and I was glad of it. Elizabeth needed some time to relax. What happened here on Sunday had to be topmost on her mind, as well as her being constantly badgered by the police and family members as to if she remembered something. When we arrived back at the hotel that afternoon, a security guard was still posted at the entrance to the driveway, but only a handful of bored paparazzi and gossipmongers remained. If the rain came, that would (hopefully) see the end of them.

Elizabeth lifted a hand, and a waiter magically appeared. When we initially sat down, Matt and Simon said they'd take care of the bill, and Elizabeth had not argued. "I'd like to return to my rooms now, Jason. If you have a moment, would you be so kind as to escort me?"

"It would be my pleasure," he said, clearly meaning it.

Simon and Matt leapt to their feet.

"Time for me to go to my room, also," Rose said.

Jason got the walker for Elizabeth and helped her stand. Rose went with them, and my friends and I headed off in search of a nightcap. A scattering of people were leaning on the bar or sitting at tables. Emma, Susannah, and Carmela among them. Emma called to us to join them, and we did so. She gave Bernie and me a nod and a discreet thumbs up. I took that to mean she'd spoken to her father, and he hadn't yelled at her too much.

"Any news from the police about how the investigation's going?" Matt asked once we were seated and drinks ordered.

"The same questions over and over again," Susannah said. "DI Ravenwood asked me if Alicia Boyle, of all people, had ever made threats against the family. I laughed in his face. Man's a fool."

"I don't think so," Carmela said. "He's checking all the angles, as they're supposed to do. You don't suppose Alicia might have taken the sapphires, do you? To give the money to some of her radical groups?"

"I do not," Susannah said. "The organizations she belongs to can hardly be called radical. Plenty of people in the UK think it's time to get rid of the monarchy once and for all and sell off all their assets."

"Do you think that?" Simon asked her.

"I might be leaning that way. Haven't entirely made up my mind. I will admit, it's not a personal thing for me. As the daughter of a daughter of an earl, I am not in line for any sort of title."

"I apologize if this is an indelicate question, Carmela," Bernie, who had never worried about delicacy in her life, said. "Do you know when you'll be able to have the funeral?"

Carmela dipped her head and gave it a small shake. "No."

"It makes things difficult," Susannah said. "No one knows whether to go home or to stay, and the reservations clerk is trying to balance extended visits with sudden cancelations and new bookings. Believe it or not, we're getting new bookings because people heard about Thornecroft Castle in the news."

"Ghouls," Carmela said.

"No publicity is bad publicity," Susannah said. "Or so they say in advertising."

"They're hoping to find the Frockmorton Sapphires among the dust bunnies under their bed or stuffed into the back of a drawer," Emma said. "Maybe we should institute a policy of searching people's bags when they check out."

"Great idea," Susannah said with a laugh. "I'll suggest it to Tony. Speak of the devil, here he is now."

Carmela's head jerked up. Light filled her eyes and a broad smile appeared on her face. "Tony! There you are, my darling. Come and join us."

He looked at Carmela, but he did not smile in return. Then he turned away and spoke to no one in particular. "Sorry, but things to do. Never stops around here, does it? That's the hotel business."

He almost ran out of the bar.

"Your brother needs to learn to take it easy sometimes," Carmela said to Susannah. "Nothing wrong with having a drink of an evening."

Susannah gave the other woman a poisonous look. "Tony *is* this hotel. If he took it easy, we'd be out of business in a fortnight."

"He's worried," Emma said. "He was called down to the police station earlier."

"What for?" Carmela asked.

"About the death of *your* husband, I'd guess. And the disappearance of our grandmother's jewels. Did he say anything to you when he got back, Susannah?"

"No," Susannah said. "I asked, but he snapped at me that he didn't want to talk about it. Very unlike Tony. We always talk things over. I could tell he was bothered by it. He was at the station for a long time, almost all afternoon. No one else, far as I know, was asked to present themselves for questioning. The detectives have always come here to talk to us. To me, anyway. What about you, Carmela?"

"Why are you asking me? They have not questioned *me*. I am, let me remind you, the widow."

"Ah yes, the grieving widow. Good thing Julien didn't have much money for you two to fight over in the divorce. Otherwise, maybe they would be hauling you downtown. Then again, can't forget about the sapphires."

Carmela stood up. "As pleasant as this conversation is, I think I'll seek company elsewhere."

"Tony's probably in his office," Susannah said. "With the door locked and bolted and that cat on guard outside."

"What is that supposed to mean?"

"It means give it up, Carmela."

Carmela walked away without another word.

"I didn't get a chance to tell you earlier," Simon said, when at last we were alone in our room, "I got a call from Genevieve, my boss at Garfield Hall, shortly after we got back from York."

"Do you have to go back? A gardening emergency?" I went to the windows and pulled the drapes against the night.

"Good thing about being a gardener, there never are any emergencies." Simon dug through the snacks left on the small side table, next to the kettle and tea things. He selected a packet of chocolate biscuits and ripped it open. "No, the police paid them a visit and she wanted me to know. Two in here. Want one?"

"No thanks. I don't like the sound of that, and I am not referring to cookies at bedtime. Was it DS Capretti?"

"No. They sent a uniform, which is a good thing, meaning more of a routine check than an interview. He asked how well she'd checked my references, and if I'd shown any signs of having criminal tendencies or contacts, either here or in the states."

"Why would they do that? You weren't even here on Sunday."

"I suspect they think you might have passed the jewels on to me."

My eyes widened. He nodded. "Fortunately, I've kept my international jewel thief background a secret. Just kidding, Lily."

"I suppose it's only logical they'd want to speak to you eventually. Bernie and I have been telling everyone we wouldn't have stolen the sapphires as we don't know anyone to give them to, and we wouldn't be able to get them out of the country."

"He asked Genevieve if I'd ever mentioned going to Thornecroft Castle, prior to this week, and if anyone from there visited me at Garfield Hall. She said she didn't know. Which is fair enough, as I don't tell everyone my personal business, and Genevieve doesn't spend her days standing on the battlements with binoculars spying on the staff. Not that I have anything to hide."

"Is this going to cause problems for you at work?"

"Genevieve's okay with it. She knows what happened here on Sunday, of course—everyone does—and I'd previously told her I was taking a few days off because my American friends would be here for Lady Frockmorton's birthday. The police are checking all angles, that's all."

I wasn't entirely reassured. Just when I'd started to think I was in the clear, I found out the police had been asking about the bona fides of my only English friend.

"What did Emma have to tell you?" He ripped open another packet of cookies. Yorkshire shortbread this time.

"Emma?"

"Yes, Emma. You and Bernie ran off after her, obviously hot on the trail. Only one reason you'd do that. Did you learn anything?"

"Nothing that provides any insight as to what happened with the murder or the theft. As Bernie told us, Emma's in a financial mess, and she confirmed that, but she didn't steal the jewels in an attempt to get out of it."

"You know that for sure?"

"Pretty sure. She called her father, very reluctantly I might add, to ask for a loan. She wouldn't have done that if she had expectations of coming into a multimillion-pound windfall."

"How do you know she called her dad?"

"She told me?" I admitted.

"Right," he said. "Sure you don't want a biscuit?"

Chapter 18

As planned, Simon and I set off for Halifax immediately after breakfast the following day. He suggested taking his motorbike, forcing me to decide which of two options I feared most: riding on the back of the bike or driving us to the nearest branch of the company we'd rented the car from so Simon could be registered to drive it.

I decided on the car.

"Speed limit's up to fifty, Lily," Simon said as we crept down the road leading from Thornecroft. The security guard was still in place, but the press seemed to have taken their leave. On to bother someone else, I assumed.

"It might be. But I am not." I turned slowly into yet another exceptionally narrow street.

"Whoa! Careful there. You're on the wrong side of the road."

I swung back into my lane as the driver of an approaching car used his horn to tell me what he thought of my driving.

I glanced at the GPS. Only ten miles left to go. I only hoped I'd live to make it.

"I will never, ever do that again," I said to Simon as I

collapsed over the steering wheel in the first available parking space at the car rental office. "If you're not here when we leave, we'll take a cab and call the owners to come and pick up the car. Never mind the cost."

He reached out and ruffled my hair. "You'll get used to it. I noticed you were almost at the speed limit on that last stretch."

"Like a horse returning to the barn, I was in sight of my destination," I said.

Car business completed, we drove into the center of Halifax, Simon at the wheel. Elizabeth suggested we start our day at the Piece Hall. Once the vibrant center of the textile trade, it's now a pleasant location with tiny stores, restaurants, and coffeehouses. The massive, three-story building formed a square around a large courtyard, which in the summer would be filled with restaurant tables, children's play areas, and seating. At this time of year, it was quiet, but we wandered through the small shops. I wanted to get gifts for Cheryl and Marybeth, my tearoom staff, and for Edna, who helped in the B & B. For Edna, who made much of the jam to accompany the scones in the tearoom, I got a selection of tiny jars of jams and preserves, thinking she might like to try something different. For Cheryl, a selection of coasters with pictures of Yorkshire sheep, and for Marybeth, I bought a decorative china plate. Then I realized I should get something for the housekeepers who were caring for Éclair, my dog, so I added several souvenir calendars for next year to my bag.

Shopping completed to my satisfaction, we headed to the town library, which Elizabeth told us had been built right into an old church. We climbed the library steps, studying the fourteenth-century stone pillars and archways, and in particular, admired the gorgeous rose window.

"So cool," I said to Simon, after we'd taken numerous

pictures of us both standing in front of the window. We then walked the short distance to Halifax Minster for a look at the church, parts of which date from the fifteenth century. When I'd had my fill of admiring the grand art and architecture, and speculating about the generations of Yorkshiremen and women who'd walked through these doors, I said, "It's coming up to lunch time. Want to find a coffee shop or something?"

"Sounds like a plan," he said.

As we crossed the pedestrian-only Woolshops shopping area near the Piece Hall, a sign in a window between a shoe store and an electronics shop caught my eye. A doctor's office, names of the associated doctors listed on the window. Including Dr. Alicia Boyle. "I remember now. Alicia told me her office—'surgery,' she called it—was in the Woolshops. I wonder if she's in."

"If she is, she'll be busy."

"Wouldn't hurt to pop in and say hi."

"Lily, that name was mentioned last night in the bar as someone who might be of interest to the police. Are you taking time out of our tourist day to investigate?"

"Kinda. I mean, if Bernie was here, or even Rose, they'd be through the door without so much as stopping to think about it."

"Bernie and Rose are not here, and you are stopping to think about it."

I looked up at him. "You want me to leave it?"

He grinned at me. "I want you to do what you want to do, Lily. Maybe one of the things I love most about you is that insatiable curiosity."

I sucked in a breath and looked quickly away. I was suddenly extremely hot in my heavy sweater and padded vest. That was the first time the L word had been mentioned between us. Did he mean it? Or was it just an off-the-cuff saying? I once told Éclair I loved her because she chased squirrels with no chance of ever catching them. And she wouldn't know what to do with them if she did catch them.

Did I "L" Simon in return? I looked at him, at his handsome face, his sandy hair, his lovely kind blue eyes, his smile. *Yes, yes, I believe I do.*

Do we love each other enough to uproot our lives in order to be together?

"You want to help, Lily," Simon went on, as though he hadn't said anything earth-shattering. "Won't hurt to ask, as you said."

I pushed aside my thoughts, to be examined at a more opportune moment, as he opened the door and we walked in. It was immediately obvious we were in the waiting room of a pediatricians' office. Colorful walls and furniture, low chairs and tables, mounds of soft toys, a play mat covered with cars and trains, boxes of puzzles, a knee-high bookcase. Only one woman was in the waiting room. Huge pregnant belly straining at her winter coat, she watched a toddler attempting to put a puzzle together.

"Good morning. Or is it afternoon already? I lose track of time some days. Can I help you?" asked the plump, pink-cheeked woman behind the reception desk. "Do you have an appointment?"

"No. We're just passing and I remembered that Alicia— Dr. Boyle—told me she worked here. I wanted to pop in and say hi."

She gave me a big smile. "From America, are you? Friend of Alicia's?" She glanced at Simon. He smiled back but didn't say anything.

"Sort of. We met at Thornecroft Castle on the weekend."

Her face darkened. "Nasty business, that. And then the coppers had the nerve to come in here, during surgery hours no less, to question Alicia. Of all people."

An inner door opened and a woman in bright pink

scrubs stuck her head around the corner. "Mrs. O'Malley, Dr. Ambrose will see Teddy now."

The pregnant woman lumbered to her feet and called to her son. He took her hand, they followed the nurse, and the door closed behind them.

"Alicia is between patients at the moment," the receptionist said. "She's having her lunch and catching up on paperwork. I don't know if she has time to see you."

"That's okay, if not. I understand. My name is Lily Roberts."

The receptionist picked up the phone. "Sorry to bother you, Alicia. There's an American name of Lily here to see you." She put down the phone and said, "She'll be right out. Take a seat."

We didn't have time to sit down before a smiling Alicia emerged from the inner sanctum, adjusting her glasses. She wore jeans with sneakers and a sweater under a white lab coat. "Lily. Nice of you to drop by. Is everything okay?" Her eyes flicked to Simon, and I introduced them.

"We're doing the tourist rounds," I said. "I saw your name on the door, so we decided to pop in. I've been thinking about you after—what happened." I glanced at the receptionist, not bothering to conceal her interest.

"Never mind Joanie there," Alicia said. "She's my very nosy older sister, and she knows absolutely everything about my life. More than I do sometimes."

"Hi," Joanie said.

"Hi," Simon and I replied.

"I thought you should know the police have been asking questions about you," I said. "But it seems you're aware of that."

Alicia rolled her eyes. "Oh, yeah. I do. Something was added to the sandwiches I helped you make, and the cops seem to be developing a fixation with me."

"With more people than just you," I said. "Ian. Me."

"Ian, I've spoken to. He didn't mention you. I'm sorry to hear that. Not a very welcoming attitude to tourists, is it?"

"It's not the police's job to be a branch of the tourist industry," Simon said.

Alicia laughed. "I told them the same as Ian told them, and no doubt what you did, too. I didn't see anyone paying any particular attention to those sandwiches who shouldn't have been. I guess it's the 'shouldn't have been' that's making them suspicious of the three of us, although a lot of people were in and out of the kitchen that afternoon."

"Was Julien's allergy generally known?" Simon asked.

"I'm sure it was no secret. Ian and the regular kitchen staff had to know because Julien often visited and ate in the restaurant. I had to tell the police I knew, although I'm not on any sort of friendly basis with the Crawfords. I'd never met the man before, and I was only at the tea because of my mother's connection to Elizabeth. This practice was my father's before me, and his father's before him. The Crawfords were their patients for many years. My grandfather signed the death certificate for Elizabeth's husband, Edward. When Julien was about seven years old, he had an incident when he was visiting Thornecroft. He had to be rushed to hospital because of exposure to walnuts. He almost died. My father attended him. Obviously, such was recorded in his medical records, and I have access to those records today. Ergo, the cops think they have something on me." She shook her head. "Taking the easy route, as usual."

"They wouldn't, if you hadn't needled the chief constable all those times," Joanie said.

"The chief constable shouldn't be so sensitive," Alicia said. "Which he wouldn't be if he wasn't such an incompetent fool."

"You don't think the police would charge you at the CC's orders, do you?" Simon said. "Without evidence?"

Alicia's face relaxed, and she almost smiled. "No, I do not. Just means I'm high on their suspect list, and they likely either got the word to give me a hard time, or decided on their own initiative to do so, to possibly score points with the big boss. As there's nothing to find—they won't find anything. I'm not worried about it."

"Do you know Josh Hansen?" I asked.

"Who's that?" Simon said.

"Someone I was talking to at the party."

"I know Josh to see him, but no more," Alicia said. "I don't keep horses, but some of my neighbors do, and Josh is a farrier. He was at the tea with his grandfather. Why do you ask?"

"It would appear he and Julien clashed several times recently. The police are interested in that."

"Don't know anything about it. Sorry. I hope the police are looking further afield than Yorkshire. Julien lived in London these days, remember. Although, if the almonds were added to the sandwiches, then the person had to be in the hotel, right?"

"Not something you can do remotely," Simon said.

"What about relations between the family members?" I asked. "I sense some—shall we say 'tension'?—between the cousins."

"I could launch into a diatribe about the evils of inherited money, but I'll save you the time and I won't. Almost everything I know about the Crawfords is from my mother's memories or the gossip I hear, in here or down the pub. Almost everyone you talk to loves Elizabeth. Even if they don't know her personally, they love her devotion to the history of the estate and to the town and people who live in it. Can't say the same for the late Julien or his father, Robert. They don't live here, and don't often visit. Robert, despite being the current Earl of Frockmorton, has little to no interest in taking over his family's business affairs. To his credit, Robert doesn't try to play lord of the manor when he does drop in, unlike Julien."

That matched what Josh had to say about Julien's generally obnoxious behavior.

"As for the rest of them." Alicia shrugged. "I can't say. Tony is in charge of the hotel, and by all accounts he does a darn good job of it. Several of my patients are employed there, and they're generally happy. Some of the longtime staffers wonder what's going to happen following Elizabeth's death, particularly, if Julien inherited it all. They feared he had plans to sell it off or to make major changes of the sort that would destroy the boutique-hotel atmosphere. No one knows what's going to happen now. Hopefully, Elizabeth leaves Tony to continue to run it as he has for a long time."

The bell over the door tinkled, and a man pushing a stroller came in, followed by a woman holding a child's hand.

"Doctor will be with you shortly, Mrs. and Mrs. Evans," Joanie called.

"Sorry," Alicia said. "I have to get back to work. Anything else?"

"No," I said. "If you want to talk things over. If you're worried about . . . what we discussed, give me a call. We're sort of in the same boat."

"Thanks," she said. "Good to know I have someone on my side."

"She's worried," Simon said to me as we crossed the wide courtyard. He'd taken my hand as we left the doctors' office.

"You think so?"

"Yeah, I do. I'm not saying the English police are corrupt, far from it. But they are massively overworked and underfunded, and if the CC is putting pressure on them to get this case solved . . ."

"Alicia is a good suspect," I said. "Except, she isn't. She had no motive to kill him. Noticeably, she referred to them as the Crawfords and used their first names, even the late earl, but it's a well-known fact she's opposed to the very concept of the aristocracy. Elizabeth would have been fully aware of that, and she invited Alicia to her party, anyway. It's been speculated that whoever added the almonds to the chicken mixture didn't intend to kill Julien, only to disrupt the celebration. Of all people, that doesn't apply to Alicia. Not if she's read Julien's medical records. Not if she knows he almost died at age seven."

"There are a lot of things you don't know, Lily. Maybe Julien was blackmailing her over something. Maybe her political involvement isn't as legal and nonviolent as everyone thinks. Maybe they were having a torrid secret affair. Is she married?"

"She is. She told me her husband was minding their kids while she was at the party. You're right, of course. So much I don't know. But I do know I'm hungry." I pulled out my phone and checked the map. "Lots of coffee shops and sandwich places around. How does that sound? We've been eating and drinking so much since we got here, I don't want a big lunch."

"Sounds good to me," he said.

We left the Woolshops and arrived at Market Street. I turned my phone upside down to try to follow the map to the coffee shop. I tilted my head. I squinted at the screen. I enlarged the image. I narrowed it again. I turned the phone right way up.

"Maybe we could try that place over there," Simon said. "The one with the sign in the window saying, coffee, soups, and sandwiches."

I looked up to see the building he was pointing at. Almost directly across the street.

I saw something else. Tony Waterfield leaving the bank. He skipped nimbly down the stairs and stopped on the sidewalk to check his own phone.

I was about to point him out to Simon when I saw someone else I recognized. Carmela Crawford stepped out from a shop doorway. "Tony," she trilled. "How nice to run into you."

A car moved between us so I didn't hear his reply. When I could see him again, it was easy to tell he wasn't pleased at the encounter.

"Come on." I half-dragged Simon across the street. Fortunately, no other cars were coming. I nipped into the doorway that previously concealed Carmela. Simon didn't quite fit, but Tony and Carmela were not paying any attention to what else was going on around them. I stuck my head out and peered around Simon.

"Carmela," Tony said. "What brings you into town?"

"A bit of shopping. I don't have suitable funeral clothes. One doesn't usually think to bring those on a family visit, does one? Do you have time for a coffee?"

"No, I do not. I have to get back."

"We need to talk things over. About the hotel, I mean. Julien and I were still legally married. That means I am his heir. And that means I have an interest in the running of the hotel. Oh, don't worry." She laughed lightly. "I have no intention of getting involved, and you have my total and complete confidence. But I would like to know what plans you have for the future of the hotel."

"Actually, Carmela." Tony's face was set, his tone so cold I wouldn't have been surprised if ice pellets began falling from the sky. "You can have as much interest as you want, but you have no financial interests whatsoever, because neither did Julien—although he certainly wanted to. I'll remind you my grandmother is still alive, as is Robert, Julien's father. As well as Granny's two other children, one of whom is my own mother. Now, if you'll excuse me." He turned to go.

Her hand shot out, and she grabbed the sleeve of his coat. "Tony, all I want is for us to still be friends. Can't you see that?"

"Your husband isn't even in his grave yet, Carmela. Give it a rest." He jerked his arm out of her grasp and walked away, his steps firm and angry.

She stood where she was, watching him until he disappeared around the next corner. Then she sighed, her shoulders slumped, and she turned around. She walked past us, without registering us. I might have seen the glimmer of tears in her eyes.

Chapter 19

"Carmela has designs on Tony, and Tony is not interested." The cold wind whipped my hair and stung my face.

"If you told us the conversation you overheard exactly as you remembered it," Bernie said, "it sounds as though she's wanting to know what's going on with the hotel. Seems insensitively premature to me, but as someone once said, the rich are not like you and me."

"Except the Crawfords are not rich," I said. "Not in cash, at any event. Obviously, this house is worth a lot, as are the farms and the dower house and probably the other rental properties. Elizabeth owns it all, but for the family to share in the wealth, rather than just the income from the properties, everything would have to be sold and the proceeds divided up."

"Which was the entire point of entail and primogeniture." Rose was heavily bundled in her wool coat, gloves, scarf, and a red hat with a purple pom-pom on top. Lissie had jumped out of an open window to follow us outside, and she was now curled happily in the warmth of Rose's lap. "The great estates continued to be great as by law they could not be divided between quarreling sons and nephews and whoever, no matter the wishes of the owners."

"Beside the point, Rose," I said. "This is all beside the point. Carmela suggested she and Tony talk about the hotel as a pretext. She is, for lack of a better word, romantically interested in Tony. They are not blood relatives, so nothing wrong with that. He's not married, she was about to get divorced, so nothing wrong there. Except—"

"Except?" Bernie said.

We were sitting on a bench in the garden maze at Thornecroft Castle House. Simon and I enjoyed a pleasant light lunch of soup and sandwiches before getting the car for a tour of Shibden Hall, home of the nineteenth-century diarist Anne Lister, now a museum, freshly popular as a result of the TV show *Gentleman Jack*. We had great fun poking around the house, with its origins in the fourteenth century, seeing the "modernizations" made by Anne Lister herself, touring the barn and other outbuildings, and wandering the extensive gardens. Back at the hotel, I impatiently waited for Bernie to return from her day's outing with Matt so I could tell her what I'd learned. Naturally, Rose wanted to hear the details as well, and as she had suggested a walk on the grounds, we did so.

"It wasn't only today's chance meeting," I said, "which I don't think was chance at all. Carmela was lying in wait for Tony outside the bank. She said she'd been shopping, but she didn't have any bags."

"She might have put them in her car before going someplace for lunch. You're overthinking this, love."

"No. I'm sure I'm on to something. Bernie, remember last night when Tony came into the bar, and Carmela just about squealed in her joy at seeing him. He turned and ran out of there fast enough. Susannah made a dig at Carmela, implying she was wasting her time chasing after Tony. Susannah and Tony seem to be close, so it's possible he told her if Carmela is being a pest. Even if he didn't tell her, Susannah might suspect. I've noticed before he seems particularly cool toward Carmela, whereas he's generally friendly to everyone else."

"Being friendly is part of his hotelier personality," Bernie said. "That's his job. Doesn't mean he likes everyone he's talking to."

"True. I suspect they might have had something going on in the past. He ended it, and she wants to pick it up again. You can't deny it's adding up."

"I can't. And I won't. I'm playing devil's advocate here. The other question the devil has is, does it matter? Carmela didn't have to kill her husband to be with Tony. This is the twenty-first century. She and Julien were getting a divorce. I suppose she might think she's in line for a cut of any inheritance as Julien's widow, whereas she wouldn't be as his ex-wife, but that seems too much of a long game for a murder motive. We can't forget Julien's father is still alive and kicking."

"It takes two to tango," Rose said. Lissie purred. "Even when one dance partner doesn't want to. Or appears not to."

"What on earth does that mean?" I asked.

Katherine Wakefield, Tony and Susannah's mother, came out of the hotel in the company of her brother, Robert. She had her arm tucked through his, and they were well wrapped against the chill. They walked slowly, not talking, appearing to take comfort in each other's company. Julien's father had aged a decade in the days since I first met him. A handful of other guests were in the garden, wandering the paths, admiring the intricate layout of the shrubs or studying the old architecture, but the temperature was dropping steadily, and no one other than us lingered.

"Are you sure Tony doesn't return Carmela's feelings?" Rose said. "Might he be pretending for some ends? She might be in on the act."

"Why?" I asked.

"You're the amateur detective, love. Find that out."

"I am not an amateur detective, and I have no way of finding out what they're thinking. Short of asking them. I suppose he could be acting, but why?"

"For them to openly appear as a couple at Elizabeth's party, in the presence of Carmela's still lawfully wedded husband, would be shockingly indiscreet. Elizabeth is exceptionally progressive considering her age, social rank, and the times in which she grew up, but that might be a bridge too far. Julien wanted to pretend the marriage was doing fine, this weekend at any rate."

"There might be other reasons," Bernie said. "Things to do with the possible inheritance, although I can't see it. It must be difficult getting to Elizabeth's age and knowing everyone around you is twiddling their thumbs waiting for you to kick the bucket so they can find out what they're going to get."

Rose laughed so hard, she woke the cat. "A fine way of putting it, Bernadette. Elizabeth is much loved by all her family, but even so, one can't forget that time is passing, and quickly."

I touched my grandmother's hand and looked into her face. She gave me a wink. "Speaking of getting old. These aging bones of mine feel the cold these days. Time for us to go in."

"We thought we might go to that pub near here for dinner," Bernie said. "Matt and Simon haven't been there yet, and we liked it. Would you like to come? We can take a cab."

"No, thank you, love. Elizabeth was singing the praises of this wonderful police show set in Yorkshire, so I'm planning a night in front of the telly, with room service for my dinner. Apparently, some of the cast stayed here while filming. Elizabeth said it was most exciting."

Simon and I arranged to meet Matt and Bernie at the hotel entrance and walk together to the pub. When they joined us, Matt said, "Dennis called earlier to let me know he checked in with Alfred. Nothing new. Alfred says there's not a whisper in what he calls the 'usual circles' about the Frockmorton Sapphires, other than so much speculation it's clear no one knows anything for sure. Mighty strange, he said. Someone should know something."

"I don't know how much faith I'd put into Alfred and his network," Bernie said. "Criminal connections shift and change all the time. The old guys die or retire, new ones take over. Not always in a friendly manner, either. Add in possibly unfriendly governments with a need for fast cash, or organized mobs, and Alfred and his drinking buddies are likely to be way, way out of the loop."

"You're probably right," Matt said. "The old guys dream of the glory days. And that includes Dennis. The sapphires are gone. Likely in several pieces by now. The insurance company will be wanting to be sure before they pay out, and that could take years."

Susannah joined us, dressed for the outdoor weather. "It's getting cold out there. No rain in the forecast, fortunately. There's nothing like a freezing cold Yorkshire rain to have me running home to London."

"Are you going home soon?" I asked as we all stepped out into the night, buttoning coats, pulling on gloves, tightening scarves.

"Tomorrow. We originally planned on leaving Sunday night, following the party, but after what happened, I asked for a couple of extra days off to be with Mum and Granny. No one knows what's happening about Julien's funeral, and I have to get back to work. My husband picked the kids up from his parents on Monday, dropped them off again today, and he's coming to get me tonight. We're leaving in the morning."

We started walking down the driveway. "Looks like we're going the same way," Susannah said. "Are you off to the pub? So am I. I told Ray I felt like the walk, so we're meeting there."

We reached the main road. Matt and Simon walked ahead, with Bernie in the middle, and Susannah and me bringing up the rear.

"It's probably impolite of me to ask," I said, "being an outsider and all, but do you have any thoughts about Julien's death, or the disappearance of the sapphires?"

"It's not impolite. None of us are thinking of anything else. I have absolutely no idea. If I was to guess, and it's only a guess, someone attempted to play a practical joke on Julien. Julien could play Lord Muckety-muck sometimes, and that doesn't always go down well these days. Whoever did it, might have thought it would be a laugh to humiliate Julien, make it look as though he was drunk, and he'd throw up in front of everyone, including our grandmother, and make a fool of himself. He had several drinks before the tea even started, and he was hitting the wine mighty hard. A practical joke, but whoever did it didn't realize just how allergic Julien was. A lot of people don't, do they? Emma's told me some stories of parents at her school who think the school is overreacting when they ban peanuts, and so they pack them in their children's lunches, anyway."

Susannah, I thought, might have a point. Members of the family would have known tree nuts were life-threatening to Julien, but perhaps not more casual acquaintances. Or even the hotel staff. Alicia Boyle knew, if she'd read her father's report on tending to Julien as a child. Josh? By his own account, Josh and Julien held a considerable amount of antagonism toward each other, and had for a lot of years. Is it possible Josh was trying to humiliate Julien and went too far? If Josh thought Julien was too high-and-mighty for his own good, might others have thought the same? Including Ian or other staff or former employees? No, not Ian. I still believed no chef would endanger his reputation that way—but others might.

Possible. Susannah seemed to be saying so.

We walked slowly, enjoying the night and the conversation. Matt, Simon, and Bernie were pulling ahead of us.

"Emma loves this place," I said. "She told me she feels rooted here. Same with you?"

"Not really. I'm a city girl, I'm afraid. Like my mother. Mum couldn't wait to leave the sheep and fields of Yorkshire behind and move to the big city. She comes back a couple of times a year to visit Granny and Tony but doesn't stay long. The history of this place and the family doesn't have all that much to do with me. Being the daughter of a daughter sometimes has that effect, right?"

"I wouldn't know," I said with a laugh. "My father's a musician and my mother's a singer and actress. Her family's from Iowa. Fields and cows rather than sheep, but much the same. I'm a city girl myself. Spent all my life in Manhattan until I moved to Cape Cod to help my grandmother run her B&B and open my tearoom."

"Manhattan. It must be wonderful living in Manhattan. Ray and I went to New York on our honeymoon. I loved every minute of it." She sighed with remembered pleasure. "Both the honeymoon and the city."

"Tony likes it here, though?" I asked.

"Tony loves the hotel, and he's protective of it as a vital part of our family's heritage. The hotel's had its ups and downs over the years, and it was struggling for a few years before he took over management of it."

"When was that?"

"About fifteen years ago. He was groomed for it. Got a degree in business, then education in hotel management, and a job at a big hotel chain to learn the ropes."

"Did he mind that? Being groomed for it? Seems rather—"

"Aristocratic?" Susannah laughed. "No, he didn't mind. He loves the hotel business. I'd say it's in the blood, but my grandparents certainly didn't expect their home would become a hotel. Tony's always been the closest of us to Granny. Her favorite, if I could use that word, even when he was a child. Something about that blond innocence." She laughed again. "Yes, he could even wind me, his little sister, around his finger if he wanted. Still can, come to think of it."

"I'm American, so I have trouble sometimes figuring out your titles and lines of succession. Emma's expecting to be Lady Emma if Robert dies before her dad, Thomas, the second son. What about you?"

"I'm Mrs. Susannah Maria Reilly and always will be, and proud of it. Emma gets a mite carried away sometimes. I can't tell you the amount of time she spends looking through old photo albums in the storage rooms, or reading up on local history, trying to find some obscure reference to the Crawfords."

"I assume Jacqueline is Lady Jacqueline, as she's the daughter of the current earl. I'm only assuming that because it's never even been mentioned. If Emma's father becomes the earl, with Jacqueline cease to be Lady?"

"No. She's the daughter of the earl and will be even when her father dies. Her children won't have titles, though, as her husband isn't titled. Much ado about nothing, in my opinion. I mean, really, no one cares anymore. Jacqueline agrees: to her the title is meaningless, so she doesn't flaunt it. Not that my cousin is some sort of radical anti-aristocrat. The title might be meaningless, but she'd be more than happy to accept her share of the family money."

I wondered if that included the sapphires. As the daughter of the earl, did Jacqueline think the jewels should eventually come to her? Did she take them to prevent them being sold? Susannah and I were chatting comfortably, so I ventured to ask about the sapphires. "Everyone says the sapphires don't have to be part of the estate."

"And they don't. Granny has never said what she intends to do with them. They haven't been seen in public for something like fifty years. Aunt Annabelle's been nagging and nagging for a chance to wear them, and Granny always refused. I figured it was because they'd been sold off years ago. I guess not. Better if they had been."

"You don't suppose Annabelle got tired of begging and decided to help herself?"

"Nah," Susannah said firmly. "The thought might well have crossed her mind, but if she had taken them, and the police and insurance company were notified, which they were, she'd never be able to wear them in public. Aunt Annabelle only wanted them to show them off to her friends, as befits the current Countess of Frockmorton. When I said no one cares any more, I wasn't entirely right. Some people care about that stuff very much. I feel sorry for her. And I don't mean just because her son died, although I do. But Aunt Annabelle longs for the old days, when she would have been able to put everyone around her in their place with a raised eyebrow and a sniff of disapproval."

I decided I liked Susannah very much. "What about your cousin, Julien? I've heard he could be the same."

"Yes, poor Julien. Uncle Robert is firmly practical about these sorts of things, but Aunt Annabelle and Julien were not. On occasion, Julien could play the viscount card a bit too much for my liking. I'm no psychologist—far from it—but I sometimes wondered if he overcompensated for the fact that Tony, not even in the line of succession to the title, was the favored grandchild, whereas he, Julien, the rightful heir, was not."

"Someone told me Julien was not much liked by the local people, because of that attitude."

"He could be all 'step aside peasants,' and he could be mighty condescending at times, thinking he was being gracious. But what of it? He lived in London and popped in now and again to check up on things."

"What about after Elizabeth dies? If Julien had taken over, he'd have trouble doing business with people who didn't like his attitude."

"There is that. And believe me, first in line would've been Tony."

The night was dark, the street lamps, few and far between. The scattering of houses along this stretch were set back from the road, and the ever-present hedges and low stone walls lined the sidewalk. Traffic was sparse, the occasional car throwing sudden pools of yellow light into my eyes and onto Susannah's face.

Up ahead the road curved slightly, and the bright lights of the pub came into view. Bernie had caught up with Matt and Simon, and Simon dropped back, waiting for Susannah and me to catch up.

I heard the roar of a car engine, coming too fast around the sharp corner, but headlights did not appear, instead a black bulk emerged from the darkness. I grabbed Susannah's arm, and I heard her gasp. The car was heading directly toward us. I felt myself frozen in place, unable to move, not sure of what to do. A solid wall was beside us. Run forward or fall backward? What would the driver do? Would he see us in time?

Susannah screamed, and I think I did, too.

Chapter 20

A solid mass hit me in the chest, and I flew backward, crashing into Susannah. My legs gave way, and I hit the ground hard. Pain streaked up my arm and into my right knee. Susannah collapsed next to me with a scream. Directly in front of us, I could see two wheels climbing the sidewalk, coming to rest only feet from my legs. Before I could regain my senses and struggle to my feet, with another roar of an engine, the car backed up. Wheels spun, found purchase, and the vehicle hit the roadway.

And then, it was gone. As though it had never been there.

"Everyone okay?"

"Oh my gosh. What happened?"

Simon held out a hand, and I reached for it. Matt was bent over Susannah, asking her if she could stand. Simon had seen what was about to happen, shoved me out of the way, and I'd fallen against Susannah.

"Lunatic!" Bernie screamed into the night. "You could have killed someone."

"I—I . . . ," I said.

"I'm fine," Susannah said. "What happened?"

"Good thing you'd stopped, buddy," Matt said to Simon,

as he helped Susannah to her feet. "When that car came around the corner so fast, with no lights, I figured something was going to happen, but I wouldn't have gotten here in time."

Simon dusted his jacket off. "All in a day's work. You okay, Lily?" He put his hands on my shoulders and stared into my eyes. I blinked. It had all happened so fast.

"I think so." I shifted my feet, and my right knee protested.

Bernie noticed my wince and said, "Are you hurt?"

"A bit sore where I hit the ground, but I'm okay." I shook my head. When nothing fell out, I realized I'd been lucky. Luck, and Simon, had saved me.

Saved us. Susannah was sobbing quietly. Spots of blood dotted her cheeks where she'd fallen facefirst into the pavement. Bernie gathered her into her arms and held her. "You're okay. You're okay."

"Let's go back to the hotel," Matt said. "You want to clean up."

I became aware of a stinging sensation in my hands. I held them up in front of me. The right palm was deeply scratched and bleeding, and when I rolled my wrist, it hurt.

"Should we call the police?" Matt said.

"No point," Susannah said. "He, whoever it was, will be long gone by the time they get here. Hopefully he gets himself home before he endangers anyone else. Rotten drunk."

"I didn't get the license plate," Matt said. "Did anyone?"

"No," Bernie said. "Dark car, a compact sedan, but I can't say what make. And as it didn't hit anyone—thanks to Simon and his quick thinking—there won't be any damage the police can use to identify it. I've lost my appetite."

Matt and Simon exchanged glances.

"What?" I said.

"You guys go back to the hotel," Matt said. "I'll go to the pub and tell them what happened. The person driving that car might have been leaving there, and they might know who it is, if it's a regular. But . . ."

"But?"

Another look passed between Matt and Simon. This time Bernie joined in.

"But," she said, "it might not have been an accident."

"If not," Simon said, "we do need to contact the police."

Not an accident? Surely Simon wasn't suggesting it had been a deliberate attack. On me? On Susannah?

"Does anyone have the detectives' phone number on them?" Simon asked. "I can call 999, but it's not an emergency. Thank goodness," he added under his breath.

I dug DS Capretti's card out of my bag, and while Matt ran to the pub on the corner, and Bernie shepherded me and Susannah down the road the way we came, Simon gave the detective a call. My nerves were on high alert, and I was aware of Bernie walking carefully, checking out every car that approached, listening for the sound of stealthy footsteps behind the walls and hedges.

Simon caught up to us as we reached the entrance to the hotel. "She's on her way. I told her it might have been an out-of-control drunk driver, but it also might have been a more calculated attempt."

"I'm inclined to agree," Bernie said. "The way they drove didn't indicate any diminished driving ability to me. Reversed in a straight line, spun the wheels, and took off in another straight line. Around the corner and gone. Lily and Susannah need to wash up and take a moment to breathe. I'll take them to your room and meet you in the bar."

Simon touched my arm telling me to hang back. "I'll be with you in a sec," I said to Bernie. She gave me a nod and accompanied Susannah inside. Simon put his hands on my arms and looked into my face. "You are okay, Lily? You're not just putting up a brave front?"

I smiled at him bravely. "I'll have a mighty sore knee tomorrow, but nothing more serious than that."

"I—I don't know what I'd do if—how I'd manage if—if things had gone the other way."

"But they didn't," I said. At least I think that's what I said. I couldn't really hear it over the pounding of my heart.

"Lily, I—"

"Simon, I—"

"Evening all." I jumped out of my skin, as a couple came out of the hotel. "Winter's on its way, I fear. Have a nice evening."

"You go with Bernie," Simon said to me. "Get cleaned up, and catch your breath. I'll tell the receptionist the police have been called and where they can find me. Let's talk later, okay. When all this dies down."

"Later," I said.

When I reached my room, I found a pale and shaking Susannah sitting on the edge of the bed, her head in her hands. She or Bernie had wiped most of the gravel off her face and hands, scrubbed her face, and tidied her hair.

I went into the bathroom and washed my own face and hands. The blood from the scratches on my hand had stopped already and the marks on my face were just tiny pinpricks. The knee of my favorite jeans was filthy and in shreds. Very fashionable, I told myself.

When I emerged from the bathroom, carrying my jeans in a crumpled ball, Susannah was on the phone. Her voice, I was pleased to hear, was steady, and she'd stopped shaking. "I changed my mind and decided not to go to the pub after all," she said. "I'm at the hotel. Text me when you get here. Love you."

She put away her phone and gave us a weak attempt at a smile. "I'm fine now. Thank you."

"Why don't you take a moment to wash up?" Bernie said. "And then I'll take you to your room, if you want."

Susannah stood up. "My husband'll be here in about half an hour. What I need now is a good stiff drink. It's not true, what they say. Your life doesn't flash before you." Her laugh was strained. "I don't recall thinking of anything at all. It happened so fast."

She went into the bathroom, and I searched for another pair of pants.

"You think—?" I began.

Bernie nodded toward the closed door. "Let's wait until we're all together. But yes, I think."

When we were once again ready to be seen in public, we headed for the hotel bar. We found Tony sitting with Matt and Simon, and he jumped to his feet when we walked in. He ran to his sister and wrapped his arms around her. "These guys told me what happened. Are you okay, Susie?"

She pulled herself out of the embrace and smiled at him. "I'm fine. Really. Ray'll be here soon."

"As we're missing dinner," Simon said as we pulled chairs up and took seats, "I took the liberty of ordering bar snacks."

"This round's on me," Tony said. "What can I get everyone?"

We gave him our orders and he went to talk to the bartender.

"I spoke to the guys behind the bar at the pub," Matt said. "They said it's been a quiet night, and no one left who appeared to be excessively intoxicated. I couldn't give them a useful description of the car and none at all of the driver, so that didn't help."

Tony and the bartender brought our drinks, and when

they'd been passed around, we raised our glasses and said, "Cheers."

"Beth told me these guys called the cops," Tony said to his sister. "The last thing we need is more police activity around here, but Matt and Simon are suggesting it might not have been a drunk driver losing control."

"What else could it be?" Susannah said with a nervous laugh. "I don't have any enemies. The mob is unlikely to have put a hit out on me."

"Are you sure they were aiming at you?" Bernie said. "Lily was directly in the path, too."

"I don't have enemies, either," I protested.

"Don't you? You've been investigating the two crimes that happened here this weekend. Maybe you're getting too close."

"Investigating?" Tony said. "What does that mean? Are you a cop?"

"She's an amateur sleuth," Bernie said.

Simon groaned.

"I'm nothing of the sort," I said, "I'm a pastry chef on vacation."

A waiter arrived with heaped platters of finger food, side dishes, and napkins, and we obligingly moved our glasses out of the way to make room.

"You have been asking questions," Bernie reminded me.

"So have you," I said.

"Maybe I'm just more subtle than you. No, Lily, this time you've taken the lead. Not me."

"This time?" Tony and Susannah said.

I picked up a crostini and thought. I *had* been asking questions. I'd talked at length to Ian about who had access to the coronation chicken sandwiches. I'd gone to Alicia Boyle's office yesterday. I'd asked Josh Hansen about his relationship with Julien. I'd spied on Carmela waylaying Tony outside the bank. I'd followed Emma to the castle and encouraged her to confide in me about her financial troubles. I'd been with Elizabeth when she discovered the Frockmorton Sapphires were missing, and I'd met with a former jewel fence.

Had I been observed Saturday night listening to Julien and Jacqueline discuss having their grandmother declared incompetent?

I put down the crostini. I'd lost my appetite once again.

"Here she is now," Tony said.

DS Capretti came into the bar. She pulled up a chair and squeezed between Susannah and Bernie.

"Can I get you anything, Detective Sergeant?" Tony asked.

"Orange juice wouldn't come amiss."

Tony didn't bother to go and get it. He called across the room to the bartender.

"Which one of you called me?" Capretti asked.

"I did," Simon said. "I'm Simon McCracken, and Lily gave me your card."

She got straight to the point. "On the phone, you said someone tried to run you down earlier. You have reason to think it wasn't an accident?"

"I do. We do." Simon told her what happened earlier. He emphasized that the car's lights were not on, that the driver appeared to be deliberately heading straight for Susannah and me, and then drove away without stopping to check if anyone had been hurt.

"Surely not," Tony said. "It had to have been a drunk driver, in shock when he realized what he'd done. Almost done. If not that, maybe a kid without a driver's license who stole his dad's car and went on a joy ride."

"Those are possibilities," Matt said. "However, we've talked it over and we have reason to believe it was deliberate."

"And you are?" Capretti asked.

Matt introduced himself as Rose's and my neighbor. He didn't mention he was a true-crime writer or that he was in England researching a book. If he'd done that, Capretti would possibly leap to the conclusion he was making stuff up.

"I can't get over what you're saying. You actually think someone tried to kill my sister?" Tony reached out and put his hand on her shoulder and gave it a squeeze. She reached up and touched his hand briefly and gave him a brave smile.

"Her or Lily," Matt said. "Kill or frighten. He, or she, didn't try to have another go. Just backed up and took off."

Tony stood up. He paced up and down the long narrow room, fists clenched. A couple of men stood at the bar with their beer, too far away to hear what we were talking about, but the people at nearby tables were trying to look as though they were not listening.

"Even if they were only trying to frighten you," Tony said when he came back, "it could easily have gone wrong. A car is not a toy, and even the best driver can make mistakes in the moment and in the dark."

"It's particularly dark at that spot," Matt said. "Immediately before the road takes a bend at the White Hart."

"Sit down, Tony," Susannah said. "I'm perfectly okay, as you can see."

"What if they try again?"

"Do you have reason to think they might?" Capretti asked.

He dropped into his chair. "No. I mean, I don't know who would do such a thing in the first place. Not towards Susannah, at any rate. They had to be after her." Tony pointed at me. "You're here with your grandmother. She and Granny are getting on like a house on fire, but maybe it's time for you to leave."

"You can't chuck us out," Simon said.

"I'm not—"

"Can anyone describe this vehicle?" Capretti asked.

We offered what limited description we could. "Sedan. Small. Dark color."

"Did you see if anyone was with the driver?"

My friends and I looked at each other. We shook our heads in unison.

"It all happened so quickly," Bernie said. "I heard the car coming and saw it take the corner far too fast. I turned around to check on Lily, not paying much attention to the car itself. You should be thanking Simon for saving your sister, Tony, rather than throwing him out. Simon moved fast and knocked Susannah and Lily out of the way."

Tony stood up. He held out his hand. "Yeah, I should do that. Thanks, mate. My sister means the world to me."

Simon got to his feet and shook. "I'm glad I was there."

Susannah looked at her brother, and the smile she gave him was warm and full of affection. "And you mean the world to me, brother dear, but not as much as my husband and children, and I suspect that's Ray buzzing me now to say he's arrived. If you don't need me any more, DS Capretti, I'd like some quiet time with my husband."

"Do you have any reason to believe anyone might have wanted to either kill or frighten you, Mrs. Reilly?" the detective said.

"Absolutely not. I'm a secretary in a law office, not an undercover agent with MI5. Like everyone else around here, I've been wracking my brains trying to remember if I saw anything that might indicate what happened to Julien or to the sapphires, and I come up completely blank."

"Good night, then," Capretti said. "As for you, Ms. Roberts, I'm reminded that the police in your town say you sometimes get involved in things that don't concern you."

"I'll admit we meaning Bernie and my grandmother and I, have been interested in what happened here. We've spoken to a few people. None of that has led to me having a clue. Both the death of Julien and the theft or disappearance of the sapphires are as much mysteries to me as they are to you."

"Assuming it remains a mystery to you, Detective," Matt said.

Capretti sipped her orange juice. "Interested in mysteries, are you Mr. Goodwill? Or should I say Mr. Lincoln Badwell?"

"I see my fame has preceded me."

"It has. As has the fact that you've been talking extensively to Dennis Pembroke, retired DI, and not only him but some of the old time lads who gather over more than a few pints to fondly remember their light-fingered days."

"A matter of public record, which has nothing to do with what happened here earlier."

"What are they talking about?" Tony asked Bernie.

"Perhaps. Perhaps not." Capretti put down her empty glass. "I wouldn't normally let myself be called out at suppertime for a motor vehicle incident which resulted in no casualties and no damage, but I find this of considerable interest in light of what went on here recently and what Ms. Roberts and the rest of you have been doing about it."

"You don't think it was aimed at Susannah?" Tony said with a noticeable sigh of relief.

"That remains a possibility. We still don't know why someone murdered her cousin, do we? Before I leave, I'd like a chat, Ms. Roberts. In private."

"Me?"

"Yes, you. If you know something that might have inspired someone to threaten you, I'd like to hear about it."

"Now?"

"Either now, in this hotel, or now down at the station."

I stood up. "Okay."

Simon also got to his feet. "I'll come."

"That's not necessary," Capretti said. "We're just having a little chat. If I have reason to ask Ms. Roberts to leave the hotel, I'll let you know."

He threw a questioning look at me. "It's okay," I said, and he slowly sat back down, not looking entirely convinced.

Before we could move, Carmela and Jacqueline came in.

"Tony, what's happening?" Jacqueline said. "I passed Ray Reilly in the hallway, and he asked me if Susannah is all right. Why would she not be?" She looked at DS Capretti. "Why are you here at this time of night? What's going on?"

"Do you have an update?" Carmela asked. "Have you arrested someone for killing my husband?"

"Routine questions," Capretti said.

"Susannah's fine," Tony said. "I don't want to talk about it. Detective Sergeant, I'll find a place where you can talk in some privacy to Ms. Roberts."

"Why's she interviewing her?" Jacqueline asked. "Again."

"Don't rush off, Tony," Carmela said. "Stay and have another drink. For old times' sake?"

"No," he said.

Chapter 21

Rather than find a private room in which DS Capretti and I could chat, Tony pretty much bolted down the hall the moment we were out of the bar.

Capretti watched him go. "Families are interesting, don't you find, Ms. Roberts? Childhood resentments, emotions, jealousies, greed, even lust, all swirling around. Always fascinating."

"What are you saying?" I asked.

"Just commenting. As our host seems to have abandoned us . . . When I came in, I noticed one of the small dining rooms was empty. Let's take a seat."

I followed her. The tables were set for breakfast, the fire allowed to die. We sat down. The detective studied my face. "If you know anything about who might have been driving that car, please tell me. Now."

"I do not."

"Okay. I'm not entirely sure it wasn't a matter of being in the right place at a bad time, but if you and your friends are right, someone might be out to get you. To kill, injure, or frighten you."

"That is a scary thought," I said. "I truly do not know.

I'll freely admit I've been thinking about the death of Julien and the disappearance of the jewelry. I've been talking it over with my friends. But I'd venture to say everyone in this hotel has been doing the same. Including those who weren't even here at the time. And yes, we went to York to talk to a retired cop and a former gem thief, but that led nowhere."

She grinned at me. I relaxed slightly. When she asked to speak to me, and me alone, I'd had a temporary fright, fearing she was about to arrest me. But then I realized I didn't sense any animosity coming from her. If anything, she was relaxed and smiling. Almost friendly. Good cop, bad cop all in one short package? Perhaps, but I didn't think so.

She believed us about the car incident, and that must mean she believed I wasn't a killer or a thief. A falling out among thieves might be possible but, aside from my grandmother, I'd been with all of my friends when the car left the road heading straight for Susannah and me. I knew no one in England I could be in cahoots with and have subsequently fallen out with.

"Is it possible, if the attempt was deliberate, they were aiming at Susannah Reilly, not you?" Capretti asked.

"Yes, it is. We were walking together. Going slowly, talking casually, not in any particular hurry. The others were faster and were pulling ahead of us. I was on the outside, nearest the road. Simon knocked me out of the way, I fell into Susannah, and we both hit the ground. Sort of like bowling pins. Do you have bowling in England?"

"We do. My grandmother is the current champion of her lawn bowling club."

"I was on the outside, but if the driver didn't much care about harming me, he could have run right over me and into her."

"You say 'he.' Do you have reason to think it was a man?"

"No. Just a figure of speech. I saw nothing at all of the driver."

"Tony Waterfield and his sister seem to be very close."

I blinked at the change of direction. "I think they are. Not excessively so, if that's what you're implying."

"I am not. After some of the things I see that families do to each other, I like to see siblings getting on. That's all."

I didn't think that was all, but I didn't get the point.

"You told me you overheard Julien Crawford telling his sister he wanted to take control of the hotel from his grandmother."

"I did. I also told you Jacqueline said it wouldn't work and they'd have to wait. What brought this to mind?"

"I've been wondering if someone else heard that conversation. Likely wouldn't matter. From what I've heard about the late Viscount Darnby, he didn't have a subtle bone in his body. Everyone would have known what he was up to. No doubt including his grandmother."

"You're not thinking Elizabeth—"

"I am not. Even if she wanted to, as has been pointed out, Elizabeth can't get around without being noticed. She did not go into the kitchen at any time, and some combination of her daughter, daughter-in-law, granddaughters, or party guests were with her in the hours before she joined the rest of the family and guests in the garden for her birthday tea. Over the time you were making the sandwiches.

"Things were beginning to come clear to me, but now I need a rethink. If the attack—if it was an attack—was aimed at Susannah, that gives me an entirely new direction to consider."

And with that cryptic comment, DS Capretti bid me a good night.

Chapter 22

I tossed and turned most of the night. My wrist was bothering me where I'd landed on it, and I had a throbbing pain in my knee that hurt when I lay on it, but that wasn't what was keeping me awake.

Did someone try to kill me? Am I getting so close to solving the crime or crimes, I have to be eliminated? Does someone think, incorrectly, I'm close to discovering the truth?

Susannah seemed to genuinely not know why anyone would try to kill or scare her. I didn't know why anyone would try to kill or scare me. I didn't know anyone in England, other than the people in this hotel.

It was possible, I suppose, the car had been driven by a drunk driver or a kid on a joyride, who lost control and took off in fright at the realization of what almost happened. But if not? Would they try again?

Had someone been following us? Or had they happened to see us out walking and decided to head straight for us on the spur of the moment?

Perhaps it was deliberate, but not aimed specifically at Susannah or at me. Someone looking for trouble who decided it would be great fun to give a couple of women a fright.

While Simon was in the shower, I'd taken out my phone and studied a map of the roads in the area. We'd been about a half a mile from the hotel, coming in sight of the pub on the corner. In the other direction, a mile past the driveway leading to Thornecroft Castle House and Hotel, an intersection met a road that circled around and joined the one running along the front of the White Hart. Traffic had been light as we walked, but the street was not empty, and I'd paid no attention to passing vehicles. It would have been possible for someone to see us as they drove toward the hotel, to decide to do—something—take the next intersection, and make a circle to come toward us again.

I thought about what Capretti asked me in the dining room earlier. Had Susannah, not me, been the target? That was as possible as anything else. Did Susannah know something about Julien's death she didn't know she knew? Might she have seen something, heard something, which pointed to the killer? If so, the attempt on her life was pretty feeble. Surely the killer would have been able to come up with something more guaranteed to succeed. If anything, the incident served nothing but to focus her mind on possible reasons for it, as it had done mine.

As for me, did this person want to scare us into leaving Thornecroft earlier than we'd planned? Seemed rather a lot of trouble to go to, considering we were due to check out the day after tomorrow. If I'd been injured in the incident, our departure would have been delayed.

Tony had pretty much ordered us to get out of his hotel, but he retracted that when reminded Simon had saved Susannah.

I went over what I knew. I had to know something. I had to have come across something someone didn't want me to figure out.

The death of Julien. The disappearance of the Frock-morton Sapphires. How were those two things related, if at all? It's possible someone killed Julien to cause chaos in order to give them time to get away with the gems, but murder did seem a mite far-fetched.

As Simon pointed out, I didn't know much about these people and their lives. All I could do was to go over, once again, what I did know.

If I considered nonfamily members, the only people I was aware the police suspected were Ian Carver, Josh Hansen, and Dr. Alicia Boyle. And the only reason I knew that was the police had told me. Ian, I dismissed, and I remained confident in doing so. No chef would poison his own food and hope to get away with it. As for Alicia, if some political shenanigans had been going on there, the police likely knew about it. Josh had freely admitted to a couple of run-ins with Julien, but if so, then it was possible, likely even, other people had also. I believed Josh when he said if he'd killed Julien, he would have been a lot more upfront about it.

As for the family, Julien and his sister Jacqueline wanted to take control of the hotel and the related businesses from their grandmother, Elizabeth. Julien was in a hurry; he wanted to do it immediately. His sister said they needed to wait.

What did take control even mean? Elizabeth was the primary owner of the businesses, but she was no longer managing things. She didn't make the decisions.

Not the day-to-day decisions, no. Tony managed the hotel, and I presumed Elizabeth had people who took care of the other interests. But if someone, such as Julien and Jacqueline, wanted to do something major, such as sell the hotel out from under her, Elizabeth could and would intervene.

I'd been told more than once the family was not wealthy. What they owned was wrapped up in Thornecroft Castle House, the neighboring farms, and some rental properties. To realize the value of those things, they would have to be sold.

The gems *were* about to be sold, which would bring a substantial amount of cash to the family and their businesses. Was it possible the Frockmorton Sapphires were fakes? Had the real ones been sold years ago and imitations substituted so Elizabeth wouldn't know? They'd been in a bank vault for decades. Who had access to the vault other than Elizabeth? I had no way of knowing or of finding out.

As for the inheritance, if someone, Jacqueline or Emma, for instance, even Tony or Susannah, wanted to get their hands on the inheritance, Julien was the wrong person to kill. His father and his grandmother were still alive. Killing Julien wouldn't benefit anyone financially. Except, I suppose, Carmela, who would not have to go to the bother of a nasty, drawn-out divorce. Regarding the claim to the title of Earl of Frockmorton, Emma seemed to be delighted that the death of Julien left Robert without a son, so upon Robert's death her father, Thomas, would become the new earl. But it was less than guaranteed Robert would predecease his younger brother.

Was Robert in danger? I hadn't had great deal of contact with the current Earl of Frockmorton, but I hadn't seen any signs of security around him.

So much I didn't know. My mind wandered. I chuckled to myself when I remembered the look on Carmela's face when Tony refused her offer of another drink and abruptly walked out of the bar. Carmela was trying far, far too hard. "For old times' sake," she'd said.

Yes, they'd had an affair at one time. Easy to assume Tony broke it off, and Carmela was not happy about that.

Still, as we all know, this is the twenty-first century. Neither Tony nor Carmela would have been disinherited and thrown out into the dark and stormy night penniless, to make their own way in the world, if news of their relationship came to light.

Not that, as far as Tony was concerned, there was a relationship. Not anymore.

What might Carmela do to woo him back? Kill her husband?

Possible. If she thought Tony left her because he didn't want to be involved in her divorce proceedings.

Rose had speculated that Tony and Carmela might be acting. Pretending to be no longer together this weekend in front of the family. But the look on Carmela's face when Tony walked out on her told me that was no act.

What might Carmela do to get Tony back? Threaten his sister?

I couldn't see that working to her advantage at all.

As soon as I thought the time was reasonably decent, I texted Bernie: **Feel like a walk before breakfast?**

The reply was immediate. **No.**

At least she was up. I was still in bed, trying to type silently without turning on the light and disturbing Simon.

Me: Gotta talk about what happened yesterday. Can't stop thinking about it.

Bernie: Fifteen minutes. Front door.

Lights were still on in the sitting room and behind the desk when I walked into the lobby, but the hotel was beginning to come to life. A vacuum cleaner roared in the hallway; cutlery tinkled in the dining rooms. The receptionist looked up from her computer and gave me a bright smile. "Good morning, Ms. Roberts. I'm sorry to say the weather appears to be turning. Rain expected later today, and temperatures will be dropping rapidly."

"Not a problem. We didn't come to Yorkshire in October for the beach and the sun."

She laughed. "True, that."

A yawning Bernie came down the hall, zipping up her padded vest. "This is supposed to be a vacation. Why am I getting up at the crack of dawn on vacation?"

"You were awake when I texted you."

"Awake, but not up. Those are different things." We edged away from the reception desk. "Okay," she said, "I have to confess I spent some considerable time thinking about what's been going on when I could have been sleeping. I've come to no conclusions. Have you?"

"No."

"Did you learn anything from Capretti after you left the bar last night?" Bernie asked.

"Nothing concrete, but she said one or two things I've been mulling over."

"Did you tell Rose what happened last night?"

"I didn't. No point in worrying her."

"It wouldn't worry her, if we could tell her it was a near miss and an accident and wouldn't happen again. Obviously, you and I are thinking such might not be the case."

Deep in my pocket my phone buzzed with the distinctive sound that told me my grandmother was texting. "Do you think she's psychic?" I said to Bernie.

"Wouldn't surprise me in the least."

Rose: My spies tell me you and Bernie are up and going out. Come to my room.

I looked at the young woman behind the reception desk. Beth gave me a guilty wince and turned away.

Spies, indeed.

Bernie and I went to Rose's room, where we found Lissie sitting patiently outside the door. I knocked and a few seconds later we, including the cat, were admitted. "I'm pleased to see you're locking your door," I said.

"Skullduggery is afoot." My grandmother was in her nightgown, her hair standing on end, her face clear of makeup.

"What do you know about that?" Bernie asked.

"I know it's easy to be a gossip and a snoop these days without leaving the comfort of one's bed." Rose nodded to the book on her side table. An earlier one of Matt's. "I came across a confusing passage in this book last night, and so I texted the author himself for clarification. He might have mentioned you returned to the hotel without dinner because everyone had lost their appetite. Naturally, that is such a rare and unusual occurrence, I asked what happened to cause it. And he told me. A near miss with an out-of-control automobile."

"I should have known," Bernie said. "After you left with DS Capretti, Lily, Matt got a text, and he came over all shifty when he was replying."

"I let you enjoy a good night's sleep, hoping your subconscious would arrive at some conclusions," Rose said. "Tea? Coffee? I have only been provided with two cups, but I can call for another."

"I'll wait until breakfast," Bernie said. "I had some of that instant coffee the other day and it was beyond awful."

"Tea for me, thanks," I said.

Bernie sat in the chair by the desk, and I plopped myself down on the bed while Rose fussed with the tea things.

"I'll have one of those shortbread cookies with the walnuts," Bernie said. "Almost as good as Lily makes."

"It's the pure Yorkshire butter," Rose said. "Beyond compare."

"Does sheep's milk make butter?"

"They do farm other animals, love." Rose poured boiling water into the small tea pot provided.

"I haven't seen any," Bernie replied. "We did see two horses, though."

Tea made, Rose poured. She added a splash of milk and a half teaspoon of sugar to two cups, handed me mine, tossed a packet of cookies to Bernie, and settled herself in the wingback chair under the window. Lissie made herself comfortable on the windowsill behind Rose's chair. The sun was coming up and the first rays warming the room. "Now, tell me what happened. Leave nothing out."

We did so. In the fresh light of a new morning the incident didn't seem so bad. No one was hurt, except for a couple of bumps and bruises sustained when I hit the ground. It's possible even if Simon hadn't shoved us out of the way, the car wouldn't have hit us. It wasn't going all that fast; it climbed the curb, but stopped short of where we'd been standing.

"A failed attempt at killing or injuring someone is still an offense," Rose said, "regardless of intent. The incident would likely not be worth concerning ourselves about except for what happened here earlier. I believe such is DS Capretti's thinking as well, as she came out personally to discuss the matter with you. What are you thinking, love?"

"First, let's go over what we know and what we don't know, and what we can guess," I said. "The motive for the theft of the sapphires is probably obvious—someone stole them intending to sell them. As for Julien, money, hopes of an inheritance, family rivalries, the settling of old scores. Might be lots of reasons. Might be none, but I can think of absolutely no reason someone would try to kill Susannah and/or me. Susannah might know something she's not telling, but I don't get that feeling from her. All she wanted to do last night was to be with her husband, not out hunting for whoever she believed tried to kill her. As for me, yes, I've been poking my nose where some might say it doesn't belong, but what of it? I've learned nothing, and we're due to go home tomorrow."

"The two incidents don't have to be directly related," Bernie said.

"Three incidents," I reminded her. "Do you think what happened last night was nothing but a bad driver?"

"I simply don't know."

"If Susannah wasn't being warned off investigating, because she isn't," Rose said, "and Lily wasn't being warned off, because she doesn't know anything, we have to ask—" She paused dramatically.

"Enough of the drama, Rose," I said. "Spit it out. We have to ask what?"

"Was a message being sent to someone else?"

"You think the driver of the car mistook us for someone else?"

"Not necessarily. Go back to your conversation with Capretti last night as you told it to us. She specifically mentioned Tony and Susannah are close, right?"

"Yes. She said it was nice to see siblings getting on. I guess in her line of work that's not the norm. So?"

"Tony was angry, naturally, at what happened to Susannah."

"I was angry at what almost happened to Lily," Bernie said. "But if someone was trying to send us a message, we didn't get it."

"Not a message," Rose said slowly, "but an attempt at getting attention. Carmela."

Bernie leapt to her feet and punched the air. "Yup, I can see it."

"Well, I don't," I said. "Carmela wasn't even there when we came in. Everyone, particularly Tony, fussed over Susannah and me, asking if we were okay. No one paid any attention to Carmela when she did show up."

Bernie paced up and down the small room. Lissie, Rose, and I watched her. "If Rose and I are thinking along the same lines, and we usually are—"

"Don't I know it," I mumbled.

"—We're wondering if Carmela would have the nerve to try to kill Susannah, hoping that in his grief Tony would reach out to her, Carmela, for comfort. She might think he'd do that."

"I'm pretty sure they were an item at one time," I said. "Could she really be that desperate?"

"Who knows? She might not have even known what she was thinking. Maybe it was a spur of the moment thing. She saw Susannah and took her chance. That you were in the way was irrelevant."

I thought about it for a long time. "She is, I believe, that desperate. There's something about unrequited love that turns some people absolutely crazy. But it's still a heck of a stretch, and I have my doubts."

"What do you propose we do about it?" Rose asked.

"Nothing we can do," I said. "All we have is a guess, and I'm not satisfied you've made the correct one. Even if we were sure about it, not only is there no evidence, no real harm was done."

"We can subtly and discreetly ask Carmela if she took a car out last night around the time in question," Bernie said.

"She's not going to tell us if she did," I said. "No matter how subtly and discreetly we ask."

"If Carmela did try to kill, harm, or frighten Susannah, for nebulous reasons," Bernie said, "isn't it possible she's also the sort to rid herself of a no-longer-necessary husband?"

"I'm still unsure about that," I said.

"It wouldn't hurt to have a friendly chat with her," Rose said. "You can subtly and discretely let her know you know and warn her off trying something like that again."

"I can do that," Bernie said.

"No, you cannot. You are never subtle, Bernadette. Lily will have to do it."

"What? How am I going to do that?"

"Make friends with her. Chat comfortably and easily. Complain you suspect Simon is about to dump you and wait for her response."

"I am not going to knock on the door to her room and say, 'Hi, let's be best friends and confidantes.' Also, let me remind you, I'm the one finding it hard to believe she's the one who drove at us."

"All the more reason for you to chat with her. You are not convinced of her guilt. As for knocking on her door, that won't be necessary. I've seen her heading into break-fast at precisely half nine, otherwise known as nine-thirty, every morning. It's eight now. You have an hour and a half to plan your approach." Rose stood up. "Bernadette and I will go to breakfast now."

"Why?"

"So we are not there at half nine , when you arrive. You can't sit all by yourself, now can you?"

"What about Simon and Matt?"

"A complication I failed to consider."

"Matt's up," Bernie told us. "He wanted to get some re-search in before we go to Haworth later, so he ordered room service. I can have room service sent to Simon. Sort of a treat, like." She reached for the phone. "Which means you're banned from your room in the interval, Lily. Other-wise, he'll question you as to what's going on, and you'll spill the tea."

"Will that be so bad?"

"You don't want him sitting on the other side of the breakfast room, trying not to look as though he's ready to pounce in case Carmela makes a threatening move toward you. Yes, I'd like breakfast delivered, please. Room seven."

I grumbled. It didn't matter. It never mattered what I

thought. Once Bernie and Rose had an idea in their heads, nothing I could say or do would convince them to change their minds.

I looked at them. At those familiar determined faces. Maybe that stubbornness is what I love about them so much.

Bernie and Rose headed for the dining room. Lissie jumped out of an open window in the hallway to check on what else was happening this morning, and I also went outside, but via the door. We were planning to go to the village of Haworth today, where the Brontë sisters had lived. Bernie was hoping the steep streets and windswept moors on which Charlotte, Emily, and Anne had wandered would inspire her own writing. I hoped it wouldn't cause her to completely change the direction of her book.

Clouds the color of the fresh bruise around my knee were forming in the west. The wind was strong, and the scent of rain hung heavily in the cool air.

I went back inside. "I know it's early," I said to the receptionist, "but I'd like to talk to Lady Frockmorton, Elizabeth. Is she likely to be up, do you know?"

"She should be. She usually goes over notes about hotel activity and issues from the day before with her tea at seven, and breakfast is delivered to her rooms around now. I can call and ask if she's available."

"Thank you," I said. "It's not urgent. I have a question for her, that's all."

She placed the call. Someone answered almost immediately. "Lily Roberts would like to have a few minutes for a chat, Elizabeth. Are you free? I'll tell her. Thank you." She put the phone down. "Go ahead. She's up and dressed."

I made my way to Elizabeth's rooms. I knocked lightly on the door and her voice called, "Come in."

Elizabeth, Dowager Countess of Frockmorton, was seated

at her desk. The computer screen showed a spreadsheet full of rows upon rows of numbers. A fine china teacup rested next to her computer. She wore a heavy wool sweater over pressed slacks, with modern sneakers of the sort that don't need laces on her feet. "Lily. Good morning. I hope everything is all right. Your grandmother?"

"She's well. She and my friend Bernie are having breakfast, but I decided to—uh, go for a walk first. Get it in while I can. They say it's going to rain later."

"In Yorkshire, one can always say it's going to rain later and have a good chance of being correct. What can I do for you, dear? Please, take a seat. Tea?"

I perched on the edge of a chair. "No tea. Thank you. I understand this is none of my business, and please tell me if you think I'm intruding, but I have been wondering about the sudden death of your grandson."

"You mean the murder of Julien. I'm sure you have. We all have, my dear. Detective Sergeant Capretti paid me a call yesterday evening. She had little new to tell me, but she did inform me that you and Susannah experienced an unfortunate incident earlier." Her blue eyes were encased in folds of skin, but the look she gave me was still sharp. "She assured me you were both unharmed."

I spread my arms out. "As you can see. A couple of bruises, but nothing more serious than that."

"And thus, you've been wondering if the incident is related to Julien's death. The thought occurred to me as well, and obviously it did to DS Capretti, but I fail to see how. If she came to any conclusions, she neglected to inform me."

"I know the police have been interested in Alicia Boyle. Dr. Boyle."

"Yes, yes. Total nonsense, as I told them. Alicia is a physician, sworn to do no harm. She has an excellent reputation as a doctor, as did her father and grandfather before her. She also has a reputation for being politically active regarding the things she believes in, and good for her. She's fundamentally opposed to the aristocracy, and I will confess that if I were not the Dowager Countess of Frockmorton, I would likely be opposed also. Such a relic of less favorable times. My late husband took his responsibilities to the community, to the people who work and live here, seriously, regardless that those responsibilities were inherited. I considered the same to be my duty after his premature death, and in that, I believe I succeeded."

"What about Robert, the current earl?"

"Robert has, I fear, little interest and even less enthusiasm about managing an historic house and a modern property company. He will do what he can. That pesky duty, Alicia and her friends are so dismissive of. Robert might not be wanting to do much of the hands-on—he has dreams of spending a good deal of his retirement years in Spain—but he's fully capable of managing people from a distance. I see no harm in telling you this, Lily. I've left the estate in its entirety, except for some provisions for long-serving staff and my great-grandchildren's education, to Robert. I see no value in breaking things up. Neither financially nor on a personal level. I've seen friends and neighbors do what they thought was best, and all it resulted in was arguments and animosity. In one case I know of, years of legal battles."

"That includes the house? It will continue to be a hotel?"

"The crown jewel, so to speak, of the Crawford family. Tony is aware of my intentions, and he's fully committed to continuing to manage the hotel under his uncle's ownership." She lifted her cup and took a sip. The china was plain white, one of the regular hotel dishes. "I'm planning on suggesting your grandmother and I go into Halifax for lunch today. She's scarcely been off the grounds since she arrived, and I believe you're going home tomorrow. Would you care to join us, dear?"

"Thank you, but my friends and I have plans." I can tell when I've been dismissed, and I'd started to stand when there was a light tap on the door.

"Come in," Elizabeth called.

Jacqueline did so. "Morning, Granny. Lily, good morning. I hope I'm not interrupting anything?"

"Lily was leaving. A day of exploring with her friends." Elizabeth let out a long sigh, the sound full of happy memories. "Ah to be young again, off exploring in the company of good friends. I believe, Lily, that's why your grandmother and I reconnected so comfortably. Neither of us have many friends left."

"I know she's very happy it happened."

"I want to take the girls to the doctor," Jacqueline said. "Is there someone near here who can see them, or should we go home?"

A look of alarm wiped the fond memories off Elizabeth's face. "Are they ill?"

"I don't know, Granny. They don't seem to be sick, but they're acting strangely. Both of them. Lifeless, not interested in anything. Not eating well, which is so unlike them, it's my biggest concern." She let out a strangled laugh.

"I'll call Dr. Boyle in Halifax, but I'm sure it's nothing. Everyone's here's been on edge since Sunday, it's bound to have a negative effect on children. They sense the tension, even if they don't understand the cause. Talk of death and funerals, people eying each other suspiciously. Not to mention police popping in and out, and questioning everyone."

"You're likely right," Jacqueline said, "but I'd like to be sure and have them checked out. They were so interested when a police officer came to the school for career day about a month ago, they talked about nothing else for days, and did nothing but attempt to arrest each other. This week, the sight of a uniform has them running to their rooms."

"It's unfortunate reality hit them at their age. I hope they didn't overhear talk of poison killing Julien. That might put them off their food."

"We've tried to keep the details from them," Jacqueline said, "but it's hard when everyone in the family is talking of nothing else."

Elizabeth swung her chair around and reached for the phone. "I'll call Dr. Boyle's surgery now. They might not be in yet, but I'll leave a message."

"Thanks, Granny. Any word yet as to when we can make arrangements for Julien?"

I slipped away. It was still only eight thirty. An hour to go until I was expected to make friends with Carmela. I couldn't go back to my room, under fear of interrogation by Simon, so I might as well have that walk before the rain hit.

Chapter 23

The lobby was busy with people heading for breakfast or checking out. I cut across the parking lot and headed for the footpath leading to the castle ruins. On the other side of the drystone wall, the sheep were eyeing the dark clouds with suspicion. I wondered if sheep minded the rain. Surely it must get heavy, carrying all that wool around if it was soaking wet.

As I walked, I thought about things other than sheep. The more I considered it, the less confident I was that Carmela had tried to run over Susannah and me last night. At least for the reason we believed. Surely, she wasn't that much of a fool to think Tony would seek comfort in her arms in his grief? Wouldn't he be more likely to lash out at her for pestering him? Yet last night, DS Capretti had specifically mentioned how close Tony and his sister were. Did that mean she was also thinking along those lines? If Carmela had a record for stalking, the police would know about it. If the case or cases had never come to court, Bernie wouldn't have come across them when she searched for information on the family. From what the detective told me, it sounded as though she'd been considering the motive had something to do with Julien and Jacqueline plotting to take control of the hotel and the businesses, but in light of the new development she was having, in her words, a rethink.

I had to believe that meant she believed the car incident was deliberate, and it was deliberately aimed at Susannah.

Could it have been a setup? The incident arranged by Susannah herself to throw police suspicion for the murder off her? I couldn't see any reason for Susannah to have killed Julien. Didn't, of course, mean she didn't have a reason. Yet, as far as I knew, Susannah had no interest in the hotel or the family businesses. She and her husband lived in London. She traveled to Yorkshire a couple of times a year to visit her grandmother, but no more than that. I suppose she or her husband could work behind the scenes, but that would hardly be a secret, and thus no reason for her to pretend to me or anyone else she was not actively involved. She hadn't been issuing orders or directing staff at the party. As for the inheritance, Elizabeth told me she was leaving everything to Robert, the eldest son. That wasn't common knowledge among the family, but surely, regarding the eventual inheritance, as the second child of the third living child of Elizabeth, Susannah was far down the scale in the traditional order of inheritance. Even her brother, Tony, was only the hotel manager; he was not a co-owner and would not be after Elizabeth's eventual death. Not if Robert inherited.

Tony and Susannah were close. That was obvious. Even I'd noticed it. Capretti had commented that it was nice to see adult siblings who cared for each other.

Last night's incident had focused police attention in a new direction.

If Tony is in possible danger . . .

I'd reached the clearing overlooking the castle ruins. The parking lot by the visitor center was empty, the gate across what had once been the moat closed and locked. Clouds were moving fast in my direction, and the first raindrops began to fall.

If Tony was in possible danger, what might someone who loved him do about it?

I stood on the hill for a long time, enjoying the scenery and thinking, as the wind whipped my hair and the sheep called to each other.

I turned and hurried back to Thornecroft Castle House. As I walked, I checked my phone. Quarter after nine. Almost time for me to "accidentally" run into Carmela over breakfast. I wouldn't beat about the bush, I wouldn't lie to Carmela about my relationship with Simon, hoping for her to confess all in sympathy. I'd come right out and tell her I knew she'd driven at Susannah last night, but I also knew she had no intention of harming Tony's sister. I'd tell her I knew why she'd done that, and I'd ask her what else she knew.

And I'd then go to the police.

The front door of the hotel opened as I reached for it, and Tony came out, dressed in a rain jacket and wool scarf. "Good morning, Lily. Looks as though we're in for some weather." He brushed past me.

"Tony," I said.

He stopped and turned to look at me, the polite hotelier's smile in place on his face. "Yes? Can I do anything for you?"

"I wanted to tell you how much we're loving this hotel. The building and the grounds themselves are marvelous, of course, but you've done so much with it. The service is impeccable, the staff genuinely friendly. I can tell everyone likes working here."

The smile he gave me in return was genuine. "I'm happy to hear that. I—I mean, we try hard."

"What will happen when Elizabeth dies? Will you be able to keep the hotel going?"

His eyes narrowed. "That's a rather insensitive comment. I'm not expecting my grandmother to pass away any time soon."

"No, but the thought must have crossed your mind. Particularly now Julien's not in the picture."

"Let's take a walk, Lily."

"I haven't had breakfast yet. Maybe later."

He took my arm. His grip was not light and friendly. "I said, let's walk. Have you visited the original Thornecroft Castle yet? Yes, you have. I've seen you and the redhead heading that way a few times."

"You've been watching us?"

"I watch everyone, Lily. Like the good host I am. You followed Emma there one day and then had a chat with Josh at the stables. You do get around, don't you?"

He started walking, almost dragging me behind him. All the people who'd been around earlier had disappeared. No cars drove into the parking lot, and no guests came out of the hotel unfurling umbrellas and heading out for the day. I could have resisted. I could have called for help. I could have made a fuss, and he would have had to let me go. Instead, I let him lead me toward the footpath.

The sheep watched us pass. They didn't intervene, either.

The rain began to fall harder. It was a cold rain, and as we emerged from the shelter of the trees onto the rise overlooking the ruins of the castle, the wind threw wet drops into my face. One car was in the parking lot, and the gate was unlocked, but no one was in sight.

"You think I questioned Emma," I said, "but all she told me is how much she loves her family heritage and how proud she is of her lineage. She's hoping her father

becomes the earl someday so she can tell everyone to call
her Lady Emma."

"Emma's a gullible, scatterbrained fool. Always has been.
She might have dreams of eventually being 'Her Ladyship,' but I can assure you no one in the family, Granny
most of all, would trust her with a penny."

"I don't get that feeling of pride in the family history
from you, Tony."

He pointed to the castle. "Bunch of old stones to me.
Old stones and old stories. The house, the hotel, as it is
now, is what I care about."

"Julien threatened that, didn't he?"

"Have you seen the castle up close? Some people find
that stuff interesting." He pulled me along after him. We
crossed the moat and stepped between the low stones mark-
ing what long ago had been the castle walls. The ruins
loomed in front of us, foreboding against the dark, tumul-
tuous sky. The crumbling old stone, the steep outside staircase, the ramp leading sharply down to the rooms beneath
the ancient structure.

I dug in my heels and tried to pull my arm free. "I'm not
going any further, Tony."

"You don't want to see inside the castle?"

"I've already seen it, thanks. I have one thing to tell you,
though, before I go. It was Carmela who drove at Susannah and me last night."

The look on his face was one of genuine surprise.
"What? Why would she do something like that? Are you
sure?"

"I don't have proof, and I didn't see the driver or details
of the car. But I've worked it out, and I suspect DS Capretti is thinking along the same lines as me."

"Was it deliberate?"

"It was deliberate, yes. I don't think she intended to
hurt us, but a car is a deadly weapon, and things can eas-

ily get out of control. If Simon hadn't seen what was happening and knocked us out of the way, Carmela might have done far more damage than she planned."

He shook his head. His grip relaxed, and I gently took back my arm. "I can see you believe me, Tony."

"I do. I mean, I wouldn't put it past her. Carmela has a screw loose, in my opinion."

"You and she had an affair. You broke it off. She didn't like that."

"How do you know?"

"I only know what I've observed." I looked into his eyes and touched his arm. "Let's head back. I'm getting wet."

He didn't move. "I've been wondering if Carmela killed Julien, although I can't see why she'd do it. They were getting divorced, but it wasn't a particularly hostile breakup."

"You didn't consider she might have killed him as a way of getting back with you?"

"No reason for her to think that. Julien knew about our affair when it was happening." He turned and retraced his steps. I walked alongside him. Neither of us was in a hurry. "The marriage was already on the skids, so he didn't much care what she got up to. I told the cops I had my suspicions about her but no proof. If she attacked Susannah that's proof enough. For me, anyway. She's obviously in a great deal of mental distress. I hope she gets the help she needs."

"Except she didn't kill, Julien, did she, Tony?"

He stopped walking and faced me. "What are you saying?"

"You killed Julien. You, alone of all the grandchildren, know Elizabeth intends to leave the hotel to Robert. She expects Robert will keep you on to manage the place, but Robert isn't interested in the business. He wants to retire to Spain. He would have left the big decisions, such as who to hire and who to fire, in Julien's hands. Julien would not have let you stay on. Even if he didn't outright fire you, you wouldn't have been able to work under him, would you, Tony?"

"You have an active imagination."

"Yes, I do. Helps me sometimes see things others don't."

He set off again, pulling the hood of his raincoat up, so I couldn't see his expression. Water streamed down my face. The path was getting muddy, and all I had on were my sneakers. "I suspect, and it is only a guess, that once Julien took control, and he fired the current manager—i.e., you—he'd find a way of operating the hotel at a loss and try to convince his father to sell it. To sell Thornecroft Castle House. You told me you don't care about the earldom and the family history. But you care about Thornecroft Castle House, don't you Tony?"

"Care about the old house? No, not really. I care about the hotel. I've worked hard to make this place one of the premier luxury hotels in West Yorkshire. I did it, not because of the legacy of my sainted ancestors, but because I'm a good hotelier, and I take pride in my work. I have plans, big plans, for expansion and improvement."

"Is that why you stole the sapphires? To get the money for those improvements?"

He turned to me again, this time his face a picture of total surprise. "Looks like you don't know everything, Lily. I didn't take the gems. I have no more idea of what happened to them than anyone else. Would have been a mighty stupid thing to do, in any event. I'd eventually realize a fraction of what they're worth. Granny was planning to sell them and put the money into the hotel and the other properties. Another reason why Julien couldn't be allowed to get his hands on the hotel. Intentionally or not, he'd mismanage it."

I said nothing. The end of the footpath came in sight.

Much of what I'd told Tony was sheer guesswork on my part. People said Tony had always been his grandmother's favorite, and Julien resented that. Childhood resentments can have a way of lingering well into adulthood, and I'd wondered if Julien would want to get the better of his rival by taking away the thing Tony valued most, the hotel. Tony was, as he said, a good hotel manager. If he left Thorne-croft Castle House and Hotel, he should be able to get a job just about anywhere. But, despite his protestations about not caring about the family legacy, I suspected he cared more than he let on. It was, after all, his heritage, as well.

To lose the job, and eventually the house itself, to a sneering older cousin, would have been a blow indeed.

Two police cars pulled up to the hotel entrance. DS Capretti was driving with DI Ravenwood in the passenger seat. Two uniformed officers were in the other car.

"I suspect they're here for you, Tony," I said.

"You called them?"

"No, I didn't. But if I guessed, they could have."

"Let's circle back before we go in. I don't understand what this has to do with Susannah and Carmela."

"Carmela knew the police are focusing their attention on you, Tony. You're the only one of the family they took down to the station for questioning. Likely the direction of some of their questions alerted Carmela to their suspicions. Previously you and she had an affair. If I may say, I suspect you took up with her because you enjoyed getting one over on your much disliked cousin."

"Not entirely, but yeah, that might have been part of it."

The detectives and one uniform had gone into the hotel. The other officer stayed with the cars. He pulled out his phone.

"When you realized not only did Julien know about the

affair, he didn't even care, you broke it off with her. When you were together, you and Carmela probably talked a lot about Julien. She knew you were worried he'd kick you out of the hotel, given half a chance. Friday night, I overheard Julien and Jacqueline talking about having Elizabeth declared unable to manage her affairs. Julien was ready to make his move. If that happened, Robert would have immediately handed control over to Julien. I believe Carmela knew that. It's possible Julien told her what he was thinking. Thus, she knew you had reason to kill Julien."

I'd accused Tony of the murder, but so far he'd neither denied it nor admitted to it, so I kept talking. "Carmela wanted to throw suspicion off you and what better way, in her mind, to do that than make it look as though Susannah knew something about what happened, and Julien's killer had to eliminate her."

"That makes no sense."

"But it does. Everyone knows you and Susannah are close. Even Capretti knows that. She told me it was nice to see. You would never risk harming Susannah. You would never try to run her down, thus you are not the killer."

"I have to say, I admire thinking like that. I never would have guessed Carmela had that degree of loyalty in her."

"You put almond powder in the coronation chicken sandwiches, didn't you, Tony?"

"Yeah, I did. I knew Julien was allergic, and I had the powder on me, hoping for a chance to use it. I came into the kitchen before tea started to check on progress and found no one there. So I took my chance. I had to move fast, and I didn't get the powder on them all. Julien was just unlucky. In all honesty, I regret it. Not because Julien died, I never could stand the smug little twat, but because other people fell under suspicion. Ian, the chef. Dr. Boyle. I felt bad when I heard the police were questioning her."

But not bad enough to come forward.

"Even you. I didn't intend that. Sorry if I spoiled your visit to Yorkshire."

"It has been interesting."

The detectives came out of the hotel. They stood in the entrance, looking across the parking lot.

"You don't know about the sapphires though?"

"Nope. A complete mystery to me." Tony walked toward the waiting police officers.

Chapter 24

News that Tony had once again been taken in for questioning, and this time in handcuffs, spread through the hotel before I so much as stepped inside. A babble of voices greeted me, everyone wanting to know what was going on.

DI Ravenwood accompanied Tony in the patrol car. DS Capretti just about dragged me into a quiet spot beneath the leaded windows. "What happened there, Ms. Roberts?" she demanded, as a circle of curious faces watched. "Tony Waterfield walked up to me calm as could be and told me he wanted to confess to the murder of Julien Crawford. I couldn't help but notice you were with him seconds before that happened."

"He told me he did it," I said. "For what it's worth, he's sorry he caused distress to other people who came under suspicion."

"It's worth absolutely nothing at all. I'm going now so I can take part in his interview with DI Ravenwood. I'll be in touch later. Please don't leave the immediate area. If Tony denies what you're saying, you'll have a lot of explaining to do."

"I'll be here," I said.

"I'll see to it." Simon slipped up to me and put his arm around my shoulders. When Capretti pushed her way through the crowd of onlookers heading for the car, he pulled me close. "Dare I ask what you've been up to?"

"Did you have a nice breakfast? Room service was Bernie's idea."

"That comes as absolutely no surprise to me. To keep me out of the way, I suppose. Let me repeat myself, what have you been up to this time?"

"It's a long story. Let's find the others and talk."

The others found us. By the time Simon and I joined the crowd, Bernie, Matt, and Rose were there.

"I need to talk to Elizabeth," I said in a low voice. "She should hear it from me, I think."

"People are saying Tony killed Julien," Bernie said.

"Looks like it."

"He took the sapphires?"

"He denies that, and I believe him."

"What happened to them then?"

"That's what I'd like to find out. Beth, can you ask Elizabeth if she has time to see me, please? It is important."

The receptionist looked at me and my friends and my grandmother. "All of you?"

"Yes," Rose said. "Please."

Beth made the call, and when she put down the phone she said, "Elizabeth will see you in the drawing room. She's asked me to order tea and biscuits. It might be a few minutes before I can find someone I can send to help her."

"I can do that," Simon said.

She nodded, and he slipped away.

"Can you ask Jacqueline to join us, if she's free?" I asked. Beth made another call.

Matt, Bernie, Rose, and I took seats in the drawing room. Lissie appeared out of nowhere, and as seemed to be becoming her habit regarding Rose, she settled on the couch next to my grandmother. Jacqueline followed the cat. "What's happening? People are saying Tony's been arrested. That can't be right."

"It would seem so," I said. "We're waiting for Elizabeth now."

Jacqueline gave me a curious look before sitting hesitantly down. Simon came in with Elizabeth and her walker. She parked the walker in a corner of the room, and he helped her to a chair. A wide-eyed waitress brought in a tray of tea things and a plate of chocolate biscuits and arranged them on the low table.

"Thank you, Irene. That will be all," Elizabeth said.

When the door had closed behind Irene, she said. "Tony?"

"I won't go into much detail," I said, "before Tony's spoken to the police, but he told me he killed Julien because, if Julien took over the hotel, as he intended, the first thing he'd do would be to fire Tony. And then he'd run the hotel into the ground and convince his father to sell it."

Bernie attempted to look wise and all-knowing.

Jacqueline dropped back in her chair with a moan. "I knew Julien considered it was long past time he took over, to assume his rightful place in the family as he called it. But I didn't realize that was his plan. I thought he only wanted to be in charge."

"But that's not—" Elizabeth began.

"Not *your* intention, I know," I said. "Suffice it to say, it will all come out soon enough. Tony confessed to the killing, but not to the theft of the Frockmorton Sapphires."

"First, Lily," Simon said, "are you telling us you confronted Tony, on your own, and accused him of murder?"

"Yeah, I guess I am."

He swore under his breath. Matt shook his head. Rose looked proud. Bernie grinned. Lissie purred in what I took to be approval.

"I didn't sense any danger from him," I said.

"Famous last words," Matt said. "I've used them more than once in my books. The paragraph before the obituary."

Simon swore again.

"He flatly denied knowing anything about the jewels, but I have some thoughts on that," I said. "For reasons we can go into later, Matt has some contacts in the Yorkshire underworld, specifically regarding jewel theft. He's been told no one in those circles has heard so much as a whisper about the Frockmorton Sapphires."

"Last I heard," Matt said. "My sources are not guaranteed to be fully informed."

"Regardless of that, I consider it to be significant. It's possible the person who took the jewels doesn't have a clue what to do with them, now they have them. It's possible the person who took the jewels doesn't need to ask around about disposing of them, because they know exactly what to do. However, it's also possible someone took them, without fully realizing what they'd done, and are now afraid of being caught."

"Okay. How do we find this person?" Bernie asked.

"Jacqueline," I said.

Jacqueline started. "Don't look at me. I didn't steal them!"

"I know you didn't. I believe your daughters did."

"That's ridiculous."

"Is it? They're seven years old. Girls that age love to play dress up, and they love nothing more than bright, sparkly things. You said they've been out of sorts since Sunday. Not eating, not playing. Not happy. Most significantly, they run and hide when they see uniformed police officers."

Elizabeth laughed. "Oh, my dear. I do believe you might be on to something. Katy and Zoe came to my room on

Friday evening as I was preparing for the drinks party. I let them wear the necklace, and they enjoyed twirling around the room and admiring themselves in the mirror. They know where I keep my jewelry, as I often open the boxes to show them things and let them try the pieces on."

"How would they have gotten into your room when you weren't there?" Bernie asked. "You keep your door locked, don't you?"

"They're bright, inquisitive, curious girls, always underfoot," Elizabeth said. "They might well have found out where the master and housekeeping keys are kept."

Always underfoot. I remembered the twins running into the kitchen, ponytails flying, snatching cookies out from under Ian's nose and running off again, yelling, "Time to get ready for the party."

"Reminds me of the time Lily's mother and her little friends took my best broach," Rose said. "The one my mother gave me when I left England after my marriage to Eric. I didn't even know it was missing until Eric found it in the vegetable patch when he was weeding the carrots."

"The twins might have initially planned to wear the jewelry to the tea," I said. "But they lost their nerve and thought better of it."

"They didn't lose their nerve, they didn't get the chance," Jacqueline said. "I told them it was time to go, to hurry up. They told me to go ahead without them. I wasn't going to do that and told them so. They didn't have a chance to put the jewelry on."

"They probably intended to put the items back later, but before they could, everything was disrupted by Julien's death. The arrival of the police and ambulance. The questioning of staff and family and guests. Searching the hotel. They might have thought at first the police had come to arrest them, and then they were afraid to come forward in case they were arrested and thrown in jail."

"Where are the girls now?" Elizabeth asked Jacqueline.

"In our room, reading books with their father. We have an appointment with the pediatrician in Halifax at three."

"Would you please ask them if they know anything about what we're discussing here?" Elizabeth said.

Jacqueline left without a word. Judging by the look on her face, if I was right the twins would be in for a stern talking-to.

"Lily, dear, would you be so kind as to pour?" Elizabeth asked.

"I'd be happy to," I said. "This is a lovely set of china. Part of the Royal Doulton Romance line, I think." A pattern of pink roses and gray leaves under a gray band and fine gold edging.

"Yes, it's the Rebecca pattern. Edward's great-grandmother's wedding china."

I took great care not to drop a cup as I passed around the tea. Simon caught my eye and gave me smile of encouragement. Bernie threw me a wink.

"Tony," Elizabeth broke the silence once we'd all been served. "I find it so very difficult to believe. Are you sure there wasn't some mistake, Lily?"

"I'm sorry," I said. "I've told you what he told me, that's all."

"I did everything in my power to try to prevent my descendants from falling into bitter argument upon my death. I'm not even gone and . . ." Her voice trailed off.

Simon put down his cup. "I've just remembered a few things I have to attend to. Some—issues have arisen at Garfield Hall. Matt?"

"Right. I've got calls to make. Bernie, you can help me."

"I can?"

"Yes, Bernie. You can."

"Okay. Helpful, I will be."

My friends fell all over themselves in their rush to get

out of the room. They must have passed Jacqueline, her husband, and daughters in the hallway. Jacqueline carried a shopping bag, containing something noticeably small but heavy.

Her husband looked confused. The twins kept their heads down, their eyes averted, and their hands clasped tightly together in front of them.

"What do you suppose we have here?" Jacqueline handed the bag to Elizabeth. The older woman took it. She balanced the weight in her hands and smiled. Then she reached in and took out the Frockmorton Sapphires. The stones caught the light from the lamp next to her, and the room seemed to almost light up in shades of white and blue. She put the necklace on the table, next to the tea things and brought out the earrings. "I'm pleased to have my things back," she said to her great-granddaughters. "But they shouldn't have been taken in the first place. Do you agree?"

The girls mumbled something indecipherable and dipped their heads even more.

"Speak up," their father ordered. "And look at the person you're talking to."

They lifted their heads. I smothered a laugh. They might have been heading for the executioner's block at the Tower of London.

"Sorry, Great Granny."

"Sorry, Grandma Elizabeth."

"You two caused a great deal of trouble and worry. I'll forgive you, because you gave them to your mother when she asked. I trust you'll never do anything like that again. You can play with my things when I am with you, but you are not to take them away. Nor anyone else's things, either. And do not, ever again, go into a room into which you have not been invited."

"Yes, Great Granny."

"Sorry, Grandma Elizabeth."

"You may go," Elizabeth said. "You may join me for tea here at four."

Without another word the girls bolted for the door, and their father followed.

"I am so sorry," Jacqueline said.

"You didn't take them, dear. No need to apologize. What's happening outside in regards to Tony? Any word?"

"Susannah and Katherine have gone to the police station. Katherine's calling around, trying to find a good criminal lawyer. Do you know one?"

"Criminal lawyer, no? But my own lawyers will know whom to use. Give them a call and have someone sent down there immediately. I will pay all costs."

I stood up. "I'll be going, if you don't need me for anything, Elizabeth?"

"No, my dear. You run along." She looked into my eyes. "I thank you for all you have done. I knew any granddaughter of Rose would turn out to be clever. Rose, will you have another biscuit? These are my favorites, although absolutely nothing can compare to the ones you made for Edward and the children. All those long years ago."

"There are some that can compare, m'lady," Rose said. "Lily makes them. Perhaps in the summer you could come for a visit."

"I'd like that," the Dowager Countess of Frockmorton said, as she passed the plate to the former kitchen maid.

Chapter 25

Our bags were packed. Bernie and Matt had left for York. Rose was having breakfast with Elizabeth in the dowager countess's rooms. My grandmother and I were due to catch a train from Leeds to London in a couple of hours and then the flight to Boston.

Simon and I walked together to the original Thornecroft Castle so I could have one last look. The day was overcast, strong winter winds blowing down from Scotland.

Time to go home.

"Home," I said. "On one hand, I'm looking forward to home. Sleeping in my own bed. Playing with Éclair. Not living out of a suitcase. On the other hand, home is work. And I never did get to see so many of the things I wanted to see."

"There will be other opportunities," Simon said. We held hands and stood close together on the human-made hill looking across what had once been the moat, to the castle ruins and the green hills of Yorkshire.

"I'd like to come back." I hesitated. Wanting to say more. Afraid to say more. I could come back for a visit another time. Would a yearly visit be enough to keep Simon and me together? Unlikely. Those things rarely worked out.

I was committed, at least in the short term, to my grandmother and her B & B, not to mention my own tearoom. Simon had his job here, at Garfield Hall, which he seemed to like very much.

He cleared his throat. "I had a word with Rose last night."

I looked at him. He was staring into the distance. "About what?"

"I asked how the gardens at Victoria-on-Sea are doing. A total and complete mess, she said. It's been a wet fall, and the weeds are out of control. The young fellow she hired to cut the grass and do some minor weeding is doing his best, but he's not a professional. He decimated the hosta bed near the garden shed, thinking they were weeds. She had to order him to have nothing to do with the roses, after she asked him to prune them and he cut a couple back almost to the ground." He cleared his throat. "I told her my contract at Garfield Hall is only for the winter. Their regular head gardener took six months off to study landscape architecture in Italy, and he plans to come back."

"Did you know that when you took the job?" I asked. For some unknown reason, my heart was pounding in my chest and my palms were so sweaty, I feared Simon would let go of my hand and reach for a towel.

"Yeah, I did. It was an opportunity too good to pass up." He took a deep breath and turned to face me. He took me by the shoulders and turned me, so I was facing him. "Rose said she'd like me to come back in the spring. I told her that would be up to you, Lily."

"Do you—want to come back?" I asked.

"I want to come back. And for far more than to whip the gardens at Victoria-on-Sea back into shape. I want to be with you, Lily. If you want me."

I couldn't find the words. Which didn't really matter, as the kiss I gave him said all I wanted to say.

Recipes

Coronation Chicken Sandwiches

Lily loved these sandwiches so much she now makes them as part of the regular rotation at Tea by the Sea. (She is very careful not to include almond powder.) The mixture can also be served as a salad atop fresh greens.

Makes 10 sandwiches.

Ingredients:
6 tablespoons mayonnaise
2–3 teaspoons mild curry powder, to taste
½ teaspoon ground cinnamon
2 tablespoons mango chutney
1–3 tablespoons sultanas (optional)
500 grams cooked chicken, shredded

Method:
Mix the mayonnaise, curry powder, cinnamon, chutney, and sultanas (if using) together, and season with black pepper.

Add the shredded chicken and stir to coat with the sauce.

Spread the chicken mixture onto lightly buttered slices of white bread. Cut the sandwiches as desired. For proper tea sandwiches, crusts should be removed.

Chocolate and Coffee Tart

This extremely rich treat is strictly for dedicated chocolate lovers. It suits afternoon tea perfectly, as one small slice is more than enough deliciousness.

Makes one 14 x 4-inch tart (about 10 bars).

Ingredients:
1½ cups chocolate wafer crumbs
½ cup melted butter
150 grams bittersweet chocolate (about 5½ ounces), chopped
150 grams white chocolate (about 5½ ounces), chopped
⅓ cup whipping cream
2 tablespoons prepared strong coffee

Method:
Preheat oven to 325°F.

Mix the wafer crumbs with the butter until moistened; press into bottom and partway up the sides of a 14 x 4-inch tart pan lined with parchment paper. Bake on a rimmed baking sheet just until firm, 10–12 minutes. Let cool completely.

In a heatproof bowl set over a saucepan of hot (not boiling) water, heat together the bittersweet chocolate, white chocolate, cream, and coffee, stirring until melted and smooth, about 5 minutes. Pour over the crust, spreading to the edges and smoothing the top. Refrigerate until firm, about 2 hours. Slice into bars.

Sticky Toffee Pudding

Lily brought this recipe home with her, but not to use for afternoon tea, as it can't be eaten with the fingers. It is, however, a great dessert dish. Note that in Britain, "pudding" is another word for dessert. This is more of a cake with sauce on the side than what Americans call pudding.

Makes one cake (about eight servings).

Ingredients:

For the cake:
200 grams pitted dates
150 milliliters hot tea, made with 1 tea bag
150 grams unsalted butter, softened
200 grams dark brown sugar
3 eggs, at room temperature
200 grams all-purpose flour
1½ teaspoons baking powder
¼ teaspoon salt
1 teaspoon baking soda

For the toffee sauce:
100 grams unsalted butter
200 grams dark brown sugar
150 milliliters 10 percent cream

Method:
Preheat oven to 350°F.
Line a 20-centimeter square cake tin with parchment paper.
Chop the dates into small pieces, then add to the hot tea. Put to one side to soak for 15 minutes.
Cream together the softened butter and brown sugar

in a large bowl, until pale and light. Add the eggs one at a time, beating well between each addition.

Sift the flour, baking powder, and baking soda onto the butter mixture and then fold in with a rubber spatula until all of the flour is combined. Fold in the dates, along with any tea that hasn't soaked in, until you have a creamy cake batter.

Pour into the prepared cake tin and bake 35–40 minutes, or until the cake is a deep golden brown.

While the cake is in the oven, make the toffee sauce. Melt the butter in a small pan, then add the brown sugar and cream, and cook over a low heat, stirring every now and then, until the sugar has dissolved. Once the sauce is smooth, increase the heat and let it bubble for a couple of minutes.

Let the cake cool for 5 minutes in the tin before turning out and cutting into squares. Serve warm with the hot toffee sauce.

Acknowledgments

My daughter Alex and I had a wonderful time in Yorkshire, scouting out locations to be used for this book. While there, we stayed at the marvelous Holdsworth House and Hotel (www.holdsworthhouse.co.uk), which dates back to 1633. Although the hotel provided inspiration for Thornecroft Castle House and Hotel, none of the people we met there appear in my book nor was there a murder in all the time we stayed.

We enjoyed afternoon tea, and discovered coronation chicken sandwiches, at the Wolseley in London (www.thewolseley.com). Thanks to Alex for driving us around. Some of Lily's terror as she drives the side roads of Yorkshire was the same as mine.

I'd like to thank my friends Dave Carpenter and Karen Ralley for letting me watch their two gorgeous horses being checked over by a farrier.

Thanks also to the good people at Kensington for believing in Lily and the gang, and to Kim Lionetti, my agent.